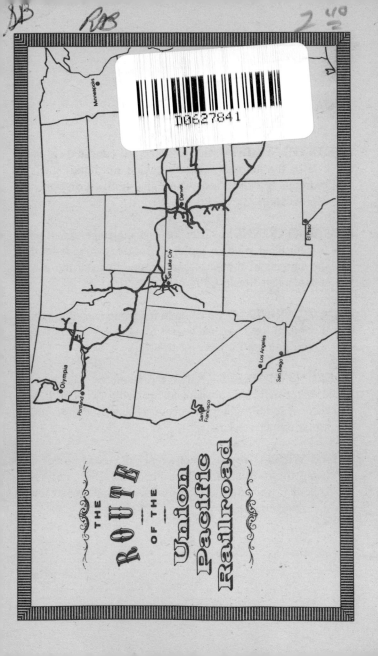

THE

ROUTE

OF THE

Union
Pacific
Railroad

THEY CAME
TO CHEYENNE...

GLENN GILCHRIST—He was a Harvard-educated engineer, one of the innovative minds behind the building of the railroad. But the West would give him a different kind of education . . .

MEGAN O'CONNELL—Her loveless marriage ended when her husband died in a flood. But Megan did not fear the dangers of the land—and dreamed of starting a new, independent life in California.

LIAM O'CONNELL—He came to the frontier to find adventure—and found he had a taste for whiskey, a quick hand with a gun, and a nose for trouble.

AILEEN O'CONNELL—Her sister stood by her when a drunken husband abandoned her with two children to feed. But following her dream west led straight to her worst nightmares . . .

EAGLE WING—He was a hot-tempered Sioux warrior who hated the railroad and all it stood for. His ambition to become a war chief made him the railroad's most feared and dangerous enemy.

JOSHUA HOOD—Chief hunter and scout for the Union Pacific. He knew the plains and the Sioux as well as any white man alive, but he was a babe in the woods when he had to talk to a pretty woman!

WILLY—A hard-living Indian fighter who fell in love with a Cheyenne beauty. They'd make a home in California—if they made it that far . . .

CASSIE—She worked the dance halls and saloons, a pretty half-breed who could satisfy any man with a few dollars to spend. When her one true love died in a bar fight, she took revenge the only way she knew how.

DOCTOR THADDEUS WISEMAN—A healer who had seen suffering at its worst on Civil War battlefields. Now his dreams lay in the open West—if he could survive a new war against the Sioux.

LEROY HAWS—A mule skinner, as tough and mean as they came. He worked for the railroad builders. But when he shot a man in a barroom brawl, he was his own boss, master of his uncertain future . . .

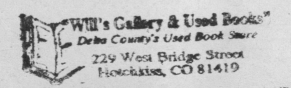

The *Rails West!* series from Jove

RAILS WEST!
NEBRASKA CROSSING
WYOMING TERRITORY

RAILS WEST!
Wyoming Territory

FRANKLIN CARTER

JOVE BOOKS, NEW YORK

WYOMING TERRITORY

A Jove Book / published by arrangement with the author

PRINTING HISTORY
Jove edition / January 1994

ISBN: 0-515-11278-X

A JOVE BOOK®
Jove Books are published by The Berkley Publishing Group,
200 Madison Avenue, New York, New York 10016.
JOVE and the "J" design are trademarks belonging
to Jove Publications, Inc.

PRINTED IN THE UNITED STATES OF AMERICA

10 9 8 7 6 5 4 3 2 1

RAILS WEST!
Wyoming Territory

CHAPTER 1

Just before sundown, the telegraph key at the Union Pacific's Plum Creek station went dead. Stationmaster and chief telegrapher William Thomas scowled, his long, supple fingers tapping the key again and again.

"What happened?" one of the repair crew asked.

"I sure wish that I knew, Milt. The line running west to the construction crews at Cheyenne is dead."

"It couldn't be wind. Our weather is perfect for this late in the year."

"Maybe buffalo have rubbed another pole down?" Thomas knew better than most how much the huge and powerful buffalo loved to use the telephone poles as scratching posts. They could be counted on pushing over dozens each year.

"Didn't see any buffalo when we inspected the line yesterday, Mr. Thomas. I got a report that they're seventy, maybe even a hundred miles to our north."

Thomas tapped the lifeless telegraph key again—still nothing. "Then it might be Sioux," he said without looking up.

"It could be a lot of things. Mr. Thomas, do we got to go out there tonight? It's pretty cold."

"I know, but I've a stack of important messages I

1

need to send along to Cheyenne. If we want to keep our jobs, I'm afraid that we have little choice but to investigate."

"Yes, sir."

"Get a spool of new wire, repair tools, and make sure that everyone has a loaded rifle," Thomas ordered, coming to his feet and brushing back his long, silver-shot hair. "We'll ride out on a handcart. Yeah, and bring along a couple of lamps because there's not going to be much in the way of moonlight."

"If we find that some itchy old bull buffalo did this," Milt snorted angrily, "we'll have us a big feast with what hump meat we can bring back to the station."

"That'd be a fair payback. Now get the men. We'll be leaving in a quarter hour."

Thomas sat back down and tried the key one last time. Nothing. It took him only a moment to rewire the telegraph and send a message eastward.

LINE DOWN WEST OF PLUMB CREEK. STOP.
GOING TO REPAIR ON HAND-PUMP CART.
STOP. COULD BE SIOUX TROUBLE. STOP.
ADVISE WESTBOUND SUPPLY TRAIN TO
EXERCISE EXTREME CAUTION. STOP.
W. THOMAS. STOP.

"Let's go," Thomas said, checking to see that his own rifle was loaded.

"We'll have a full load," Milt said, "barely enough room for all of us and the repair wire and tools."

"There is safety in numbers."

Will Thomas rubbed his hands together briskly to stir circulation. It was November and cold. There was a chance of snow, but it still felt more like rain coming unless the temperature dropped another few degrees. He was a tall, orderly man in his forties who took great pride in his work and responsibility as supervisor of this isolated Union Pacific train station and telegraph office. He'd been raised in Connecticut, but he'd come west after the war and had already fallen in love with the solitary beauty of the Great Plains. He paused to look up the line and the view was spectacular. The huge orb burning fire was diving into the table-flat western horizon and the sky was a smeared artist's palette of magenta, gold, and lavender.

"Hop on board, sir," Milt said to his grumbling repair crew. "With any luck at all, we'll find the break and be back within an hour."

"There's another supply train not far behind us," Thomas said, focusing his mind to the work that lay ahead. "I'd like to be here to relay any messages when she passes through to Cheyenne."

"It'll take a little luck. Might have to buck this heavy cart off the track and let that supply train roll on past. But at least there are plenty of us to lift this pushcart back onto the track, Mr. Thomas."

Milt grabbed one side of the pump handle and another repairman grabbed the other. Slowly at first, then gathering momentum, the car began to roll toward sunset which Thomas watched until it sank into the west and died.

Twenty miles east of the Plumb Creek station, Aileen O'Connell Fox was filled with anxiety as the Union Pacific supply train hurdled westward into the brilliant, bloodred sunset. The Nebraska prairie was magnificent with its buffalo grass gilded by the fading sunlight. Aileen had never seen anything so immense and glorious as these vast plains. Small wonder that the Sioux and Cheyenne had vowed to forever stop the Iron Horses of the Union Pacific Railroad. Aileen knew that the Army had vowed to protect the railroad crews and passengers such as herself, but she had also heard that a nearly bankrupt post–Civil War Congress had been unable to supply and garrison the lonely western military outposts. Indian attacks were on the rise and the Union Pacific was under constant siege.

"Are you feeling any better, Mommy?"

"Much better, Jenny," Aileen said, forcing a smile.

"If you were sick all the time on this train, why didn't we go back home?"

"Omaha wasn't our home," Aileen explained patiently. "We were just staying at the hotel in Omaha waiting for Aunt Megan to send for us."

"And she did?" Jenny asked, fingers absently toying with the yarn hair of her raggedy doll.

"Well," Aileen hedged, "not exactly. We are going to *surprise* her."

"I like surprises!"

"So do I," Aileen replied, afraid that Megan would be very upset about their unexpected arrival at the Union Pacific Railroad's newest hell-on-wheels tent city.

Megan had been sending Aileen money ever since she'd left to serve the construction crews with her tent saloon. But Aileen vowed that was going to stop. Guilt-ridden by her sister's charity, Aileen had decided that it was high time she ought to also follow the rails west and do her share of the work instead of remaining in the relative comfort and safety of Omaha.

Jenny stood up on her wooden bench seat and gazed up and down the coach. "Where is Uncle Liam? Is he hiding from the Indians, Mommy?"

"Certainly not! Your uncle is back in the caboose with the workmen," Aileen said, knowing full well that her irresponsible younger brother was gambling and drinking.

"But isn't Uncle Liam afraid of the Indians too?"

Aileen was distressed by the question. Back in Omaha, there had been almost daily reports of the Indian deprivations against the struggling work crews. Some of those reports went into the gory details about the Sioux and Cheyenne killing and scalping but Aileen had tried very, very hard to keep her young and impressionable daughter from hearing such frightening news. She thought that she'd been successful—until now.

"Jenny, your uncle Liam isn't afraid of Indians."

"But they shot him with an arrow. He told me so."

"That's . . . that's not quite true." Aileen did not want to elaborate, but Jenny was looking at her so intently she was compelled to explain.

"Jenny, your uncle was shot in the hip by an awful man who was himself killed. But your uncle is fine now and eager to get back to work. That's why he's with us and how we were able to gain passage on this construction train. Otherwise . . . well, we are very fortunate."

Jenny nodded. She was a sweet and precocious child, the light of Aileen's life. Without Jenny, Aileen felt as if her existence would have no purpose. Last year a springtime flood had wiped out Omaha's Irish shantytown and made both herself and Megan widows. Since then, Aileen had devoted herself to her five-year-old daughter and convinced herself that remaining in Omaha was her duty as a responsible parent. Her young son, alas, had perished in a flu epidemic two months earlier. Aileen had been devastated, but knew she had to get on with her life.

Nearly as bad, her bakery had continued to wither along with Omaha itself as the Union Pacific construction crews had departed to lay track westward. Only Megan's charity had kept them fed and sheltered through this past winter. All that time Aileen had fretted as her sister's rail-town saloon had become the victim of a "whiskey price war" instigated by her main competitor, Ike Norman. Thanks be to God, Ike Norman's ruthless price war had failed. But all the worry and wondering had convinced Aileen that even her strong, self-reliant sister needed support.

Gazing out the window into the glow of a fading sunset, Aileen thought about how *she*, being the older, was supposed to be the strong leader. Yet, there was no sense in trying to delude oneself—Megan had been blessed in abundance with nerve, strength, and determination. Some might say even pigheadedness, but Aileen knew that an unfair description.

"Hey up there!" a loud voice boomed from the back of the empty passenger coach. "You two girls gettin' lonesome yet?"

Aileen and Jenny turned around to see Liam. One look at her brother told Aileen that he was almost drunk. Liam came lurching up the aisle favoring his bullet-shattered hip that had left him with a permanent limp.

"Hi there, Jenny!" Liam boomed into the coach that was empty except for his sister and niece. "How's your luck today?"

"Liam!" Aileen said sharply. "Don't tease the child."

Liam scowled. He was tall and devilishly good-looking, which Aileen considered a flaw because it always got her brother in trouble with the wrong kind of "ladies."

"I'm not teasin'," Liam protested, reaching over and lifting the child up.

Jenny squealed with delight but then she wrinkled her nose. "You smell awful, Uncle Liam!"

"Aw, just a little whiskey and tobacco. Someday, when you grow up and find a husband, you'll learn to accept those smells, honey."

"I hope not," Aileen said with stern disapproval.

"Aileen," Liam said, absently setting Jenny down, "I've had a streak of bad luck at cards but that's changing. Say, can I borrow . . ."

"No!" Aileen glared at her brother. "I won't be a party to gambling and carrying on. And furthermore, I don't understand how employees of this railroad are allowed to drink and gamble when on duty."

"Aw," Liam said, trying to look as if his feelings were injured, "there's just a few of us back there playing a little low-stakes poker. No harm."

"There *is* harm! You shouldn't be squandering your money and those men should be busy."

"There's nothing else to do!"

Liam stared out the window to the south where the cottonwoods huddled, their naked branches shivering in the frosty evening air. "Barely even any moonlight or I could take potshots at buffalo or antelope. Only thing to do is to gamble and have a few drinks to stave off the boredom."

"You could all at least try and watch for trouble."

"There ain't no trouble out here! Why, end-of-track is clear to Cheyenne in the Wyoming Territory! That's well over a hundred and fifty miles. And we ain't going to get there until late tomorrow."

Aileen didn't want to alarm Jenny, but she felt it her responsibility to point out the dangers of frontier travel to her drunken brother. "This is *still* Sioux country. You ought to know that."

"Not much longer, it ain't. Besides, Chief Red Cloud and the rest of them cowardly Sioux always attack the advance survey and bridge-buildin' crews. They wouldn't dare mess with this Union Pacific supply train."

"Please," Aileen said, glancing at her daughter who was listening to this discussion with great interest. "We can talk about this later."

Liam found a cheap tin flask in his inside leather coat pocket. He thumbed back his slouch hat, then uncorked the flask and took a long, shuddering drink.

Aileen wagged her finger at him. "Liam, I swear that you've got Uncle Patrick's sickness for drink. Have you forgotten that it killed him when he went west to join the California gold rush in 'forty-nine."

Liam made a sour face. "Uncle Patrick wasn't willin' to work! I'll work."

"You'll only do what you want and call it work."

"The devil you say!" Liam patted the six-gun strapped to his hip and leered. "Why, Mr. Joshua Hood hisself chose me to be one of his scouts and buffalo hunters. And I didn't even know how to ride a horse nor shoot—but he could see that I was strong and hardworkin' enough to learn. Brave as they come too!"

"I don't want to argue. Go back to your friends."

Liam sniffled, then wiped his nose again with his coat sleeve. "You didn't work so hard back in Omaha. If'n you had, you'd still be there and not expectin' more charity from Megan."

Aileen glared at her brother who she had never really liked. "Uncle Patrick ran off to California crowing that he'd find gold and send for the whole family but I'll bet that all he ever found was whiskey and misery. And I'll bet he's buried in a pauper's grave—if he got buried at all."

"Maybe he *did* find gold and never told us."

"Ha!" Aileen's eyes flashed with righteous anger. "Mark my words, Liam. If you don't mend your evil ways, the same fate awaits you."

But now Liam wasn't listening to her. He was staring out at the dying light, mesmerized as if by some inner vision.

"Liam?"

"Aileen, you should have been here last summer when I rode out hunting buffalo with Mr. Hood. We shot about fifty head just over there in them low, dark hills. We just passed the Elm Creek station. Next up is . . . Plum Creek. Mr. Hood named it hisself on account of we found a couple of wild plumb trees growin' along the Platte River."

Liam expelled a deep, happy sigh. "God, didn't we have ourselves a fat feast!"

"I'm sure that it was all very delicious," Aileen managed to say without visible enthusiasm for the idea of devouring anything's tongue made her stomach lurch.

"Two dollars," Liam said, snapping his attention from the fading landscape to his sister. "Loan me a lousy two dollars and I'm out of your hair. I'll pay it back. I promise and I'll give you a share of my winnings."

To get her brother out of the car quickly, Aileen gave him the two dollars. When Liam was drinking, he was obnoxious and thoughtless. He wasn't mean, but he was loud and relentless.

"Thanks," Liam said without gratitude. "I guess this money really comes from Megan, huh?"

Aileen bit her lower lip to keep from telling Liam to go straight to hell.

Liam chuckled. "Thank God for good old Megan! Hell, she's worth more than the both of us."

"Go on," Aileen said, pulling Jenny close. "And don't come back until morning when you're sober."

Liam wiped his nose with the back of his sleeve. "You ain't so prissy, Aileen. You forgettin' that I knew your husband 'bout as well as a brother. He weren't no saint either. He drank and cussed ten times worse than me!"

"Go away."

Liam jammed the money into his pocket and said, "I'm gonna hunt Indians and buffalo again when I return to the end of the track. Ain't no bullet can keep me from the excitement. But what the hell are you coming out here for?"

"I told you—to help Megan."

"Ha! A fat lot of help you'll be! She'll wind up nursemaiding you. That's what'll happen!"

Despite all that she could do to stop it, Aileen could feel her eyes begin to sting with tears. She gritted her teeth but her chin was trembling and her hands were bloodless and clenched tightly.

Jenny hugged her neck. "Don't cry again, Mommy."

"Jezus!" Liam said, his voice dripping with disgust.

"Is Megan ever going to be revolted."

"Go away!" Aileen cried, bursting into tears.

A shadow of guilt passed across Liam's face but so fleetingly that it vanished in a moment and he turned and headed back to the caboose and his poker game.

"Don't cry," Jenny pleaded. "Uncle Liam didn't mean to be nasty."

Aileen sniffled. "I know that. He never means to do harm, but he does. You uncle is . . . well, never mind."

Aileen hugged Jenny and then she found a cheap cotton handkerchief and dried her eyes. The sun was almost down and it frightened her to be out here in this huge and hostile darkness. Aileen gripped the arm of her wooden bench seat and told herself that she had to learn to control herself around Liam and not let him upset her so. His remark that Megan would be revolted by her weak behavior struck a very sensitive chord. Megan was not a crier and it was true that she did not approve of tears or any outward sign of weakness.

But dammit, sometimes a lady couldn't help but have a good, honest cry.

CHAPTER 2

"You see anything yet!" William Thomas demanded, his breath driving steamy clouds from his mouth.

The repairman raised the feeble kerosene lamp a little higher. "I can't seen more'n ten feet ahead. Darker than the bottom of a well tonight."

Thomas looked up at the slice of cold, thin moon that kept dipping in and out of the low ceiling of clouds. There wasn't even any starlight. For the past hour, their little repair crew had been pumping and bumping along on the Union Pacific's new rails, stopping at every telegraph pole and carefully inspecting it before climbing back onto the pump cart and continuing westward. Thomas estimated that they were now at least five miles from Plumb Creek.

"Mr. Thomas?"

"Yes?"

"How far are we going to go tonight?" Milt asked.

It was the question Thomas had anticipated and yet could not satisfactorily answer. "I don't exactly know. A little farther. If we don't find the break in the next mile or two, we'll turn around and head back out at first light. At least this way, I can tell management that we tried to find the break and get it repaired."

"That's all anybody could do," one of the repairmen offered. "I think we've already given it a real honest try, Mr. Thomas."

It was true. They weren't all that far from the next telegraph office at Willow Island and Thomas knew that each foot they traveled diminished the chances that the break would be his repair crew's responsibility.

Over the clackety-click of the rails, Thomas heard a coyote's mournful howl. Off to the north he could see a glittering splinter of lightning reach down out of the heavy cloud cover and stab the dark plains. The wind was picking up and the temperature was dropping. Thomas thought that he could smell the approach of a storm. Snow would be more tolerable than a wet, bone-chilling rain. And even this late in the year, it could still rain buckets on these open plains. Thunder could clap louder than cymbals. Men could be killed by lightning. It had already happened to three unlucky Irishmen on Dodge's surveying crew in the Wyoming Territory.

For the next quarter of an hour, the men were silent, perhaps awed by the fury of the approaching storm. They marveled as delicate spiderwebs shivered against the backdrop of an indigo sky. Occasionally, a huge lightning bolt would pierce the heavens and strike the earth, then a moment later thunder would resound across the flat plains.

It was awesome and frightening.

William Thomas could feel the repairmen growing anxious for their safety. You couldn't shoot and kill a lightning bolt. Not like you could an Indian. He was about to say that it was time to turn back when suddenly the man holding the lantern cried out a warning. An instant later Thomas heard a sharp, whirring sound like a pheasant launching into a hard wind. Only it wasn't a pheasant and when the man screamed and staggered, Thomas experienced a moment of sheer terror. The lantern and the man pitched off the hand-pump cart an instant before it struck a barricade and overturned.

Thomas lost his rifle in midair. He hit the rails and felt his ribs snap. A second scream erupted from his throat and he struggled to get up and fight, or—God forgive him—run for his life.

But something was wrong with his knee. It betrayed him as he tried to rise and before he could quite gain his senses, he saw a shadow and heard the scream of a Sioux warrior. He twisted around and looked up to see a silhouette blacker than the angry sky.

"No, please!" he cried.

He punched upward and struck the Sioux warrior in the throat. The Indian's upraised war club chopped downward into his shoulder, causing it to go completely numb. Thomas heard other men howling in pain and terror. There were two gunshots . . . or was it the thunder of the storm?

Thomas broke away from the gagging warrior and tried to run but his knee folded like paper and he spilled from the roadbed into the deep prairie grass. He began to scramble away on his hands and knees, his mind threatening to unravel like a spool of twine. Maybe he could escape into the grass. Somehow reach the Platte River and . . .

But the Indian was on him again. Thomas heard the Sioux's war club whistle as lightning flashed behind his eyes. He felt his long blond hair being pulled violently upward until a moccasin on the back of his neck drove his face into the dirt muffling his screams. He lost consciousness as the Sioux warrior took his scalp.

Thomas awoke bathed in a halo of fire. He did not want to awaken and was sure that he was dead. For long, agonizing minutes he lay still, feeling the wind freshen with the approaching storm. Over the roll of thunder he could hear the ring of hammer striking steel. He raised his head as a bolt of lightning speared into the water-loving cottonwood trees clogging the banks of the Platte. One of the naked cottonwoods ignited like a pitch torch and Thomas witnessed the Sioux using the repairmen's tools to uncouple the rails and then twist them apart.

Dear Lord! These bloodthirsty savages *knew* that a westbound supply train was coming and were determined that it should be derailed! Thomas rolled onto his stomach and wiggled deeper into the grass. His heart was pounding and his face was a mask of caked blood. All that he knew for certain was that he had to somehow warn the onrushing train's engineer that the tracks were separated. Otherwise, the train would derail and any survivors would be slaughtered just like his own repair crew.

Thomas reached the trees. He grabbed one and used it to pull himself to his feet. His knee was either broken or dislocated. He didn't know which and it didn't matter. He was afraid to touch what had been his scalp and could not even imagine what he must look like as he clung to the tree fighting the whipping wind and a deep belly sickness.

He tried to leave the tree with the idea of finding a stick to use as a crutch or a cane. But the moment he began to leave, another bolt of lightning illuminated the surrealistic scene of the Sioux warriors dancing and howling in the storm. Thomas felt his bowels flood with paralyzing fear. This fear crystallized and shattered when he heard the lonesome whistle of the approaching train. Mindless of all else, he tried to intercept the train but fell. Pushing to his feet, he began to hop toward the blossoming oil-fired headlamp, bellowing a warning that could not possibly be heard by the engineer.

Only the Sioux heard his shouts. Three dashed to their ponies and came racing in to kill him before he could reach the tracks and warn the supply train.

Somehow, Thomas did reach the tracks. With the onrushing locomotive bearing down on him, he began to wave and hop up and down on one leg. The engineer saw him but only a moment before he could apply the brakes and then Thomas was struck by the cowcatcher that spun his broken body high into the air. The tortured screech of iron on iron overrode the rumble of the summer storm and did not end until the train slid off the twisted rails and crashed over sideways like a team of lung-shot horses.

Six cars back in the only passenger coach of the Union Pacific freight train, Aileen heard the terrible protesting screech of the iron wheels as they smoked and burned against the rails. At the same instant, she was hurled forward from her bench seat and slammed hard against the sidewall. A moment later the world seemed to tilt crazily and then a scream filled Aileen's mouth as the coach yawed to the right, balanced on one set of wheels, then shuddered and rolled into a nightmarish darkness.

"Jenny!" Aileen cried as she felt herself being lifted high into the air and then hurled downward. A crushing weight landed on her chest and Aileen struggled to breathe as she reached blindly for her daughter. "Jenny!"

Jenny began to cry somewhere. Her thin howl infused Aileen with new life and she managed to throw off whatever had pinned her to the side of the coach. Clawing her way through the twisted benches and baggage, she found Jenny. Pulling the terrified child to her bosom, she rocked Jenny. Outside, they could both hear the triumphant howls of the Sioux and the pitiful death cries of the supply train's crew.

"Oh, my God!" Aileen prayed. "Jenny! Liam! God, help us!"

In the darkness and chaos of the overturned caboose, Liam found the money he had just lost at poker as well as a good deal of the winners' money. All around him frenzied railroad men were shouting and smashing at the windows and jammed doors. Liam had no doubt that they would escape the caboose only to be cut down by the Sioux. His own plan, as soon as he'd groped around and was sure that there was no more loose money lying about, was to reach Aileen and Jenny, then try to hold out against the savages as long as there was any hope of rescue.

Glass shattered. Somewhere in the confusion an apparently dying man kept groaning. Liam's fist closed on a few last dollars. He stuffed them into his pockets along with two pints of liquor. The men in the caboose broke through the jammed door and poured outside. Liam crouched and listened to the pounding hooves of the Indian ponies. He did not even want to think about what was happening to the men who had just departed.

With one coat pocket full of money and the other filled with whiskey, he crawled to the door and watched as Indians on foot and on horseback raced up and down the overturned train. Several of the coaches were already engulfed in flames. The thought that Aileen and Jenny might be trapped by a raging inferno brought Liam to his feet. Taking a deep breath and drawing his six-gun, he jumped outside and ducked in close to the smoking wheels. When there was an opening, he raced forward like a rat sprinting for its hole. A Sioux noticed him, yipped in joyous anticipation, and unleashed an arrow. Missing, he yelped in rage and his heels pelted his pony as he raced at Liam, intent on running him down.

Liam ducked under a smoking train wheel. The Indian jumped off his pony, drew a knife, and charged. Liam set himself and waited until the Indian was almost on top of him before driving the heel of his boot into the Indian's gut and stopping the attacker in his tracks. An instant later Liam's fist smashed into the warrior's face. The Sioux collapsed and Liam grabbed the Indian's hair and used his knee twice with bone-crushing effect. The Indian flopped over onto his back twitching.

Moments later Liam burst into the overturned passenger coach. Fire and smoke filled his nostrils and burned his lungs. "Aileen! Jenny!"

He staggered forward, beating at the smoke and coughing violently. Over and over he called their names. Once, he came so close to the flames that his pants began to smoke. Reacting with fear, he staggered backward knowing that Aileen and Jenny were gone.

Liam escaped through a window and threw himself up against the underside of the passenger coach. A sound close by sent his hand flashing for his gun.

"Don't kill us!" Aileen exclaimed out of the darkness.

Liam blinked with surprise. "Where are you?"

"Liam? Liam, we're back here under the coach. You've got to help us. We're both hurt."

Liam pushed up hard under the coach and groped for the pair. No wonder they had not been found and scalped.

"How badly are you hurt?"

"I don't know!" Aileen whispered, throwing her arms around his neck and beginning to weep.

"Aileen! You've *got* to get ahold of yourself!"

She drew back. Liam could not see her face but he could imagine how frightened his sister must be as the Indians raced up and down the length of the train, killing the last of the white trainmen and smashing out windows with their stone war clubs.

"What on earth are we going to do?" Aileen asked in a trembling voice.

"I'm not sure yet." Liam reached out and his hand touched Jenny's skin, which was cold. "Is she alive?"

"Yes, but she's hurt. I don't feel any bleeding but . . ."

"Shhh!"

Two warriors ran past, their legs flashing less than a yard from where Liam, Aileen, and Jenny crouched in hiding. Liam mopped a sheen of fear-sweat from his brow. "We've got to get away from this train. If we can reach the river, we've got a chance."

A huge bolt of lightning flashed across the sky and the thunder that followed boomed so hard that even the Iron Horse trembled.

"Can you do that, Aileen? Can you run for the river?"

"My ribs are broken!"

Liam's hand locked on Aileen's shoulder and his fingers bit into her flesh until she whimpered. "Listen to me, dammit! If we don't get out of here before daybreak, we'll be slaughtered like everyone else. Is that what you want?"

"No, of course not!"

"Then broken ribs or not, you're going to run for those distant trees like you've never run before. I'll carry Jenny."

Aileen fell silent. Finally, Liam released his grip on her shoulder and said in a low, encouraging voice, "You escaped that burning coach and you're still alive. You can also get to the river, Aileen. We can do it together."

She nodded woodenly, but somehow found the courage to say, "Yes. Yes we can!"

"Good." Liam rolled off his backside onto the balls of his feet. "Hand Jenny to me."

"We're going to go now?"

Liam stuck his head out as far as he dared. Most of the Indians appeared to be gathered up by the overturned locomotive tender around a huge bonfire. They were dancing around the fire, but a few were still on horseback, racing up and down the tracks looking for one last white man to kill.

Well, Liam thought, it won't be me.

"Give Jenny to me," he ordered, stretching out his arms for the child.

When Aileen dragged her daughter into a sitting position, Liam placed his ear to the child's breast.

"What are you doing!"

"I'm listening for a heartbeat."

Aileen's fragile composure shattered like a crystal goblet. "She's alive! And even if she weren't, I'd never leave her."

"Shut up!"

Aileen covered her face and fought hysteria.

"All right," Liam said, lowering his voice, "she *is* alive. So let's get out of here while we can."

Liam threw Jenny over his left shoulder and drew his gun. His knees felt weak and he wanted to vomit from fear and whiskey but he couldn't afford that luxury.

"Let's go!"

He didn't wait to see if Aileen was following him but ran as hard as he could for the distant trees. His lungs were quickly on fire and his leg muscles burned. Liam was sure that the Sioux would see him and Aileen, but there was no time to even throw a quick glance toward the overturned locomotive. It seemed as if he ran a thousand miles before he threw himself headlong into the trees. Rolling Jenny off his shoulder, he crabbed around to see Aileen about forty yards behind. She was bent over and staggering.

"Come on! Come on!"

But Aileen couldn't move any faster. Even at a distance and over the sounds of the Indians and the storm, Liam could hear her ragged breathing. He stood up and began to move toward his sister but something caused him to turn his head. A lone warrior had spotted Aileen. Unnoticed by the other Sioux, this man had ranged out farther from the train tracks just in case someone had crawled off to die or to hide.

And now he saw Aileen and was rewarded.

Liam watched the Sioux's heels drum against his pony's ribs. Saw him raise a feathered war lance and come racing at Aileen who seemed oblivious to everything except reaching the cottonwood trees.

Liam swore in helpless fury. He didn't dare use his gun. That would certainly attract the war party and then there would not be enough trees in the entire territory to save his scalp.

Liam fumbled around in the dark forest until his hands found a heavy broken limb. He picked it up and as the mounted Indian bore down on Aileen, he rushed out of the trees and attacked.

The warrior was so intent on skewering Aileen that he did not see Liam until the last instant. The Indian tried to rein his horse at Liam but it was too late. The heavy limb caught him a glancing blow across the side of the head and the pony ran out from under him to crash through the trees and then into the Platte River.

Liam never gave the dazed warrior a second chance. He jumped onto the man's chest and beat his face until the Indian went limp. Jumping up, Liam ran back into the trees.

"We've got to get that pony!" he cried.

The Indian pony was spooked. It was standing knee deep in the slow but freezing current and when Liam rushed to the edge of the riverbank, the pony snorted with fear and edged deeper into the water.

"Whoa!"' Liam said. "Whoa."

The horse snorted again. It did not want to go deeper into the river but neither did it seem to want to have anything to do with the white man who looked and smelled strange.

"Easy," Liam crooned, remembering how the Union Pacific's Joshua Hood had showed him how to calm a spooked horse.

He waded into the river, gritting his teeth against the cold. The thought entered his mind that he should retrieve Aileen and Jenny and then they would all wade downriver, being careful not to leave any tracks on the shoreline. But the Plumb Creek station was at least six or seven miles away and Liam did not think that he could carry Jenny that far or that Aileen could bear up to this bone-chilling water that long.

They needed the horse. Besides, after all they'd just been through, Liam was of the opinion that he richly deserved the glory of capturing a Sioux pony. It would be a fine thing to ride the animal all the way to Cheyenne wearing its Indian saddle. A fine thing that would turn heads and not be soon forgotten.

"Easy, horse," he crooned, slowly moving out into the swift, icy water.

Moments later he had the animal by its horsehair bridle. There was no moon or starlight but the glow from the inferno now rapidly consuming the supply train was enough to reveal that the pony was a chestnut, one of his favorite colors. Liam rubbed the animal's neck and spoke softly to it. After a minute the pony nuzzled him and sighed. It dipped its head and drank deeply from the river.

Liam led the Indian pony back to the shallows noting with satisfaction that the Indian saddle had stirrups and a pad.

"Aileen, have you ever ridden a horse before?"

"You know that I haven't. And certainly not a wild animal like that one! Anyway, I can't . . ."

Liam reached out and grabbed his sister. She was thin and worrisome and it was easy to swing her up onto the pony's back. Aileen clutched at the animal's mane. It snorted and danced.

"Easy!" Liam said to his sister. "You're scarin' this horse and we need him."

Aileen bowed her head and took deep breaths. "What about Jenny? We're not leaving her."

"Of course not!"

Liam picked up the child and eased Jenny onto the pony's sharp withers. "You hold her and I'll lead the horse downriver so that we leave no tracks."

"But they'll find its owner in the morning! They'll know that we escaped."

"You're right," Liam said. He led the pony over to a half-submerged tree and tied it. Then, ignoring Aileen's protestations, he sneaked back out to where the unconscious Indian lay. Grabbing up the man's war lance, he buried it into the Sioux's chest, then grabbed the dead Indian by the hair with one hand and collected his lance in the other before returning to the river.

When Aileen saw the body and realized what her brother had done, she turned away and began to retch. Liam ignored her. He dragged the Sioux's corpse out into the strong current and let it float away.

"He'll beat us downriver to Fort Kearney, if that's how far we got to go for help."

When Aileen kept retching, Liam shook his head. "Hang on just as tight as you can to Jenny," he advised before he started leading the pony downriver.

Liam knew that he had left tracks on the riverbank and that the Sioux would pick up those tracks at first light. That's why they had to reach safety before morning.

A bolt of lightning struck and ignited another cottonwood. The pony tried to pull away. Aileen whimpered in fear until Liam got the pony back under control. He was so cold that his teeth were chattering as he watched the burning tree and as the heavens opened up and sleet began to sweep across the Platte River.

It was miserable. Worse than miserable. The cottonwood branches overhead began to whip at the driving sleet and the wind moaned.

Good, Liam thought as he led the frightened pony out of the river, it will drive the Sioux to shelter and maybe even cover our tracks.

CHAPTER
3

Megan O'Connell pressed her gloved hands hard against the small of her back and closed her green eyes. Outside, she could hear the wind blow and she hoped her saloon tent was staked down tight because this threatened to be a hard, bitter storm.

"Uhhh," she groaned as she stood in the center of her saloon tent amid stacks of wooden boxes, "my back feels like a broken matchstick."

"What's the matter?" Rachel Foreman, her friend and employee, asked with an all-too-cheerful smile. "Is this packing and unpacking finally wearing you down?"

"It is," Megan admitted, arching her back and then tossing her mane of red hair. "How many times have we set up a new saloon since leaving Omaha? Twenty?"

"At least." Rachel began to rattle off the names of the rail towns at which they had set up their saloon for the Union Pacific's boisterous construction workers. "Let's see, first there was Columbus, then Jackson, Lone Tree, Grand Island, Pawnee, Wood River, Fort Kearney . . ."

"Enough," Megan said. "I've already lost count. Just hearing all those names makes me realize how hard we've been working for our money."

Rachel reached into the pine box filled with sawdust and unpacked another bottle of good Irish whiskey. "At least we have the protection of the construction crews and we don't have to worry about getting scalped. Did you hear about what just happened at Plum Creek?"

"Who hasn't heard of it?" Megan replied. "That's all the crews are talking about. A lot of them knew Will Thomas and those poor repairmen."

"Damned Indians!" Victor Boyette grumbled as he used his hammer to pry open more boxes for Megan and Rachel to unpack. "I wished that I had one of them Sioux right here so that I could wallop him in the head with this hammer."

Megan and Rachel exchanged glances but remained silent. Victor was a sweet lad and a hard worker but he was often troubled and childish. Unwilling to confide to anyone about his past, he had arrived in the rail camps and became devoted to Megan and to working in her tent saloon. Megan wouldn't have fired Victor for anything. And despite the fact that he could get very emotional about Indians and was forgetful, Victor was also completely honest and good-hearted. The dark-haired lad with no past was their friend and as long as Victor wanted a job, it would be waiting for him at track's end.

Megan stooped and continued to unpack. The sawdust was an ideal packing material not only because it protected her drink glasses, liquors, lantern globes, and other fragiles, but it also served as flooring.

Rachel unpacked a lamp, dusted it off, and then carried it to the bar. "Megan, I understand that the Indians were led by a fierce war chief named Eagle Wing and that he stole all manner of valuable supplies."

"Joshua Hood and his men will catch him."

"Wish that I was riding with him," Victor said. "I'd sure beat hell out of 'em with this hammer or a gun, if'n I had one."

"Of course you would," Megan said.

"When are Joshua and his scouts leaving?" Rachel asked.

"Just as soon as the next supply train heads east. Glenn told me that he and his men will load their horses and provisions into a rail car and ride it back to Plum Creek."

Rachel returned to her unpacking. "There's something I don't understand, Megan."

"What's that?"

"Why isn't the Army doing more to protect the Union Pacific and its crews?"

Megan shrugged. She was a tall, handsome woman with a face and figure that caught and transfixed the eye. Irish born and Irish raised, she and Aileen had both married young and unwisely. Now recently widowed during the springtime flood of the Missouri River, Megan had no interest in tying herself to any man. Her dream was to reach California and start a new and independent life. And now that she was making money again after her main competitor had been forced to end his whiskey price war, Megan was determined that by the time she reached California, she would never have to worry about finances again.

"The Army is stretched much too thin," Megan said. "They don't have enough officers and soldiers on the frontier. Mr. Dodge has pleaded with the Army but it hasn't done a lot of good."

"After what happened at Plum Creek last night," Rachel said, "I'll bet that Mr. Dodge could raise an Irish army to go after those Sioux Indians."

"And what good would that do?" Megan asked. "The Indians would just ride away and not be found while the Irish would tromp around until they froze to death."

"I wouldn't freeze," Victor said. "I'd wear me gloves and a buffalo coat like Mr. Hood. I'd have me a skin cap and leather breeches too! And a big rifle."

"I'm sure that you would," Megan said tolerantly. "But I still think that hunting Indians is best left to the professionals."

Megan was just about to say more when the tent flap was thrown open and Assistant Chief Surveyor Glenn Gilchrist strode inside. The handsome and well-dressed young survey engineer tied the flap down to keep out the blowing snow, then dusted himself off and removed his hat. Megan knew at once something was wrong because of the way his knuckles whitened as he wrung the brim of his hat.

"What's wrong?" she asked, stepping away from her unpacking. "More Indian troubles?"

"Yes." Glenn cleared his throat and came over to Megan. He placed his hat down on a packing crate and gently took her hands into his own. "Megan, I'm afraid that I have some bad news."

Her heart froze. "Say it quickly."

"Your family was on that supply train that was supposed to arrive here from Omaha this afternoon."

"Aileen, Jenny, and Liam!" Megan staggered backward, hand flying to her mouth. "What . . ."

"They're all right."

Glenn took her arm and led her over to a card table and chairs while Rachel and Victor crowded around. "Please sit, Megan."

"I'd rather stand. Rachel, *you* sit."

But Rachel shook her head. She had been in love with Liam ever since he had saved her life during that Omaha flood. "I'll be all right. I just want to hear the rest, Mr. Gilchrist."

"It's my fault they were on board that train," Glenn began, meeting her eyes.

"Your fault?"

"Yes. It was a supply train and normally would have carried a number of workmen back from Omaha. But for some reason, there were none and so when Liam telegraphed me saying that they wanted to rejoin us here in Cheyenne, I thought—sure."

"But why!" Megan cried. "Why ever would Aileen be foolish enough to come out here! It's no place for a child or a delicate woman like my sister."

Glenn gathered her hands into his own. "Megan, listen to me. Your sister *insisted* that she join you. She refused to take your charity any longer. And with her business failure, well, I thought that it might—"

"*You* thought!" Megan tore her hands free and jumped to her feet. "Glenn Gilchrist, what right did you have to presume to decide things for my family!"

"None at all. But your brother and sister decided they were coming—by wagon if necessary. I just helped them find a safer, easier way."

"Well, as it turned out, it wasn't one bit safe."

"No," Glenn admitted, "it wasn't. But that's one of the only times an entire supply train has been attacked.

If they were determined to make the journey out here, that was the best way."

"Where are they now?" Rachel interrupted.

"After the train was derailed, Liam managed to get Aileen and Jenny away. They showed up back at Plum Creek and by then the telegraph lines were repaired. We just received the message a few minutes ago that they are injured but are insisting that they be allowed to come here and join us."

"The nearest hospital is back in Omaha!"

"I know," Glenn said. "And that's why I'm here now. I took matters into my own hands when I arranged their passage on that supply train. Now, it's up to you."

"Megan?" Rachel said anxiously. "Thaddeus . . . I mean, Dr. Wiseman is as good as any they'd find at the Omaha hospital and he's a lot closer to Plum Creek."

"I know that," Megan said, "but what will Aileen and Jenny do out here! I don't think that my sister has any idea how rough it can be in a construction camp."

"Then she needs to find out."

Megan raised her eyebrows. "And what about the child? Jenny is only five years old. Does she also need to 'find out'?"

Tears sprang to Rachel's pretty blue eyes. She was a short and buxom little blonde that attracted a lot of business for Megan. And now, her feelings were bruised for no good reason.

"I'm sorry," Megan said. "It's just that I think Aileen would be shocked and very unhappy out here living in a tent and—"

"Excuse me," Glenn interrupted, "but weren't you living in some pretty rough conditions in that Irish shantytown while waiting for spring?"

"It wasn't so bad," Megan said defensively. "There were more families. Here, it's just hundreds of rough, women-starved men and a few of the worst kind of women."

Glenn consulted his Ingersol pocket watch. "Listen, Megan. I promised that I'd send your answer right back to Plum Creek. I think that Aileen will never forgive you if you tell the railroad that you do not want her to come farther west. And Liam will come either way."

Megan pushed past them and walked to the tent's entrance. She tugged the canvas flap aside and stared out into the driving snow. "They'll be miserable out here."

"That should be *their* choice!" Glenn lowered his voice and came to stand beside Megan. "This storm will pass and the sun will be shining tomorrow. But today, your sister needs a good doctor. I've already spoken with Thaddeus and he said he would be ready to do whatever was necessary."

Megan turned and looked up at Glenn. "I don't see that I can possibly send them back to Omaha under these circumstances. I couldn't bear to remain here while Aileen was suffering."

"Then I should wire them to come along?"

Megan dipped her chin. "How long will it take?"

"A replacement train will be arriving at Plum Creek in another hour and"—Glenn studied his watch and mentally worked the Union Pacific's timetable—"fifteen minutes. I know that a repair crew is at the accident site replacing the damaged track and clearing the wreckage. That will take at least three or four hours."

"How long?"

Glenn frowned. He was an engineer and liked to be precise in his figures and estimates. "Plum Creek is two hundred and fifty miles from here. I'd say that your family will arrive about this time tomorrow."

"And Aileen will be without benefit of a medical doctor until then!"

"No," Glenn said quickly. "What we are proposing to do is to rush a train eastward with Dr. Wiseman and a relief crew within the hour. Believe me, it will be going full steam and will meet the westbound train before this day is over. Joshua Hood and his men will have horses on that train and they'll be dispatched to pick up Eagle Wing's trail. The doctor, of course, will attend to your sister and anyone else who needs medical attention."

"I'm going," Megan said, untying her apron. "I'd go crazy waiting here."

"I expected that would be your answer. I wish that I could accompany you."

"I'd also like to go along," Rachel said.

"I'd prefer that you stay here and oversee the saloon," Megan answered. "Glenn, you didn't mention that Liam was hurt."

"He's not. I specifically had the telegraph operator at this end inquire and he is fine."

Megan forced a smile and laid her hand on Rachel's shoulder. "I promise that we'll be back by tomorrow."

"All right," Rachel said. "When you see Liam, tell him to come right by and I'll pour him our best."

"I'll do that," Megan promised as she hurried for her heavy woolen overcoat.

Fifteen minutes later Megan was saying good-bye to Glenn at Cheyenne's temporary train depot. "I'm sorry that I became so upset with you, Glenn."

"Me too. But under the circumstances, I should have expected it. I had no right to try and surprise you with the arrival of your family. But Liam's telegram said that they wanted it to be a surprise."

"Oh," Megan said, "it is! I just can't believe that they were lucky enough to survive. How many men were killed by the Sioux?"

"At least five repairmen on the first hand-pump cart. That includes poor Will Thomas. Another ten have been accounted for on the train that was derailed."

Megan shook her head. "How did Liam, Aileen, and Jenny possibly manage to escape?"

"I don't know," Glenn said. "The telegram was very brief. It just laid out the fact that they had arrived in Plum Creek injured but alive."

"And it didn't say how injured?"

Glenn shook his head. "No, but if they were in critical shape, I think the telegram would have said so."

"I pray that's true," Megan whispered. She raised up on her toes and kissed Glenn's lips, a quick kind of I'm sorry kiss, and then she climbed onto the train and was ushered back to the passenger coach.

It was crowded with Union Pacific workmen and every last one of them was armed with a rifle. At the far end of the coach, Dr. Thaddeus Wiseman rose to his feet. He was a huge, gentle man standing six feet five inches tall with broad shoulders and hair as amber-red as Megan's. Thaddeus motioned her to come and join him and Megan hurried up the aisle with the smell of unwashed workmen filling the cramped car.

"Thaddeus!"

He wrapped an arm around her shoulders. "Don't worry, my dear. I'm sure that they would have let me know if it was truly an emergency concerning your sister and niece."

Megan laid her head against the doctor's chest and fought back tears. Thaddeus had asked her to marry him as had Glenn and even the wild and dashing Indian scout and Union Pacific's head buffalo hunter, Joshua Hood. They were all dear and brave men of character but very different. But for some reason, Megan found it easiest to drop her defenses with Thaddeus. Perhaps because he was a wonderful doctor and very sympathetic to both emotional as well as physical suffering. He had large, lovely brown eyes and when Thaddeus spoke about his horrifying experience as a Union Army battlefield surgeon, Megan could see how much this man had suffered and that suffering had beautified rather than scarred his great soul.

"I don't know how badly she was hurt," Megan whispered. "She might have taken an arrow."

"No, I'm sure that is not the case."

"And what about poor Jenny? Can you imagine what a small child like that . . ."

"My dear lovely woman," Thaddeus said, "don't you know how very, very resilient children are? I would be willing to wager that the child hasn't suffered nearly as much emotional trauma as her mother."

Megan smiled. "When you went to medical school, did they train you to speak so wisely?"

Thaddeus chuckled. "I'm not wise in the least, Megan. It's just that I've been much around children. I like them."

Megan sat up and looked out the window. "They say that it doesn't snow in the warm valleys of California."

"So I've heard."

"That's where I dream of settling." Megan waited and when the doctor had no response, she looked up at him and said, "What about you? How does the sound of California strike your fancy, Thaddeus? What do you think of when that word comes to your mind?"

"California," he said, closing his eyes and stroking his handlebar mustache that flowed into his luxurious beard. "Well now, Megan, let's see. When I envision California I see Spanish missions fallen into ruin. I smell the pines of the mighty Sierra Nevada Mountains which the valiant Chinese laborers are even now struggling to conquer for our Central Pacific rivals."

Thaddeus grinned. "I also confess that California brings to mind golden nuggets as big as chicken's eggs that glimmer in crystal-clear mountain streams. And over all that, I can hear the raucous cry of sea gulls as they squabble about the wicked and notorious Barbary Coast with its swaggering sailors, the children of every great seafaring nation in the world."

Thaddeus opened his eyes. "That's what California brings to my mind."

Megan laughed. "You possess a lively and vivid imagination. All I see is warm valleys, flowers in wintertime, fruit to be plucked from the vine the year around, flowery meadows, sun-drenched valleys, and happy people."

"Do you see me, Megan. More to the point, do you see us walking in those great warm valleys together?"

Megan's smile died. "I see . . . I don't know. Maybe."

"Yes," he said, "maybe."

Thaddeus turned to look out the window. Megan could see the reflection of his face and his expression was somber. What was he thinking? He had already proposed marriage once. Would he ever again, and if he did, would her answer be the same?

"Thaddeus," she said in a low voice meant for him alone. "I think I can see you and me together in California. I'm not sure, but someone is there because I'm never alone. Someone big and strong and gentle."

He turned back to her and when he looked deeply into her eyes, Megan kissed his lips, not caring in the least that others might be watching. And afterward, she leaned against his broad shoulder and gazed out the window at the blowing snow. She could not imagine how terrible the train wreck must have been for poor Aileen. Perhaps now her sweet but foolish older sister would understand why it was far better to have remained in Omaha where there was nothing to fear.

CHAPTER
4

"Megan? Megan!"

Both she and Thaddeus must have been dozing because they each awoke with a start to look up and see Joshua Hood. He was frowning.

"If I'd known that my girl was sleeping in another man's arms, I'd have left my men and horses in that freezing boxcar one hell of a lot sooner."

Megan rubbed sleep from her eyes and sat up straight. "Hello, Joshua. I'm sorry you've been cold."

"I'm not," Thaddeus said flatly.

Joshua barked a loud laugh. "Mind if I squeeze in between the pair of you and thaw out for a little while?"

"I do," Thaddeus said, only half teasing. "As you well know, I am one of your many admirers, Joshua, but that would be pushing even my limits. Besides, this seat is full."

"Then I'll take this one," he said, whipping off his hat and slapping it against his thigh to send a spray of icy water across the floor. "It's just nice to be among friends again."

And they *were* friends, Megan thought. Joshua was outrageous and as bold as brass, but he was fun, brave, and a good man. And despite all his rough edges and bravado, Megan had once seen him cradle a bullet-wounded Indian child and weep for the hatred that pitted men against innocent children.

"Joshua, can you tell us anything more about Plum Creek?" Thaddeus asked.

Joshua drew out one of his black and twisted cheroots that Megan detested. He struck a match, lit the damn thing, and inhaled deeply but was courteous enough to blow his smoke at the ceiling where it hung over their heads like a storm cloud.

"I read the last dispatch that the train scooped up passin' through the Lodge Pole station about an hour ago. You might both find that to be of some interest."

"It would be," Megan said, leaning forward anxiously.

"The message said that eight more men died on that supply train, most of them scalped. The engineer was impaled on the throttle and the fireman was crushed under the same load of wood that the Sioux used to warm themselves after the wreck."

Megan paled. She glanced at Thaddeus who said, "Any idea how Liam, Miss O'Connell, and her daughter managed to escape with their lives?"

"Nope." Joshua leaned back in his chair. "But I hear tell that they arrived at Plum Creek early this morning on a Sioux war pony."

Megan's jaw dropped. "That means that . . ."

"It means that Liam killed at least one Sioux warrior," Joshua said with a chuckle. "Hard to imagine considering what he was when I first saw him in Omaha eighteen months ago. Liam was green . . . boy was he green! Didn't know nothin'! Couldn't shoot, ride a horse, read a track . . . nothin'!"

"He has certainly changed," Megan agreed, knowing how much this chief Union Pacific scout was responsible for the good changes that had occurred to her young brother. "He's still pretty wild and—"

"Aw, hell, Megan! If a man hasn't got some wildness in him, he might as well be gelded and put out to pasture."

"Mr. Hood," Thaddeus said sternly, noting how Megan's cheeks colored with embarrassment. "Please remember the company we keep."

"Oh, yeah. Sorry, Miss Megan. Damn sorry."

"You aren't sorry at all," she said. "One of your great joys in life is to try and shock the ladies."

Joshua grinned boyishly and did not deny Megan's charge.

"Tell me, Joshua," Thaddeus said, "have you ever heard of Chief Eagle Wing?"

"He's not a chief," Joshua said, pulling his eyes from Megan. "He's just a hot-blooded buck that led a successful raid on the Union Pacific. I imagine his standing has gone up with the Sioux, but he's not a chief."

"You've actually met him?"

"Yes," Joshua said. "I lived with Red Cloud's people once, but that was before this railroad began to cut across their hunting grounds and sever the migrating trail of the buffalo."

"You sound as if . . . as if *we* are at fault here," Thaddeus said.

"It's not a matter of their fault or our fault," Joshua reasoned, "it's just the way of life. Weak animals fall prey to stronger animals. Stronger people have always conquered weaker people. The Sioux would be the first to admit that they drove the Cheyenne and Arapaho off their best buffalo hunting grounds."

"And now it's our turn to be the bully?" Megan challenged him with her eyes. "Is that what you're saying?"

Both men looked at her with surprise. Thaddeus spoke first. "Megan, is that what you think we are—bullies?"

"I don't know," Megan finally confessed. "Especially in light of what just happened to those poor trainmen who were scalped. All I'm saying is that my ancestors hail from Ireland where we have a history of bloody oppression by the English and I cannot, in conscience, blame a people for fighting for their land and their way of life."

Joshua raised his rough hands and clapped loudly enough to turn heads.

"Hush!" Megan said with embarrassment as she grabbed his hands and pinned them together.

"All right, I'll behave," Joshua promised, grinning around his stinking cheroot. "But your sentiments echo mine only I couldn't have put them into such fine words."

Megan blushed at the simple, heartfelt compliment. "If you catch those Indians, Joshua, will you try to kill them?"

Joshua's grin faded and he looked outside, his face turning as bleak and wintery as the landscape.

"Mr. Hood?"

"I heard her question, Thaddeus." Joshua turned back from the window. "I just can't give you a firm answer on that, Megan."

"Why not?"

"Well, it's like this." Joshua scowled and struggled hard to put his thoughts into words. "You see, some people look at things sort of either yea or nay. Yes or no. Black or white. But I've this troublesome habit of examining everything from everyone's point of view."

"There's nothing wrong with that," Thaddeus said.

"Well, maybe and maybe not. But I view the Indian's way of looking at this just clear as a quartz stone in shallow water. The Iron Horse is bringing more white men who shoot the buffalo for food but also for hides and sport. There are still a hell of a lot of buffalo, but those Indians are smart and they know that the white men will eventually kill them all if they aren't stopped."

"But we can't be stopped," Megan argued.

"I know it, Thaddeus knows it, and everyone on this train knows it. But you can't tell Red Cloud or old Sitting Bull or Crazy Horse that they might as well give up their land without a fight."

"We had a truce," Thaddeus said. "You and General Dodge had a truce with the Sioux leaders."

"That's right," Joshua said. "And then First Lieutenant Edward Hale out of Fort Kearney attacked and slaughtered a group of Sioux hunters and any chance we had for peace vanished like smoke in the wind."

"He was under Captain Medgar Taney's command, was he not?" Thaddeus asked with obvious distaste.

"Yep."

"That fool got himself and his soldiers slaughtered for nothing. Taney *deserved* to die, but his troopers didn't. I had the sad task of examining their mutilated bodies." Thaddeus patted Megan. "I'm sorry to have brought that back to memory."

"That's quite all right," Megan said. "The only thing nearly as inexcusable as murder is to allow it to be repeated over and over again. They avenge their dead, we reciprocate and avenge our dead, and so it tragically goes around and around. Joshua, that's why you need to stop it now!"

"I can't let Eagle Wing and his followers go unpunished," Joshua said quietly.

"But why! It has to stop with one side or the other. Both sides have blood on their hands. Why not forgive if it brings an end to the bloodshed?"

"Because it *wouldn't* end the bloodshed," Joshua tried to explain. "In fact, it might even give the Sioux the idea that we've lost the will to fight. That would be the wrong kind of a message."

Megan shook her head. "So there's no solution?"

"I don't think so," Joshua admitted. "You see, one of the biggest problems is that the Indians don't have a single leader, like we now have in President Andrew Johnson. That means that you can make a peace with one Sioux chief but it'll probably be ignored by the others."

"Yes," Thaddeus said, "I've heard that before. But dammit, why can't there be a gathering of chiefs and Army officers? And then some general consensus reached?"

"Does consensus mean sort of an understanding?"

"Yes. I'm sorry."

"That's all right," Joshua said. "What you say makes sense to white folks, but not to the Indian. In our own

Bill of Rights and Constitution we have a lot of fancy words telling us we can be individuals. But the Indians, well, they don't have it down on paper, but they do a lot better than we at treating each other like individuals. Every single one of them makes up his own mind on things. And if they don't all agree, then the individual has the right to do what he wants."

"It seems to me that they are carrying the individual rights thing too far," Megan decided after a moment's consideration.

"That might be the case," Joshua said, "but that's how they've always done things and it's worked for 'em across generations. I think most of 'em would rather die true to their way of life than change because we tell 'em they must."

"And so," Thaddeus intoned, "they are as helpless as the buffalo caught in the unwavering sights of a Sharps rifle."

"That's about the size of it," Joshua agreed as the three of them lapsed into a long and troubled silence.

Their train passed through the sites of the now mostly abandoned construction towns that had once teemed with Irish workmen and where the money and the whiskey had flowed around the clock. At most of these sites, there was nothing at all to give any indication as to the former presence of a town unless it was the piles of rusty tin cans, bedsprings, and broken, useless pieces of wood and iron.

At Julesberg, the only spot where the Union Pacific line actually touched the Colorado Territory, a fine young man named Sean O'Sullivan had caught pneumonia and asked for Megan to hold his hand during his final hours and sing him a few Irish songs as he passed into eternity.

At Big Spring, the Indian child wounded by Army bullets was attended to by Thaddeus, pronounced fit to travel and then Joshua had returned him to his people with half the Irish construction crews cheering and the other half cursing.

At Ogallalla, an estimated eight hundred mounted warriors had arrived and defiantly pulled up a mile of surveyor's stakes while the helpless surveyors watched.

At Brule, the temperature had dropped to thirty-seven degrees below zero during a blizzard that froze the train to its tracks and caused Megan's tent to become as brittle as glass.

Now, all gone. The good and the bad reduced to a few scattered and well picked over piles of rusting junk.

"Excuse me," Joshua said, "I'd better check in on my men and horses to see if they're frozen solid yet."

"I hope they're not," the doctor said. "If so, bring them in and we'll thaw them out beside our potbellied stove—the men, that is—not the horses."

"Sure." Joshua laughed as he strode away.

"Quite a man," Thaddeus said, watching Megan closely. "Much deeper than he appears."

"Joshua is unschooled but he's very intelligent." Megan saw Joshua turn at the back door of the coach to brazenly blow her a kiss a moment before he ducked outside and was gone. "But he does have a certain flair."

"Yes," Thaddeus said, "I've noticed. I'm sure that he is quite a ladies' man."

Megan looked back at the doctor. Had she detected a note of cynicism? "Are you jealous?"

"Ha! Of course I am! Joshua Hood is handsome and has a rough frontier charm that I couldn't emulate if I practiced for a hundred years."

Megan took the doctor's hand. "You have your own qualities, Thaddeus, and they are very, very dear to me."

He started to say something but the conductor entered their coach and called, "North Platte. Prepare to stop for one hour."

"One hour!" Megan exclaimed. "Why in heavens would we do that when Aileen and perhaps others are wounded?"

"I don't know," Thaddeus said. "But since when does the Union Pacific answer to our questions?"

"Never," Megan said with resignation. "I just hate the thought of waiting here an entire hour knowing that Aileen and Jenny need my help."

"What about Liam?"

"He hasn't needed anyone's help since he was about ten years old," Megan said. "Well, at least he doesn't *think* he needs help. Actually, the best thing in the world for him would be Rachel."

"But he doesn't see that."

"No. For some reason, the harder Rachel tried to attract Liam, the less interest he showed. And frankly, she is far better off without him."

"That's a rather hard assessment about your own brother."

"I know," Megan said, "but Liam has a hard head. He's not bad but he sure manages to be difficult. The only one that I've ever seen him listen to is Joshua. He thinks Joshua is . . . well, like a god that can do no wrong."

"That's unfortunate for them both."

"Why do you say that?"

Thaddeus shrugged his huge shoulders. "No man is infallible or godlike. Sooner or later, even our dashing and intelligent Joshua Hood will disappoint your brother. When that happens, it will have a devastating effect—perhaps on them both."

"I just hope," Megan said, "that when Joshua makes that mistake, it isn't fatal because of the Sioux."

"I'm sure it won't be," Thaddeus said with reassurance. "And perhaps everything I've just said was balderdash. In fact, I'm certain that it was."

But Megan knew better. Joshua was impressive and Liam idolized the man and thought he could do no wrong. He talked constantly about Joshua and even mimicked his rough frontier mannerisms. The last time that Megan had seen her brother, he'd worn a gun just like Joshua and the same leather buckskins. No, Megan thought, it wasn't entirely healthy the way that Liam idolized Joshua Hood.

As they neared North Platte, Megan pushed those troubled thoughts out of her head and gazed upon the frontier railroad town with interest. Unlike all the other towns where she'd once staked her tent along with the construction camp followers, North Platte had actually survived and even flourished. Big canvas tents like her own had been replaced by permanent rock and wooden homes and businesses. The town was still rather modest but Megan could see several buildings that were being framed and that told her that North Platte was betting on a future.

Yesterday's storm had passed and the sky was cold but clear and Megan's eyes followed the snaking North

Platte into the distance, realizing that its previous miles and miles of cottonwood trees had been axed and now served as the railroad ties that this coach was resting upon.

"The river is frozen solid already," Thaddeus said. "It appears to have fallen since we were here last winter."

"I think that it is down a little," Megan agreed, recalling how often she had stood outside of her tent that long last winter and watched as the Casement brothers oversaw the building of the bridge over the Platte as well as the first phases of construction on a huge, granite twenty-stall roundhouse, a blacksmith and machine shop. It was clear that North Platte, like Cheyenne, loomed large in the Union Pacific's future plans.

When they pulled into the train yards and depot at North Platte, Joshua came striding back into the coach with a grin on his face. "Megan, this is the end of the line for you and the doc."

"What do you mean?"

"I mean that we're ready to meet the train carrying Aileen, Jenny, and Liam."

Megan shot out of her seat. "It's here!"

"Yep."

Megan almost shoved Joshua down the aisle of the passenger coach and she was standing on the unloading platform before they even ground to a stop.

"Take it easy," Joshua said, grabbing her arm to keep her from leaping onto the depot. "Getting your leg broke ain't going to bring your family here any sooner."

"No," Megan said anxiously. "I suppose not."

But the very instant that the train stopped, Megan was the first one off.

"Megan!"

She turned to see Liam striding toward her and was shocked by how thin he appeared and how his gait now had a hitch, the result of his hip being shattered by a white man's bullet. But Liam was grinning loosely and even before she threw herself into his arms, Megan could smell the whiskey.

"Good to see you," Liam said, pushing her back and grinning. "You better realize that you're hugging North Platte's biggest celebrity."

"Is that so?"

"Yep! I killed at least four Sioux and stole the last one's pony so that Aileen and little Jenny could escape with their scalps. And I got the dead Indian's lance and pony to prove it!"

"My," Megan said, noting her brother's flush cheeks and seeing how proud he was of himself. "You have turned into quite a man."

Liam actually blushed. He puffed up tall and smiled so hard his face looked as if it might split across the middle.

"Howdy, Liam."

"Mr. Hood!" Liam's expression did a complete change. "Why, Mr. Hood! I never expected you to come all the way to congratulate me! Jezus! What a—"

"Actually," Joshua said, "I did want to congratulate you. I haven't heard any of the details but . . ."

"Well, let me tell you both all about it!"

"Liam," Megan interrupted, "this is Dr. Thaddeus Wiseman. He's come to treat Aileen, Jenny, and any other survivors who might require his medical attention."

A shadow of disappointment crossed Liam's pinched face. But he recovered quickly. "Sure, Megan. Follow me."

"Wait a minute. How is Aileen!" Megan cried, grabbing her brother by the arm and dragging him to a stop.

"They'll live," Liam said, shrugging her arm away. "And that's a hell of a lot more than I can say for anybody else except myself who was on that death train."

Liam's lungs expanded and he threw his shoulders back. "Mr. Hood, all them other fools panicked and ran outside to be slaughtered like sheep. But not me! Oh, no! I'm way too smart."

"I expect so," Joshua said quietly.

Megan turned away in disgust. She wanted to strike out at Liam. It was clear to her that a close brush with death hadn't changed him in the least. And hero or not, he was still insensitive and obnoxious.

CHAPTER

5

Megan saw her niece first. Little Jenny was sitting on the front porch step of a boardinghouse with several other children. She looked perfectly happy and normal. Megan was flooded with relief.

"Jenny!"

When the child looked up and saw her aunt Megan, she let out a squeal and came racing to Megan.

"How are you?" Megan gushed, sweeping the child into her arms and joyfully whirling her around.

"I'm fine. But I have a big goose egg on my head. You can really feel it."

"I can see it," Megan said, noting the large knot just over the child's left ear. Megan gently touched the lump. "Oh, that is something! Thaddeus?"

The doctor introduced himself and then said, "May I have a look, Jenny?"

"Mmm-hmmm."

After a moment Thaddeus said, "Well, pretty girl, you're just fine."

"I know, but my mommy doesn't feel well."

"Then we'd better go inside to cheer her up," Megan said, carrying Jenny into the boardinghouse.

"She's in the second room on the right," Liam said,

hanging back until they'd passed into the room where his sister lay resting in bed.

The door was open and when Megan stepped inside, she hardly recognized her sister. Aileen was so pale and drawn and she seemed to have aged ten years since last they'd seen each other. Her sister was staring out the window and there were dark circles under her eyes.

"Mommy! Mommy! Look who's come to visit us!"

Aileen turned her head on her pillow and when she saw Megan, her face was transformed with happiness.

Megan set Jenny down and rushed to her sister. "Aileen, welcome to the wild West."

"Wild is right," Aileen replied as she clutched Megan's hand like a lifeline. "We were hoping to surprise you but never thought something like this would happen."

"It *does* happen," Megan said. "The trains are attacked often but rarely with such success. Aileen, I'm so sorry about what happened."

"Not as sorry as I am," Aileen whispered. "Megan, I apologize for all the trouble and worry I've caused."

"That's not important." Megan turned to motion Thaddeus closer. "Aileen, this is my dear friend, Dr. Thaddeus Wiseman."

"Yes, you've written about him quite often," Aileen said, giving him both her hand and a warm smile. "And he's every bit as handsome as you described him to be."

Thaddeus glanced at Megan but it was clear that he was pleased by the remark. "And, my dear, you are as lovely and delicate as a rose in the springtime."

"Oh, he *is* sweet," Aileen whispered, hanging on to Thaddeus's hand longer than was necessary.

"Now," Thaddeus said, carefully extracting his great

paw, "I'd better examine you, Mrs. Fox."

"Miss O'Connell," Aileen corrected. "Just like my sister, I lost my husband during the Omaha flood. And like Megan, I've reclaimed my Irish maiden name."

"And quite properly so," Thaddeus said, removing his coat and handing it to Megan before he opened his medical kit and removed a stethoscope. "This might be a little cold so I'll warm it in my hand for a moment."

Megan tried to smile but it wasn't easy. Aileen's fragile appearance really was shocking. Her sister had never been robust but now she looked downright sickly and although they were both taller than most women, Megan guessed that her sister could not weigh more than 110 pounds.

"There," Thaddeus said, looking into Aileen's large, sunken brown eyes. "I think this will be warm enough. I need to listen to your breathing."

"But it's my *ribs* that are broken."

"Yes, but you sound to me as if you are having some difficulty breathing. Isn't that so?"

"I have some phlegm in my lungs and I've been coughing quite a lot," Aileen admitted. "Last night was terrible and there were times that I thought we would either freeze to death or be murdered by the Sioux."

"I wouldn't have let that happen," Liam said defensively from the doorway where he stood watching. "There wasn't a minute that I was worried about the Sioux."

Thaddeus turned to Liam. "I'm sure that you're eager to talk to Mr. Hood about those Indians. He's going to be heading out after them."

"He is?"

"Yes."

"Then I'm going with him."

Aileen cried out in protest. "No, please, Liam! It's a miracle that we're even alive. Don't push your luck."

Liam sneered. "Hell, it wasn't luck. I understand Indians and Mr. Hood will be needing all the good men he can find if he intends to track down and kill that bunch of murdering redskins."

"I wish you'd stay with us," Megan said. "As soon as Aileen is able, we'll be returning her and Jenny to Omaha and—"

"No!" Aileen protested before she broke into a deep, racking cough that frightened Megan.

"Thaddeus, do you have anything for that terrible cough?"

"Some plasters and hot vapors should help, but her lungs will not clear themselves overnight, Megan."

"However long it takes, that's how long I'll stay," Megan said, taking Aileen's thin hand.

When the coughing spell ended, Aileen was very pale and her eyes were wet with tears. "Please," she begged, "I can't go back to Omaha. Jenny and I want to go west with you!"

Megan could see that argument, given Aileen's feeble condition, was out of the question. "All right," she said, intending to take up the matter again when her sister was stronger, "we can talk about that later."

"I won't change my mind. And Jenny wants to be with you as well. Please, Megan!"

Despite all good sense, Megan nodded because she knew Aileen well enough to understand that her sister could not survive any longer without her assistance.

"Very well. We'll stay together."

Now tears really did well up in Aileen's eyes and slid down her cheeks. Thaddeus, bless his heart, had his silk handkerchief out along with a kind, understanding smile. "Now that all this other business is settled," he said with a wink, "can you ladies please allow the doctor to conduct his examination?"

"This is where I get out," Liam said, turning to leave. "I'll see you later."

"Are you going to look for Joshua?"

"Yep! He may be gettin' his scouts ready to ride. I need to borrow a rifle. And a saddle for that Sioux Indian pony that carried Aileen and Jenny into Plum Creek."

Before Megan could protest, Liam was gone and she could hear his footsteps stumping down the boardinghouse hallway.

Megan started to go after him but Thaddeus stopped her. "Megan, I'd prefer that you remain here to assist and to keep us company."

Megan had only taken a couple of steps but now she retraced them to the bedside. Of course Thaddeus would need her help. He might have to do a fairly complete examination and Aileen would be upset enough without a woman's presence.

"Now, Miss O'Connell," Thaddeus said, "if you'll . . ."

"Please, Doctor. Call me Aileen."

"All right, Aileen, tell me where you hurt the most."

"My ribs," she said without hesitation. "I think several are broken. I've also got a nasty cut on the back of my scalp."

"Let's have a look at that first. I saw Jenny's head and she took a very hard rap but the skin wasn't broken and she appears to have recovered completely."

"She's as tough as her aunt Megan," Aileen said proudly. "I wish that I had their strength and resiliency. But I just don't. Megan takes after our father. Father was tall and strong, not quite as tall and strong as you, Doctor, but he did have a robust constitution."

"That's good. Now, if you—"

"But Mother, bless her soul, was always delicate. She died when we were quite young. But I guess that Megan must have told you all about our childhood."

"Not really," Thaddeus said with a grin. "Are you always so talkative, Aileen?"

Aileen blushed. "I'm sorry! There's just something about you that instills . . . trust. And makes a woman want to confide. Isn't that right, Megan?"

"It is," she heard herself say, amazed because Aileen was usually quite reserved with people until she knew them well.

"All right, ladies," Thaddeus said, "any more of this sugary pap and I'll become swell-headed and forced to buy a new hat. Now, Aileen, let's take a look at that scalp. Just turn your head a little to the right."

"Ouch!"

"Yes," he said, gently parting the hair, "I can see that you did indeed receive a very serious laceration. What did you strike this on?"

"I don't know. It happened when the coach overturned and rolled. Jenny and I were tossed around and we both lost consciousness for a few moments. Perhaps even longer."

Aileen's eyes grew misty again and her voice became husky with emotion. "When I awoke, the train was on fire and—"

"Please," Megan said, taking her sister's hand, "you're getting all upset. Just relax and let Thaddeus do his job."

Thaddeus peered intently at the wound. "It's rather deep," he said finally, "and it should be cleaned out and sutured."

"You mean stitched!" Aileen shrank into the bed with horror.

"I'm afraid so."

"Please, Doctor. I don't care if you clean it out, but it would hurt something terrible if you used a needle and I'm not very good at suffering pain."

She threw a beseeching look at her sister. "Am I, Megan?"

"No," Megan agreed, "you're not. But you are brave and that's why I know that you'll allow Dr. Wiseman to do whatever he thinks is best."

Aileen nodded, barely.

"Let's take a look at those ribs now," Thaddeus said, wanting to divert her attention away from the thought of sutures.

Thaddeus rolled down the coverlet and said, "Aileen, I'm going to need to have you pull up your gown a little so that I can see your ribs."

"Pull it up?" Aileen's eyes widened and she glanced at Megan, looking for help.

"Just a little over the ribs," Megan said reassuringly. "Come on now, he *is* a doctor and those ribs must be examined."

Aileen gulped and looked quickly away. It occurred to Megan that her sister might never have seen a doctor before and that certainly no man had seen her exposed ribs.

"Why don't you help her?" Thaddeus suggested, stepping back and moving over to the doorway to wait.

When Megan saw her sister's ribs, she had to stifle a sharp intake of breath. The ribs were black and there was a great deal of puffiness. "Thaddeus?"

He came over quickly and Megan watched to see if she could read his reaction, but there was none. "All right, Aileen," he said, "I'm going to palpitate these ribs a little and it is going to hurt, but the hurt won't last but a few moments and then this will all be over."

Aileen nodded and bit her lower lip. When Thaddeus began to press down on the ribs, Aileen buried a cry in her throat.

"Broken," Thaddeus said to himself as his fingers lightly tap-danced across Aileen's purplish ribs like a pianist testing a new keyboard. "Broken. Broken. Broken and . . . yes, also broken."

Thaddeus tugged up her gown a little and examined the other ribs. "This set is quite lovely," he said in an attempt at humor that Aileen missed completely.

Aileen sniffled and accepted the handkerchief to dry her eyes. "Well, Doctor?"

"Five broken ribs and perhaps some sternum damage."

"Is that bad?"

"It's not good but it's certainly not fatal. I'll need to wrap those ribs and keep them immobilized. And Aileen will require plenty of bed rest."

"Then we'll remain in North Platte a good long while," Megan said, trying to hide her disappointment.

"That won't be necessary," Thaddeus replied. "I

wouldn't allow your sister to climb back on that Indian pony and ride, but we can safely transport her on the train."

"To Cheyenne," Aileen said, looking right into Megan's eyes. "That's what we've just agreed upon. Isn't it, Megan?"

"Yes," Megan said hesitantly.

Aileen sniffled and then brightened. "I'm sorry for being such a bother but I swear that I'll make it up to you! In a few weeks, I'll be able to work in your saloon."

"*Our* saloon," Megan corrected, because the money that had allowed her to get started had come from a joint settlement for the death of their husbands during that flood. Back then, Megan had convinced the Union Pacific that she would generate a blizzard of negative publicity for the railroad if they didn't agree to at least offer some compensation to the survivors who'd lost their households and family members in that terrible Omaha flooding.

"All right, then, *our* saloon," Aileen said. "And I will be a good worker and try not to complain."

"I'm not worried. You're a grown woman. But what about Jenny? What kind of a life will it be for a child out at the end-of-track? There are rough men out there, Aileen. They cuss and they fight. They get drunk, gamble, and they . . ."

"They what?"

"They whore," Megan said, spitting out the word. "The railroad life turns a lot of very good men into terrible sinners."

Aileen blushed. "I know that."

"And you'll have men lusting for you," Megan said,

embarrassed because of Thaddeus's presence but determined to get it all out so that Aileen would understand exactly what was in store for her if she traveled on to Cheyenne and then raced the rails westward. "Some will say things that will make your cheeks turn red but they will not lay a hand on a lady—unless they are drunk. And then other men would beat them to within an inch of their lives."

"I'm glad to hear of that," Aileen said, a little breathlessly.

"Jenny will see things that a child oughtn't see," Megan persisted.

"And what do you think she saw in the shantytown at Omaha?"

"All right," Megan conceded. "But she'll have to be watched at all times."

"We'll be together," Aileen said. "We'll take care of each other. Even Liam. Why, Megan, when I thought sure that Jenny and I would be found hiding under that overturned train and then scalped, it was Liam who came to save us."

Aileen shook her head with evident amazement. "Can you imagine, our Liam? That's when I fully realized that what is left of our family has to stay together."

Aileen looked at the doctor. "Are you finished?"

"Yes. But I'll need to bind those ribs. And to do that, it would be best if you sat up in bed. Afterward, we'll clean that scalp wound."

"But no sewing."

"For now, no sutures."

Aileen extended her hands to Thaddeus and he pulled her upright. She gasped with pain and her jaw muscles corded but she did not utter a whimper.

Thaddeus was impressed. "You're a stronger woman than you give yourself credit for, Aileen. Much, much stronger."

"No."

"Yes," Thaddeus insisted. "In the terrible circumstances I've heard described about that Indian attack and train wreck, many women would have panicked and been killed. But not you. You kept your wits and survived."

"Thanks to Liam."

"And to your own presence of mind," Thaddeus added. "And I've seen grown men howl with pain when I've examined ribs that weren't as badly broken as your own."

"Really?"

"Yes, really. You handle pain and tragedy much better than you think."

"My, my," Aileen said, her face actually lighting up with pride. "Did you hear that, Megan!"

"Of course I did. And it's true."

A tear slid down Aileen's cheek but she was smiling and Megan had never been prouder of her sister. Maybe, she thought, Aileen would survive the railroad's godless and roaring end-of-line construction camps.

CHAPTER
6

Liam could barely contain his excitement as he hurried down the street. People called his name, shouting congratulations for saving a woman and child from Eagle Wing and his band of bloody Sioux. Liam felt proud enough to bust his britches. When he arrived at the livery where he'd left the Indian pony, he swaggered up to the corral surrounded by a crowd of admiring boys.

"That's quite some Indian pony, ain't he!"

"You bet!" the biggest boy, a strapping lad of about fifteen, said. "Tell us again how you captured him, Mr. O'Connell!"

Liam needed to find Joshua Hood and join the head scout's foray after the Indians but how could he disappoint this legion of young admirers?

He brushed the butt of his six-gun and stretched to his fullest height. "Well, boys, there were four Indians that broke away from the train and came racin' after me, my sister, and little Jenny. I could see that we didn't have a prayer in outrunning them on foot. And furthermore, it was clear that we had to have at least one horse because my sister and niece were hurt."

"So you drew that big gun and shot all four of the Sioux just like bang, bang, bang, bang!" a smaller boy exclaimed.

Liam grinned and mussed the little kid's hair. "Naw, young fella. I shot two right away but the other pair were on me so fast that I had to use my Bowie knife on the first one. I jammed it into his gizzard and he howled like a dyin' dog, then I grabbed up his spear and skewered the last one to a cottonwood tree."

"You mean you sorta nailed him to that tree with his own lance?"

"Yep."

"Wow!" The kids stared at Liam as if he were immortal and it was almost embarrassing until a buck-toothed kid asked, "But how come the other ponies didn't run back to the train and cause the rest of the Indians to come after you?"

Liam blinked. "What do you mean?"

"Well, my pa and I break horses. You separate one from the others, he'll run right back to the band. That's the way it always happens."

The other kids nodded in agreement and looked to Liam for an explanation. "Well," he stammered, his mind groping for a plausible answer, "I . . . I caught them loose ponies and tied them in close to the river. Right down among the thickets where they couldn't be seen."

The kids nodded and Liam was feeling very good about his quick thinking excuse when the buck-toothed boy said, "Then how come you didn't keep *two* of them Indian ponies instead of just this one? Wouldn't it have been easier than you walkin' all the way back to Plum Creek?"

Liam took an instant dislike to the beaver-faced kid. "You'd a had to have been there with all them howlin' devils so close to understood why I hid them other three ponies along the river. And . . . well, my sister was in rough shape and couldn't control this spirited pony so I decided to lead him."

"Yeah," the biggest boy said, "and I'll bet if the Indians would have spotted ya, you'd have sent your sister and that girl off and made a stand to the death. Right, Mr. O'Connell?"

Liam grinned. "You got that right. I was prepared to die to save my sister and poor little Jenny. But the Good Lord has other important plans for me, I reckon. Like going along to make sure that Mr. Hood and his men have a fightin' chance when they overtake Eagle Wing."

"Well," a voice said from the barn, "I'm sure glad to hear that."

Liam spun around and gulped. "Mr. Hood! I didn't know that you were waiting in the barn for me."

"I wasn't," Joshua said. "One of my Arapaho scout's horses was lamed up in the boxcar that brought us to North Platte. I was trying to talk Mr. Watt into either lending us a spare horse or buying one and billing the railroad."

"I couldn't lend an animal," Watt said, scratching his bald pate. "You'd have to have a good animal to go after the Sioux. A good animal is worth sixty dollars."

"Hell, a twenty-dollar horse is good enough," Joshua scoffed.

But Watt pretended not to hear. "And then too, you're probably wanting a saddle, bridle, blanket, and bit."

"Why of course! Even an Arapaho wants a saddle under him if he's going into a fight."

"Well then there you have it," Watt said. "You're

asking for a sixty-dollar animal, a twenty-dollar saddle, bridle, blanket, bit, and all . . . it'll tally up to about a hundred dollars."

"Oh, buffalo balls!" Joshua snorted. "A fifty-dollar outfit is good enough for any of my men."

Watt drew back and did his best to look insulted. "In that case, Mr. Hood, I suggest you go down the street, find an old nag and battered-up saddle, then offer its owner fifty dollars. I'm sure that you can find a horse for that price that is capable of walking a few miles before it goes lame—or quits."

"I don't *have* fifty dollars to spare," Joshua said. "Besides, the horse is needed for railroad business, not my own personal use."

"Then it's the railroad that ought to be here dickering for an outfit," Watt said.

Joshua stepped forward, hands balling at his sides. "Listen here, you. I need a horse right goddamn now! And I'm taking one and if you try and stop me, I'll put a bullet in your foot and you'll be jumpin' around and around in this barnyard like a goddamn cricket!"

"Now wait just a minute here!" Watt cried, backing up with alarm. "What you're proposing is horse stealing!"

"No it ain't!" Joshua stormed. "The Union Pacific will pay for the horse and you'll make a big profit. That ain't stealing a damn thing."

"No money, no damned horse!"

In reply, Joshua hauled out his six-gun, cocked it, and said, "Now, are you going to get me a good horse and outfit so that I can try and bring Eagle Wing and his boys to justice, or am I going to put a bullet through the top of your goddamn foot?"

"I . . . I got a great buckskin!"

"Fine. Let's take a look," Joshua said, winking at Liam. "Maybe if I like him enough, I'll use him myself. What about a saddle?"

"Got an old McClellan."

"My Arapaho will appreciate that very much," Joshua said as he started to turn away.

"I need a saddle and bridle too!" Liam called, hurrying after Joshua. "Mr. Hood, I also have need of a bedroll and rifle."

Joshua turned. "What for?"

"Well . . . well didn't you hear me talkin' to them boys out there by the corral?"

"I heard a pretty good windy. That's what I heard. Four Sioux? Come on, Liam. I'm not some dotin' kid that will believe any old story."

Liam withered under Joshua's penetrating stare. They were both six footers and Joshua wasn't but five or six years Liam's senior, but the man was intimidating.

Liam giggled nervously. "Well now, Mr. Hood. You know how it is. Them kids, they need to look up to men like you and me. What with the killing and stuff by the Indians, it's important that they understand there are white men who'll outfight any Indian."

Joshua snorted. "Is that the way that you see it, Liam?"

"Well, yes, sir! Don't you?"

Joshua shook his head. "Liam, I think it'd be better if you stayed with your sisters. They'll either be going back to Omaha or—"

"No, sir!"

Joshua's face hardened. "What?"

Liam gulped. "Mr. Hood, my sisters are going back to Cheyenne. Dr. Wiseman said it was all right and Aileen doesn't want to return to Omaha."

"What happens to the child?"

"She'll be watched, sir. Jenny is smart and she won't be no bother."

Joshua frowned with evident disapproval. "I don't understand why those ladies would drag a little girl along but I'll take your word for it. Still doesn't change the fact that you ought to stay with your sisters. I got enough seasoned men and you're lookin' pretty damn weak."

"Weak? Weak! Mr. Hood! I'm a little off on my weight, but I'm plenty strong. Haven't you heard what I did yesterday?"

Joshua nodded. "And the tellin' gets better every time I hear the story."

Liam blushed. He could feel the eyes of the young boys burning into him and sense the change in their respectful attitude. "I . . . I maybe lost count of the number of Indians I killed, Mr. Hood. But me, my sister, and Jenny were the only three that got out of that train wreck alive. And it was me that took charge and killed the owner of that Indian pony."

Joshua's face relaxed. "Yes," he said, "it was you and you've got every right to feel proud of yourself. But I also have a responsibility and that doesn't include taking a man into a fight that isn't up to the mark."

"But I *am* up to the mark!" Liam realized that he'd become so upset that he was shouting. He lowered his voice and struggled for control. "I'm sorry for losing my temper, Mr. Hood. But I been laid up with this bad hip for months and pining to get back and ride among your men."

"Can you ride with that bad hip?"

"Yes, sir! I rode this Indian pony around this very morning."

"That's not what I mean." Joshua heaved a deep sigh. "What I mean is, can you ride hard for days? Will that hip hold up to the pounding it'd take if I agree to bring you along with us?"

"I'm sure that it will!"

"If it didn't," Joshua said, "I'd have to leave you alone and unprotected out there. I've got orders from General Dodge to find and punish Eagle Wing and his warriors."

"I can keep up and that Sioux pony isn't tall, but he's sound and as tough as rails." Liam swallowed noisily and lowered his voice. "Please let me come."

"I think you need to help your sisters."

"They got more help than they need already. Dr. Wiseman is fawnin' all over the both of 'em. When they get back to Cheyenne, there's Mr. Gilchrist who's after Megan like a lovesick calf. And there's Rachel, Mr. Harrison, the gambler who works Megan's tables, and Victor."

"Victor can't hardly take care of himself," Joshua said.

"Maybe not, but believe me, sir, Megan and Aileen will be just fine and so will little Jenny. Fact of the matter is that they don't need me at all."

Joshua scowled. After a long, silent deliberation, he said, "I guess we can scare you up another rifle and a saddle. Mr. Watt, you must have an extra old saddle lyin' around that Liam can use on that Indian pony, don't you?"

"I . . . sure," Watt said, his resistance completely broken.

"Good! Now let's see that buckskin horse you had mentioned."

Liam expelled a deep breath. He wanted to let out a wild whoop of joy that he'd won permission from Mr. Hood to accompany him and the scouts on the trail of Eagle Wing. But the boys were watching him slowly and Liam knew that his credibility was already in question and that he needed to maintain his dignity.

"Well," he said, "I guess I'd better get ready to ride that Indian pony. You boys run along now but don't you forget us brave men who set out today to even the score."

"I think you're all pretty stupid," the buck-toothed kid said. "There's a lot more Indians out on them big plains than there is of you."

"Yeah? Well, maybe so, but we're a lot tougher."

The kid rolled his eyes and walked away while Liam followed along after Joshua and Mr. Watt into the barn to inspect the buckskin.

An hour later they were all saddled and ready to ride. Joshua had a pair of Arapaho scouts named Oshat and Red. They looked to be brothers, but then most all Indians looked pretty much the same to Liam. Only one stood out in his mind and that was the Indian that he'd driven a spear into while the man lay beaten unconscious on the dead prairie grass beside the Platte River. Liam guessed that he would remember that Indian's bloody face until the day that he died.

Killing a man, even an Indian, was easier done than

forgotten. But maybe, if this chase resulted in a hard fight, there would be a lot more Indian killing and the faces of the dead would all blend together and become indistinct.

Liam hoped so.

CHAPTER
7

Before leaving North Platte, Joshua Hood and his seasoned buckskin hunters had paraded back and forth on Main Street for a huge and enthusiastic crowd. Liam had thought it exceedingly grand to see all those cheering, adoring folks come streaming out of their homes and businesses to line the slushy avenue and cheer. Joshua had, of course, ridden at the head of his men and he'd waved to the crowd and raised a clenched fist causing them to cheer all the more lustily. Women—even the married ones with babes in their arms and husbands at their sides—had blown kisses and waved. Megan had brought Jenny out to watch and Liam had given his sister the Sioux lance that was now his most prized possession. Megan had raised the lance and the crowd had gone wild.

Yes, it really had been a fine farewell and while parading up and down the streets of North Platte, they had felt themselves invincible, like crusaders going on to a holy war. But now, under a leadened sky and riding into the face of a cold, whistling wind, that feeling of invincibility was gone, smothered by the hostile elements and the huge emptiness that might swallow forever even the dust of their bones.

Liam pulled the collar of his coat up high and humped his shoulders so that the lower part of his face was protected from the biting wind. He leaned forward on the Sioux pony and wondered how Joshua Hood or the Arapaho trackers could find anything out on this frigid, snowswept prairie.

When they reached the site of the train wreck, it was nearly sunset and Liam was appalled by the devastation. Up until this moment, he had seen the wreck only in fire and starlight. Now he saw it clearly and the impact was much more powerful. The trainmen's mutilated bodies had already been removed as had personal belongings discarded by the Indians. All that really remained was the train, the ashes from the immense bonfire fed by the wood tender and whatever else the Sioux had pitched upon the fire.

"It's getting late," Joshua yelled into the wind. "We'll make camp in the lee of these overturned cars. Some of you might even want to scoop out the char and sleep inside. Either way, there's probably some wood inside to burn."

Liam was not pleased. He looked up at the sky and decided it might even snow. Frankly, the very last thing that he wanted to do was sleep beside the overturned coaches where he had struggled to survive. No one else, however, seemed to mind and so Liam slowly dismounted. He could feel his hip socket slip painfully and he forced back a groan. The hip had begun to bother Liam after a few hours of hard riding but he'd kept hoping that it would adjust to the pounding.

"Liam!"

He turned to see Joshua staring at him. "Yes, sir?"

"How's the hip?"

"Just fine, sir."

"You're not lying to me, are you?"

"Oh, no, sir!"

"All right then, let's lend a hand and make camp."

"Yes, sir."

That night the wind howled out of the north. The horses, at first spooked by the overturned trains, quickly lost their fears and crowded in under their flooring heedless of the grease and smell of smoke and death. Liam and the others found two supply coaches that had escaped being gutted and they piled their bedrolls inside. But it was not easy to sleep because the overturned trains actually rocked to the fierce blasts of wind.

In the morning, each man ate what he'd brought and then the horses were saddled. The storm had passed south and the air was clear but very cold. So cold that the wind caused Liam's eyes and nose to stream. The Arapaho scouts had no difficulty in picking up Eagle Wing's tracks and they rode north.

It was a hard and misery-filled day for Liam. His hip pained him constantly and once, when Joshua had ordered a stop in a clump of trees beside some nameless stream, Liam had ridden off by himself to dismount. The hip was on fire and it seemed to have locked into a frozen position so that he had to stand beside the Sioux pony and cling to its mane. The stop had been brief and they'd ridden back out onto the exposed plains. No one had to explain that Eagle Wing and his men had a big head start and that there was a very good chance that the Indians would not be overtaken.

Deep down inside, Liam was not sure that he cared. He tried not to think about what might happen if they got into a bad fight with a superior force and he had to dismount and perhaps scramble for cover or, worse yet, fight hand to hand with the Indians. He feared that his hip would betray him and he'd fall and probably be scalped alive. He recalled the horrible screams of the trainmen who had been slaughtered after the wreck and that memory made his blood run cold with fear.

The second night was clear but extremely cold. The temperature plunged to nearly zero and no one slept much. The only good thing about cold weather was that Liam's hip quit throbbing. The scouts fed the fires all night long but both men and horses suffered. They left at first light, grim, stiff, and somehow knowing that if the Sioux did not kill them, the weather might render them helpless.

But later that morning when Joshua's Arapaho trackers suddenly appeared from the direction of the northwest, Liam knew that they had sighted the enemy because they were running hard over the crown of a hill and they kept glancing back over their shoulders.

"Dismount and grab your rifles!" Joshua shouted, flying off the buckskin. "Liam, grab and hold the horses!"

Liam didn't have time to think or to feel anger or bitterness at being asked to do less than fight. He jumped off his horse fully intending to follow Joshua's orders but his hip betrayed him and he collapsed, barely able to control his own excited Sioux pony.

"Dammit!" Joshua bellowed, grabbing Liam by the arm and dragging him up onto one leg. "Why in damnation didn't you say something! Willy, hold the horses and don't let them get away or we're dead!"

Willy was not much older than Liam but he was seasoned and sound. He shot Liam a look of disgust, then tore the reins from his hand as Liam yanked his rifle from its boot. In less than twenty seconds, Willy held the reins of every horse and was wrapping them around his wrists so that they'd have to drag him to death before they could break free and escape.

Liam felt his blood run cold as the Sioux boiled over the ridge in full pursuit of the two Arapaho trackers. There were at least two dozen and what impressed Liam the most was that the Sioux appeared to be physically joined to their racing ponies. Liam had never seen such horsemen or known that a man and an animal could fit together so perfectly. They were dark men dressed in flowing skins with many feathers spinning in the wind. They wore no war paint and Liam could see that a few of them had bows and arrows but that most had rifles.

"Hold your fire until I give the order to shoot!" Joshua ordered, stepping out in front of the others.

Everyone except Liam was armed with the new Winchester repeating rifles, thanks to General Dodge's appeal to the factory back east. These rifles were a huge improvement over the older single-shot percussion rifles used up until recently but they were shorter ranged with their .44-caliber rimfire self-contained cartridges. Had they been still armed with the older Sharps, the firing would have already begun, but now Joshua held steady in the face of the unnerving Sioux charge.

"Easy now!" he ordered, laying his cheek against the stock of the rifle and taking aim.

Suddenly, Arapaho Red's pony stepped into a hole and somersaulted. They all heard the poor animal's leg bone snap like a branch. Red was hurled forward to strike the prairie and roll over and over. The other Arapaho sawed on his reins and tried to reverse directions.

"Oshat!" Joshua shouted. "It's no use!"

But the Arapaho refused to listen. Liam watched with a pounding heart as Oshat managed to turn his horse around and race toward his fallen companion.

"The goddamn fool!" a man at Liam's side swore.

Red staggered to his feet just as Oshat reached and tried to pull him up onto his own pony. But Red was obviously hurt and dazed. He couldn't seem to get onto the pony and then Joshua Hood's rifle boomed and the lead Sioux warrior was knocked from his racing horse. Liam saw the man's body bounce like a rock skipping across a pond.

"Fire!" Joshua cried and the Union Pacific scouts unleashed a powerful volley. Liam fired too, but knew that he had missed. Their targets were at the very extremes of their range and only a an expert marksman like Joshua could have felled his target. Still, through the swirling gunsmoke, Liam saw five riderless Sioux ponies stampede to the south.

He turned to watch as the Sioux overran Red and Oshat. Liam sucked in a quick breath as a Sioux pony slammed into the Arapaho and knocked Oshat's horse tumbling. The Sioux dismounted and swarmed over the Arapaho in a wild and bloody flurry. Liam saw war clubs rise and fall, then the Sioux were leaping to their horses again.

Liam's blood turned to ice. He tried to reload his old percussion rifle but knew that he would never finish the task before the Sioux were upon him. He placed his rifle butt solidly on the ground and leaned on it like a crutch, then yanked his Army Colt out of its holster and took aim.

A horse next to him went down and he heard Willy shout for help but Liam did not move. He was lame and useless on foot but while he'd been in Omaha, he'd practiced most of his waking hours with this six-gun and he knew that he was fast and very accurate. And while his trusty Army Colt was a percussion weapon, it was also a proven, hard-hitting six-shooter and Liam intended to make every shot count.

"Ahhhh!" Joshua grunted as he was spun completely around. Liam saw that the man's upper thigh was torn open by a bullet. Joshua's complexion turned tombstone white but he replanted his feet and resumed firing.

Liam saw that there were not so many onrushing Sioux now, but everything was happening so quickly and the air was so fouled with gunsmoke that nothing was distinct. He could feel the earth shivering beneath his boots under the pounding of Sioux ponies and he wiped his running eyes and nose, wondering if he were about to die.

"Shoot, gawddammit!" the scout next to Liam cried. "Liam, you gawd damn . . . uhhh."

Liam glanced sideways to see the man slam over backward with his lower jaw completely blown away. Liam gagged, then turned back to the charging Sioux and steadied himself. At one hundred yards, he cocked the hammer of his Colt, took aim, and fired. A Sioux was jerked from his racing pony like he'd struck the end of a rope. Liam shifted the muzzle of his pistol a fraction of an inch and fired again with the same results.

A bullet creased his cheek but his face was so numb from the cold that he barely felt the wound. He kept firing. And then, before Liam quite realized it, there was nothing left to shoot. Only scattering Indian ponies and still brown bodies whose animal furs and feathers rippled in the cold prairie wind.

Liam's gun was empty and like the men around him, he quickly reloaded because there was always the chance that more Sioux were ready to attack from just beyond the next rise.

"Has everyone reloaded?" Joshua asked after a few hurried moments.

The men nodded as Joshua untied a red bandanna from his neck and stanched the flow of blood from his leg wound. He raised his head and then his eyes counted the dead among them.

"Could have been a lot worse," he said finally.

Liam wholeheartedly agreed. There were six standing, four dead, one dying. Liam felt his knees begin to knock so he wheeled about and hobbled over to his Indian pony.

"I'll take my pony now, Willy."

"I was watchin'," Willy said, looking right into Liam's eyes. "I thought at first that you was too scared to shoot. But when you did, you killed a bunch, Liam. You killed as many with that there Colt as anyone else with a rifle."

"I've been practicing," Liam said quietly.

"Well, it worked."

"Let's see if we killed the right Indians," Joshua said, extending a hand to Willy for the reins to his buckskin. "But I'm going to need to ride."

"Ya bet, Joshua!"

Joshua took his reins. "You better ride too, Liam. The more riding you do, maybe the better that hip of yours will feel."

"Yes, sir."

Liam eased his rawhide reins over the Indian pony's head, and somehow, he managed to climb back into the saddle although his hip hurt so bad that his eyes ran.

"Here," Joshua said, reaching down and picking up one of the new Winchesters. "I reckon that Micha Cobb isn't going to be needing this anymore."

Liam's eyes flicked to the jawless Micha Cobb who lay on his back staring up at the scudding clouds. "No, sir, I don't guess he will."

"Joshua."

"Sir?" Liam didn't understand.

"Liam, from now on, you can call me just plain old Joshua."

Not trusting his voice, Liam nodded and looked away to watch the riderless Sioux ponies graze on the brown prairie grass.

CHAPTER

8

There were no cheering crowds when they rode back into North Platte. Icy sleet was falling and had been for better than twenty-four hours. Joshua was clinging to his saddle horn, half delirious with pain, blood loss, and exhaustion. Liam wasn't much better. Their wounded man, Art Peat, had fallen off his horse and had died. They'd buried him near the site of the train wreck and followed the tracks to North Platte.

When the Indian pony followed the other horses into the livery barn, Liam was so numb from the cold that it took him a few moments to react. Then, he sort of slid his leg over the back of his horse and fell to the ground.

"Here," Willy said, "let me give you a hand."

"I can get up," Liam said, struggling to his hands and knees.

Willy grabbed him by the collar and helped him to his feet. The other men were pulling their saddles off their horses and leading them into stalls.

"Give me your reins," Willy prompted. "Your horse and mine get along. I'll put 'em in the same stall and pitch 'em a big stack of dry hay."

"Thanks," Liam said, his teeth chattering as he hobbled over to an upright support and steadied himself.

When Willy returned, he said, "Liam, we always stay at the Roper Hotel. I guess it'd have been better if you'd just ridden over there and fallen off that pony. Someone would have carried you to a room inside."

Liam swayed uncertainly. He looked around at other survivors and saw that none of them were in a whole lot better shape than himself. And for some reason, that made him feel better. Joshua had accepted a little help from his men and was being helped out of the livery barn, no doubt to be taken to see Dr. Wiseman.

"Might be a good idea to follow 'em to the doc," Willy suggested, taking his elbow and steering him toward the door.

"Why? I didn't take a Sioux bullet or arrow."

"You'll want to have your hip examined."

"It'll be all right." Liam pulled away and almost fell. "It just needs some rest, Willy."

"It needs for the doctor to take a look," Willy argued. "Might just as well do it now as later."

"All right," Liam agreed, too cold and hungry to mount a good argument. "Let's follow them."

It was about that time that Mr. Watt, the owner of the livery, appeared. "Hey, you boys hold up a minute! I ain't feeding all your horses for free. And why the hell are you putting them Sioux Indian ponies inside! Get 'em out of here!"

Joshua had taken about ten hobbling steps out into the driving sleet, but now he turned and hobbled back, his men still holding him upright.

"Mr. Watt, we killed Eagle Wing and his Sioux responsible for that train wreck outside of Plum Creek. I lost four . . . make that five men a couple of days ago and those of us lucky enough to get back here are about half dead from cold."

"Well, I'm happy you killed those Injuns, but that don't mean that I'm willing to spend my money on feedin' your starvin' horses."

Joshua inhaled deeply and then he pushed his supporters out at arm's length. For a moment Liam thought that the Union Pacific Railroad's chief scout was going to either kill Watt or else topple over in a dead faint because of all the blood he'd lost. But Joshua did neither. He just drew his gun and without seeming to aim, he put a bullet through the toe of Mr. Watt's round-toed work boot.

Watt screamed and Liam stared with morbid fascination as blood began to leak from the boot. Watt wasn't a young man but he sure could hop up and down fast.

"Guess you might as well come along too," Willy said when the wounded liveryman finally collapsed to the dirt, still kicking and howling. "We're all going to find Doc Wiseman."

"Get out of here, you dirty sonsofbitches!"

Willy shrugged. "Well, I don't reckon one measly bullet could have blown off more than a couple of your toes anyway."

Thaddeus Wiseman cut Joshua's leather pants leg away despite his protestations. He studied the wound and said, "This leg is in poor shape. Could be that you might already have a touch of gangrene."

"Can't be so!"

"Yes, it can." Wiseman gripped the torn flesh and squeezed suppuration from the wound while Joshua drew his lips back from his teeth and beads of sweat erupted across his forehead.

"Jezus, Doc! That ain't a piece of meat you're grabbin'!"

"The bullet needs to come out. Afterward, we'll just have to have a look and see if the leg can be saved."

"It'll be saved, by gawd!"

The doctor was just about to say something when Megan rushed inside. She took one look at Joshua's thigh and her hand flew to her mouth.

"It's going to be all right," Joshua said, "if the doc quits squeezin' and gets to digging that bullet out so he can put a patch on the damned thing."

Thaddeus turned to Megan. "Can you help me?"

"Of course."

"Boil water and bring it along as quick as you can. In the meantime, let's take a look at that hip of yours, Liam."

Liam stepped forward.

"You'll have to drop your pants."

"But . . . but I got nothin' on under 'em."

"Drop them anyway," Thaddeus said, stepping in front of the door. "Megan isn't going to get past me."

Liam removed his six-gun and cartridge belt and draped them over the back of a chair. He turned away from Joshua and Willy and hoped that they could not see his embarrassment. The doctor's examination was mercifully brief. "You can pull up your pants and strap back on your gun now, Liam."

"Well, Doc?" Liam asked as he hastily buttoned his fly. "What's the verdict?"

"Your wound has healed cleanly but there must be some jagged, floating bone fragments loose that are causing you a great deal of pain."

"Will they settle?"

"Not unless you rest that hip."

"How in blazes can I do that!"

"Stay off a horse. That's the number one thing. I'd also advise you to keep your weight off that leg, but I know that you'd ignore the advice."

"Hell yes I would!"

Thaddeus shrugged. "You'll do what you want until that hip begins to pain you so bad that *it* decides what you are or are not going to do."

"But, Doc, I *got* to ride a horse! How else can I be a scout and a buffalo hunter for Joshua?"

"You can't," Thaddeus said in a flat, uncompromising voice. "Can you read and write?"

"Yes, but . . ."

"I would imagine that we could find a sedentary job for you on the Union Pacific. Or at least one that requires a minimum of standing and walking."

Liam blinked. "I ain't going to take no 'sedentary' nothing!"

"Suit yourself," Thaddeus replied. "But given time and enough pain, you'll have a change of heart."

"That'll be the day!" Liam snapped. "I'm a buffalo hunter, a scout, and a pretty damn good Indian fighter, ain't I, Joshua!"

"You are," Joshua agreed. "But if you can't ride a horse, I'm afraid that I can't use you."

Liam had expected Joshua's full-hearted support. He couldn't believe what he'd just heard coming from the man's mouth. "Joshua!"

"Look," Joshua said. "You have to be able to ride."

"Well, what about you!" Liam cried. "What will *you* do if the doc saws off *your* leg!"

Joshua wearily brushed a hand across his face. Pain and worry for his men had caused him to age dramatically in just the few days that they'd been gone after Eagle Wing and his marauding Sioux warriors.

"Liam," he said as patiently as if he were speaking to a child, "go get drunk. As soon as the doc digs out this bullet, I'll come along and we can talk."

Liam was shaking with anger. He could not believe that Joshua had let him down and would actually refuse to allow him to continue as a buffalo hunter and scout. "Goddammit, I will just do that!"

Joshua turned. "Willy?"

"Yeah?"

"You and Liam stick together. I guess that when the townspeople hear what we did to Eagle Wing, they'll be buying all you boys drinks."

Willy nodded eagerly. "Well, I guess they might at that, Joshua."

Liam stumped outside into the sleet and since he was almost a head taller than Willy, Liam would have made him run to keep up if it had not been for the fire in his hip. It made him roll from side to side, listing like an old ship in high seas.

"Why'd you get so mad!" Willy demanded. "Joshua was just lookin' out for you."

"Well I don't need him to look out for me! I can pull my own freight with no special favors," Liam raged. "And I damn sure would have thought he'd have seen that out there during that fight."

"Yeah, you shot more Indians than any of them, but—"

"But hell! Is that how Joshua Hood repays one of his very best Indian fighters!"

"Of course not."

"He acted like I was nothin' but some used-up rag that he'd toss away."

"Liam, you got it all wrong." Willy shook his head. "You're just not seeing things straight right now."

Liam stopped, so upset that his anger overrode his pain. "I thought a man earned respect by fighting like I fought yesterday."

"Liam," Willy said, "you're out on your feet and upset. But it ain't going to be so bad. They'll find you a good safe job, probably a lot better one. You'll make more money, have regular meals, and sleep in a tent or in one of them big sleeper cars. You won't have to worry about freezin' or gettin' scalped."

"Dammit, I like being a scout and hunter!"

Willy raised his hands and let them fall helplessly at his sides. "Why don't we just go ahead and get drunk. Huh?"

Liam managed to nod his head.

"You got any money just in case nobody wants to buy us drinks?"

"I got maybe five dollars but I damn sure don't expect to do any buyin'."

Willy yanked his hat down tight on his forehead and together they headed down the boardwalk, hobbling and huffing. The first saloon that they found was called the Silver Dollar and when they banged inside, there were at least a dozen men and several prostitutes either playing cards or leaning on the bar. They all turned when Liam slammed his fist down hard enough on the bartop to rattle glasses.

"We killed Eagle Wing and his murderin' pack of Indians. Who's gonna buy us drinks!"

The bartender was a thick wedge with muttonchop whiskers and a round Irish face. "Boys, I'm afraid your friends already been here and got a couple of free rounds."

"What!"

"That's right. And *they* all claimed to have been the ones that killed Eagle Wing and his pack of murderin' Sioux."

Liam blinked. "Hell, I shot at least four of them all by myself!"

"Sure you did." The bartender grinned, winking at a couple of his regular clients.

"Jezus and Mary!" Liam cried, looking to Willy. "These people don't even recognize me. I'm the man that saved his sister and that little girl the night of the train wreck!"

The bartender peered at Liam. "You look different. Was you wearing a beard then?"

"No, but . . ."

"I don't think you're the same fella. And anyway, so what? That's history. What about your friend here?" The bartender studied Willy. "And how many Sioux are you claimin' to have killed?"

"Well, I didn't actually shoot any Indians," Willy said a little sheepishly. "I was too all-fired busy holding our horses."

This confession was greeted by loud guffaws. Liam couldn't believe these people. He'd risked his life to make sure that a bunch of bloody Indians had tasted the hard edge of justice and now these people were making fun of him and Willy.

Snatching a bottle of whiskey from the bartop, he growled, "I guess this bottle will be on the house.

We need two glasses. And, mister, make 'em clean ones."

The bartender underwent a dramatic change. His lower jaw shot out like that of a bulldog and his fists knotted. "Now, sonny, I'm sure that you are a brave boy but also an intelligent one. And there'll be no more free drinks on the Silver Dollar so hand that bottle over, *if you please*."

"Well, I damn sure don't please!"

Willy nudged him with his elbow. "I think we'd better try another saloon, Liam."

"Very good idea," the bartender snapped. "And also a very healthy one."

But Liam shook his head. He remembered how this town had given him and the other men riding for Joshua Hood a hero's farewell when they'd ridden out after Eagle Wing. Now, however, they were too cheap to even give him a few swallows from a second-rate bottle of house whiskey.

Liam uncorked the bottle. His hip was paining him in the worst way and he desperately needed to get drunk. "Mister," he said, "this bottle *is* on the house, glasses be damned."

"Liam, I . . ."

Willy didn't have time to say anything more because the bartender's hand shot out and tore the bottle from Liam's grasp. Liam stepped back and his right hand flashed to his gun. The Army Colt came up smooth and fast and before anyone quite realized what was happening, the bottle exploded in a shower of glass and liquor. The bartender staggered backward holding the shattered neck of the bottle and he stared at Liam's smoking gun, jaw hanging open.

"Now, sonny," he stammered, "I didn't mean no offense!"

"Another bottle—your good stuff—and two clean glasses, you ungrateful sonofabitch."

The bottle materialized in an instant and it was followed by two glasses that the bartender could not shine fast enough.

Liam pushed around slowly, his hip on fire. "Anyone else think that I didn't kill a passel of Sioux?"

No one said a word. The poker players went back to playing and the men at the bar shifted away and most left the Silver Dollar looking for a healthier watering hole.

Liam holstered his six-gun. "Bartender, you pour."

The man nodded and smiled as he poured. "You're awful damn quick with that six-gun, young fella."

"Yeah."

"Maybe you'd like to make some money in North Platte."

"Nope. I got a job as hunter and scout for the Union Pacific Railroad and it's the best damn job in America."

"What kind of money were you talking about, mister," Willy asked.

The bartender didn't even look at Willy. He was judging Liam. "I'm talking about more money than you could possibly make riding after buffalo or Indians. I could use a kid with a fast gun. So could my competitors."

Liam tossed the contents of his glass down his gullet. The whiskey burned all the way to the base of his belly and it felt wonderful. "Pour again and keep talking."

The bartender shrugged. "People saw you shuck that six-gun and they were at least as impressed as I was.

I'm not asking you to shoot anyone. All you'd have to do is just hang around and let people know that you're a friend of the house. That's all."

Willy poured his own and drank it in a gulp. "I'm pretty good with a gun too. How much would being a friend of yours pay?"

"It's not you I'm interested in hiring. It's Liam. And if I could get the other saloons to go in with me, I'd say twenty-five dollars."

"A month, why . . ."

"A week."

Liam was about to raise his refilled glass but now he set it down on the bartop. "A week? You mean a hundred dollars a month?"

"That's right." The bartender grinned. "Providing, of course, that you not only can draw that gun in a big hurry, but that you can also hit what you aim at."

"I'm a good shot. A real good shot."

"You'd have to demonstrate that to the others."

Liam drank again. He remembered how Joshua had failed to support him and even implied that he might not be physically fit to be a scout anymore. That memory hurt worse than his hip.

"We can talk tomorrow," Liam said. "Right now, you pour and we drink."

"Why sure," the bartender said. "And by the way, my name is James Flannigan and I'm the owner and manager of the Silver Dollar."

"Good for you," Liam said, still burning over the way that Joshua Hood had so easily dismissed and betrayed him. He looked over his shoulder at the room. "What about them whores? Any of 'em work for you?"

"All of 'em. And if you go to work for me and the other saloon owners, you can have your pick, if you aren't too greedy."

Liam could already feel the whiskey starting to take effect on his empty belly. He chuckled, glad that his anger was gone. "What is the name of that pretty girl with the yellow hair and that pretty purple dress?"

"Crystal. Pretty, ain't she?"

"Yeah," Liam said, sticking out his empty glass for yet another refill. "Why don't you call her over and make the introductions."

"What about me!" Willy whispered.

"Which one you like?"

"The short one with the black hair. The one that looks like a half-breed girl."

"She is a half-breed," Flannigan explained, "but, Willy, I'll say for certain that she isn't going out back with you or anyone else for free."

"Tonight she is," Liam said, looking right into the bartender's eyes.

The saloon man sighed. "All right, Liam. One night for him, maybe a lot of nights for you, Liam. Agreed?"

Liam licked his lips and swallowed, already feeling a hard knot of desire building in his groin.

"Call 'em over, Jim, and let's get this hero's party started."

When the bartender bent the crook of his finger and called their names, the two whores came swaying across the saloon and Liam knew that he was going to go to work for Jim Flannigan at least until Joshua Hood told him straight out that he was finished as a scout and hunter. After all, a man still had to make an honest living.

CHAPTER
9

"Here they come!" Rachel cried, clapping her hands together and jumping up and down at the Cheyenne passenger depot. "I can hardly wait to see them again! Aileen, Jenny, and Liam. Seems like years since we've all been together."

"It's been exactly seventy-three days," Henry Harrison Armbruster said, pulling out his heavy gold pocket watch, "and sixty-seven minutes."

Glenn chuckled and looked down at the short, nattily dressed little man at his side. Henry was barely over five feet tall and he had a withered right leg. Yet despite those physical shortcomings and his frail appearance, he managed to seem quite the elegant gentleman. Henry wore a tailored suit of charcoal-colored broadcloth, a silk vest, and a maroon cravat with a sparkling ruby stickpin. His hat was low-crowned beaver of Planter design and his delicate, almost womanish hands that could play magic with a deck of cards were protected by expensive kidskin gloves.

"Well, Henry," Glenn said, "I imagine that you are very eager to have Megan back again."

"I am, Glenn! I never enjoyed managing anything other than my own affairs. But I have had a rather good run of luck here in Cheyenne and a handsome profit for our lovely Miss O'Connell when she has time for an accounting."

Rachel laughed. "Henry has been just awful to work for. He's about driven Victor and me crazy because he's such a perfectionist. But he's made Megan a nice gambling profit."

Glenn nodded. He had already suspected that part of the reason that Henry was waiting here to greet Megan was due to the large sum of money he'd been able to win at cards. Henry's arrangement called for him to oversee the gambling and give her fifteen percent of his profit. It was an arrangement that benefited both parties because Henry was both an expert gambler as well as being scrupulously honest while Megan had no expertise or interest in the tables whatsoever. Glenn knew that it was not uncommon for Henry to win a thousand dollars in a single night at Megan's tables, which translated into a far larger profit than she earned selling her undiluted whiskey.

As the train began to slow and prepare to stop, Glenn thought about what a great distance the Union Pacific Railroad had come in less than two years since leaving Omaha in the spring of 1866. It hadn't been easy crossing the Nebraska Territory because they'd had to fight the Indians. The predominantly Irish construction crews had faced not only the wrath of the Sioux Nation, but also the blistering heat of summer and two frightening prairie fires, as well as last year's terrible winter. And things were not going to get any easier in this ruggedly beautiful Wyoming Territory. But, somehow, the Union Pacific under Grenville Dodge and the Casement brothers would manage to keep laying track westward despite all the obstacles.

Further complicating things were the politics that were being played in Washington by Union Pacific's vice president, Thomas Durant, and the congressmen who both opposed and supported a transcontinental railroad. No one had to tell Glenn that both the Union and Central Pacific railroads were always short of money and supplies. Right now, for example, the Union Pacific was having a great deal of trouble finding enough wood both to fuel the locomotives as well as to cut railroad ties.

"Is Dr. Wiseman returning too?" Henry asked.

"He is," Glenn replied. "Apparently, Aileen is a long way from a complete recovery. And I'm sure that you heard about the bullet that Joshua took in the leg when his men defeated Eagle Wing and his warriors."

"Yes," Henry said, "that must have been a very nasty encounter out on the plains. I think that our friend Joshua sometimes pushes his luck too far."

"I wouldn't disagree in the slightest," Glenn replied. "But we haven't had any Indian attacks for two weeks now and I'm hoping that the Sioux have gone north to their winter grounds. They know that it isn't wise to be caught out on the plains in one of these blizzards."

Henry nodded and looked up at Glenn with a curious smile. "I expect it has not been easy for you, knowing that Megan was surrounded by both the doctor and Joshua. From the letter she sent, it sounded like Megan has done little else but take care of her sister and the Union Pacific's chief scout. That could be a serious threat to your romantic intentions, my friend."

Glenn looked down at the dapper little gambler who was not joking. "Listen, Henry. Megan's heart won't be won overnight. And as soon as we are together again whatever advances those two men might have gained will be lost."

"Oh," Rachel said with a laugh. "Aren't we the ever so confident one!"

Glenn blushed. "You're a betting man, Henry. I'll bet you a thousand dollars that I'm going to marry Megan someday. She might not yet know that, but it's true. All that is required is that I keep my wits about me and everything will turn out just fine."

"You've got a bet," Henry said. "Remember, Megan dreams of California."

"California would suit me just fine."

"You'd work for the Central Pacific?"

Glenn laughed outright. "Of course not! Credit me with having some loyalty to this railroad. After all, every mile of track that the Central Pacific lays is one less mile that we will be able to profitably lay. I hope our competitors never break over the Sierra Nevadas."

"They will," Henry said. "I've heard that their construction boss—a tall, hard man named Harvey Strobridge—is a slave driver. He's determined to beat those mountains and race us into the Utah Territory."

"Then we'll have a race!" Glenn exclaimed. "But I'll take our brawling, brawny Irish and Civil War veterans any day over the Central Pacific's little Chinese coolies."

"They are tough people."

"How do you know?" Rachel asked. "Did you watch them do your laundry once upon a time?"

Henry scoffed. "The Chinese have never known anything but adversity. They're strong, resilient, and they are clean-living people who don't drink."

"But they do smoke opium."

"Sometimes," Henry conceded, "but I doubt very much that they are allowed to do so as long as they are employed by our competitor. I lived among the Chinese for a short period after the California gold rush. They are exceptional gamblers and gambling is in their blood."

"Why didn't you stay among them?" Glenn asked.

"They're too good," Henry replied as the train pulled in to Cheyenne. "Why should I play serious, sober men who live to gamble and gamble well when I can play against the reckless Irish who bet with their hearts instead of their minds?"

Glenn didn't have an answer but he still didn't think that the Central Pacific Railroad's Chinese work gangs could compete with the Union Pacific's own American crews.

Even before the train came to a complete stop, Megan was jumping into Glenn's arms. He drank in her scent, kissed her mouth, and then threw back his head and laughed. "I just bet Henry a thousand dollars you'll marry me. Say yes!"

"Glenn Gilchrist, how could you make such a ridiculous bet!" Megan cried, pushing him away. "I'm not marrying anyone."

"Not ever?" Glenn asked, his laughter dying.

"Someday, perhaps."

Henry giggled and rubbed his hands together. "Might as well pay me now, Glenn."

"Not a chance. I've still got a long time to work on her heart. We're only just getting into this race."

Megan hugged Rachel. "How are you?"

"Better now that you're here." Rachel looked up, eyes searching for Liam. "How is Liam?"

"He's . . . he's decided to stay in North Platte for a little while."

Rachel's face dropped. "North Platte! But why?"

"It's a long story and I'll explain in a little while. For right now, though, I will say that I expect him to return to the end of the track and rejoin us in the spring."

"Oh."

"Aileen!" Glenn shouted, moving past Megan to help her sister down from the train. "You look . . . wonderful."

She kissed him and smiled. "I know that I look anything but wonderful. The real wonder is that I'm even alive. I owe everything to Thaddeus."

Dr. Thaddeus Wiseman took Aileen's arm. "Easy, my dear. We'll get you and Jenny a coach. Joshua, you can ride with us."

"I'll be damned if I'll ride a coach. Where's a horse?"

"You stay off a horse or that leg will bust open and I really will cut it off next time."

Joshua said something under his breath and looked into Glenn's eyes. "How are you, college man?"

"I'm fine, Joshua. Sorry to hear about your leg."

"It's healing. In another week or two, I'll be back to work."

"Another month or two," Wiseman corrected, his voice quite serious. "The best thing that you can do is to hole up until spring and then we'll see how that leg is mending."

Joshua growled and pushed on by Glenn saying something about getting drunk with his men.

Glenn reached down and picked up Jenny. "Do you remember me? We were friends back in Omaha."

"I remember," she said shyly. "You were nice to my

mommy and Aunt Megan. Do you have any candy?"

"Jenny!" Aileen cried. "That's not very ladylike."

"She's not a lady," Glenn replied, digging into his coat pocket. "And I do have some licorice."

Jenny beamed and Glenn set her down on the passenger dock. He looked at Aileen, Thaddeus, and Megan before he said, "It's good to have you all back together again. It's like a family reunion and half the people in Cheyenne are planning a little celebration at your saloon tonight, Megan."

"We'll be there," she said, turning to Henry. "How are you, Henry?"

"Very well," the little man said, bowing slightly. "And I want you to know that your saloon clientele have missed you and have lost prodigiously at your card tables. I've amassed a tidy profit for you, Megan."

She took his hands and squeezed them tightly. "Henry, the day that you chose to work with me instead of Ike Norman was the luckiest day I've had in a long, long time. I don't know what I'd do without you, Rachel, and Victor."

She looked around. "Where is Victor?"

"Someone had to remain with the tent," Rachel said. "Victor volunteered, but only on the condition that I bring you by directly to say hello."

"Then let's get Aileen to a bed and . . ."

"Oh, please," Aileen begged, "I do so want to see your tent saloon. For weeks I've done almost nothing except to lie in bed. Please, Megan. Jenny also wants to visit your saloon."

Megan frowned. "A saloon is not a place for a small girl but since it will probably be empty, I suppose this would be as good a time as any for her to visit."

Jenny clapped her hands with excitement. Glenn said, "I've got a carriage waiting to take us up the street. Come along."

On the way to Megan's tent saloon, the conversation was animated. Megan, Thaddeus, and Aileen were founts of information concerning the battle between Joshua's men and the Sioux warriors guilty of wrecking the train outside of Plum Creek.

"That was a terrible fight from what I heard," Megan said. "Liam emerged a hero again."

Rachel smiled sadly. "I thought sure that he would come on to Cheyenne and visit."

"He was offered a position in North Platte by the saloon owners."

"To do what?" Henry asked, his eyebrows lifting. "I didn't know that your brother was an expert gambler."

"He's not," Megan said, her voice turning very somber. "But I guess while he was recovering from his hip wound he became quite the shootist."

"He would practice constantly," Aileen said. "He was always borrowing money from me for bullets and black powder. He wore one Colt out completely and bought another. I've seen him practice the draw. His hand is a blur and he can hit most anything he wants."

"Yes," Megan said, "and that must have been dramatically demonstrated because he was hired by the saloon owners in North Platte to keep the peace. He and a friend named Willy."

"I know Willy," Glenn said. "He was also one of Joshua Hood's scouts and buffalo hunters."

"Well no more," Megan said. "I don't know how Willy got the job but he is Liam's assistant. Willy admits that he can't use a six-gun but he can shoot a rifle. Anyway, Liam told me that he and Willy are going to be well paid."

"Much too well paid," Thaddeus said before he looked away. It was obvious to Glenn that the doctor did not approve of Liam or his newfound profession. That told Glenn that Liam and Willy were probably headed for trouble and that Thaddeus was concerned about how their new livelihood would affect Megan's and Aileen's happiness.

Rachel was also upset. "Liam could get killed!"

"I very much doubt that," Megan said. "But I am afraid that he and Willy think that all they have to do is swagger around North Platte on their reputation as Indian fighters. I pleaded with Liam to turn down the job and come back here with us, but Joshua had hurt his pride and he turned stubborn."

Rachel looked as if she might burst into tears and Megan wrapped her arms around the girl. "Don't you worry, dear. Liam is as stubborn as a mule but he learns. He's also a survivor and he won't last long on that job before he realizes that being a hired gunman is not as glamorous as he imagines."

"I'll pray that the both of them come to their senses," Rachel said.

"All right," Glenn interrupted. "If you'll all come along this way, your carriage is waiting."

Megan forced a smile. She looked all around for the first time and said, "I can see big changes are taking place here in Cheyenne. The town is growing, even in wintertime."

"It's here to stay," Glenn said. "Right now, the tracks are halted up near Laramie Summit in the Laramie

Mountains about forty miles west of here."

"You mean that is the end of the track?"

"Sort of," Glenn admitted. "But the snow is so deep up there that the Casement brothers have actually leapfrogged the summit and are surveying and preparing to lay track on the western slope of those mountains."

"They don't waste any time at all, do they," Wiseman said.

"No," Glenn replied, "they don't."

Glenn got everyone loaded into the carriage and they drove up the muddy streets of Cheyenne until they came to Megan's tent saloon. The sun was just starting to dive into the western horizon and there was going to be a spectacular sunset burning across the Laramie Mountains within the next few minutes.

"Where is Ike Norman's tent?" Megan asked.

"He moved up the line almost two weeks ago to Red Buttes. Snow is about four feet deep up there. We didn't see any point in hauling your saloon up the mountain yet."

"We've got to go where the construction crews are working."

"That's the point," Glenn said, "until the weather clears and the snow melts down a little, there is no work except what is being done by the surveyors and bridge builders beyond the Laramie Mountains."

"I see," Megan said, deciding that she would need to get more information later. Also, she had to take Aileen's and Jenny's health into consideration. She would not, under any circumstances, risk her sister's fragile health in the higher mountains.

When they all arrived at Megan's tent and unloaded

from the carriage, Rachel ran up to the tent and lifted its flap. "Step inside, Megan!"

Megan had no inkling of the surprise that awaited her. Inside her tent saloon were about a hundred Union Pacific track layers and construction crewmen. When they saw Megan, they all erupted into cheers and raised their glasses in salute.

Tears sprang up in Megan's green eyes and she smiled happily. "Friends, it's good to be back!"

The men cheered even louder when Megan introduced her sister and little Jenny. Several of the more exuberant men wanted to dance with Aileen and Megan but they both declined. Even so, they poured a couple of rounds of whiskey on the house and the men began to dance with each other as they had always done in the western mining camps before the railroads.

"I can't tell you what a thrill it is to be here with you and a part of this great adventure," Aileen said breathlessly. "I wish that I had not missed a day of this."

Megan was delighted to see her sister so happy. However, she was a little worried about Aileen's sense of reality. Right now, they were part of a celebration. But out here on the western frontier with the Cheyenne and the Wyoming winter ready to come sweeping in on them without a moment's notice, this kind of celebration was a rarity.

"Aileen," Thaddeus said, "I think that you and Jenny have had enough excitement. It's been a long train ride and I don't want your health taxed."

"Oh, please! Can't we stay a little longer?"

"I think not," Thaddeus said with furrowed brow. "You need to rest now and regain your strength. Glenn, where will they be staying?"

"I expected them to stay in Megan's tent."

But Thaddeus shook his head. "That's not a very good idea."

"Why not?" Megan asked. "I have a stove and . . ."

"It's too close to this saloon," Thaddeus said protectively. "And too noisy. We'll need to find other accommodations."

Megan looked to Glenn with a question in her eyes. Glenn shrugged. "I guess we can find something else. Perhaps a railroad car compartment until the weather warms."

"My thoughts exactly," Thaddeus said with a vigorous nod of his head.

Aileen smiled wanly at the doctor. "You take such wonderful care of me, Thaddeus. I declare that I don't know what we would do without you."

"Well," Megan said, an edge creeping into her voice, "you might have to find out. You see, Thaddeus is the only real doctor out here and I'm sure that he is going to be very busy with his other patients, many who have probably been waiting to see him while you were leisurely recuperating in North Platte."

Aileen blinked and her face flushed with anger. "Well I never meant that I should demand all of Thaddeus's attentions! I only meant that . . . well, never mind what I meant. Really, Megan! I don't know why you had to speak to me so sharply."

"I didn't speak sharply. It's just that you've had Thaddeus at your beck and call for over two months and there are a lot of other people that need his attention. That's all that I meant."

Glenn could see that the doctor was as embarrassed by this clash of wills as himself. Moving in between the sisters, he said, "Megan, I'm sure that you'll want to remain here with your friends. Thaddeus will be happy to find Aileen and Jenny more suitable accommodations."

"Yes," Thaddeus said with relief. "I'll try to return before long."

When they were gone, Megan looked upset despite the many friends who celebrated her return. "Megan," Glenn whispered when they had a moment alone, "what is wrong?"

"Nothing."

"Sure there is!"

"Well, it's just that Aileen is so possessive of Thaddeus's time now. She demands his constant attention."

"That will change as her condition improves."

"I hope so. Thaddeus is not the kind of a man who wants to be clung to and Aileen has that tendency."

Glenn nodded. It was true that Aileen was clinging but what surprised him was hearing Megan say as much. This was, to say the least, quite disturbing.

"Are you . . . jealous of your sister?"

Megan's eyes widened. "Jealous? Of Aileen! Ha!"

And before Glenn could say another word, Megan stomped away. Henry Harrison came over and said with a wink, "I couldn't help but overhear that little exchange of pleasantries. Tell me, Mr. Gilchrist, would you like to raise that bet we have as to your possible marriage with Miss O'Connell to, say, two thousand dollars?"

"I don't even have the one thousand, dammit!"

"I'll take your credit. And besides, I happen to know that you do come from a rather well-to-do banking family back east. I'm sure that they would cover your bet."

"Go to hell."

Glenn stomped out of the tent. The sun was down and there was just the trace of gold filigree across the highest peaks of the Laramie Mountains.

"By damned," Glenn muttered, "she *is* jealous of her sister! She is smitten with that oversize doctor!"

It was a rude awakening for Glenn and one that he found profoundly depressing. Well, what had he expected? Megan had been working practically night and day for Dr. Wiseman while they were together in Cheyenne. Naturally, they'd gotten very close and she must have been very impressed by his medical skills.

Glenn gazed up at the first star in the night sky. His breath made dragon clouds of steam and he knew that tonight's temperature would fall well below freezing.

"Megan," he whispered. "Megan, my Megan."

And then, with a sad shake of his head, he walked toward the railroad and his warm but lonely bed.

CHAPTER
10

Liam stepped out of the Silver Dollar Saloon and heard the call of wild geese on the wing. He looked up and saw a wedge of them heading north and he guessed that was as good a sign as any that the winter was about over. You could also tell it by the cottonwood trees along the river that were just starting to bud out and by the way the snow had all melted and the main street was a thick, churning gutter of mud.

What time was it? He had been up most of the night moving from saloon to saloon with Willy marching along at his side. Then, he'd had a few drinks and gotten into another card game and lost all of his wages again and finally he'd wound up fighting with Crystal who had booted him out of her room shortly after daybreak. After that, he'd had a few more drinks and gone to bed.

Liam reached for his pocket watch but then he remembered that he'd lost it at the card tables a few weeks earlier. He felt awful and he was dead broke, hung over from the whiskey, and Crystal had vowed to shoot him if he tried to get back into her bed. Hell, he'd been a lot better off as a thirty-dollar-a-month scout and buffalo hunter under Joshua Hood. Only Joshua was in the Wyoming Territory and didn't want him anymore because of his bad hip.

The sonofabitch.

"Ahhh," Liam groaned, pressing the palms of his hands against his temples. He needed another drink.

"What the hell is the matter with you!" Flannigan demanded, stepping out of the Silver Dollar with his hands on his hips and looking angry. "I got an earful from Crystal about you this morning. She wants me to fire you, Liam."

"Jim, if you want to fire me, do it. Willy can take my place."

"Willy can't handle a six-gun."

"He's tough," Liam said. "He ain't big, but he's quick and he'll not back down. Besides, I've taught him how to use a six-gun and he's fast."

"He is?"

"That's right. He's got a reputation of his own now."

"For a fact?"

"Yeah."

Liam knew that he was talking himself right out of a hundred-dollar-a-month job, but he didn't give a good gawddamn. He felt terrible and couldn't even buy a drink to stop his shakes. Night after night he'd gambled and drank his wages away in the saloons he was supposed to protect and on several occasions, he'd almost gotten himself killed. In fact, he would have been killed if it hadn't been for Willy and his rifle.

"Maybe I'll give Willy a couple of nights on trial," Flannigan said, studying Liam with a look of pity. "We sure aren't happy with the way that you're doing the job."

Liam's lip curled. "Hell, Jim, you're winnin' back all your wages at the tables. All I been doing these past four months is working for you and Crystal."

"What you spend on Crystal is your own damn business," Flannigan snapped. "And as for losing money at my tables and your bar bill, well, I'd rather have you sober and reliable. As it is, I never know if you're going to be fit to work. You drink too much, Liam. It's going to get you killed and I don't want to have that on my conscience."

When Liam said nothing in his own defense, Jim Flannigan pushed back the bowler hat he wore and said, "I believe I will try Willy for a couple of nights. If he works out, fine. If he doesn't, I expect that you both ought to go back to pluggin' buffalo instead of expensive whores."

"Get out of here, Jim. I don't need your damned advice. I need a drink."

"Not in my saloon."

"Come on!" Liam cried. "At least loan me a few dollars for a bottle."

Flannigan sighed. "Here," he said, digging change out of his pocket and jamming it into Liam's hand. "Get yourself some coffee and a good feed. Then sleep it off. You'll feel better tomorrow. Maybe . . . well, maybe you'll start showin' some sense. You've got ability, Liam. And I like you. But you don't show good sense when you drink."

"Shut up."

"If you keep this up . . ."

Liam's hand dropped to the butt of his six-gun. "Jim," he said, his voice ragged and raw with rage, "I told you to shut up! Now, just turn around and march back into that stink hole saloon of yours and leave me be."

Flannigan took a deep breath and expelled it slowly. "Where can I find Willy?"

"He's probably sleepin' with Cassie, that half-breed bitch."

"She's all right," Flannigan said, becoming defensive. "What's she ever done that you should call her a bitch?"

When Liam just glared at him through bloodshot eyes, Flannigan turned on his heel and went back into his saloon. But at the door, he paused and said, "You're no good, Liam. Not in town with so many temptations. You're better off out there on the plains hunting and trying to hang on to your damned scalp. At least out there you'll be sober."

"Are you gawddamn through!"

"No," Flannigan said. "You're fired. If you see Willy, tell him he can start proving himself tonight."

Liam wheeled around and looked for the geese but they were long gone.

Later that night, Willy carefully tucked his new shirt into his new pants and patted the six-gun on his hip. He wished that he had a good hat and pair of boots, but he'd have them for sure after his first hundred-dollar payday.

"Well, Cassie, how do I look?"

The slender, dark-haired girl nodded her head. Her mother had been a Cheyenne, her father a French trapper. Cassie didn't know her birthday, nor was she exactly sure of her exact age but she thought that she was about twenty-four. That was old by the standard of most working girls and she was starting to see wrinkles in her brown skin that gave her cause for alarm. She remembered her mother saying that the white men wore out an Indian woman long before her time. Well, maybe the white men also wore out half-breed girls before their time too.

"Cassie?"

She looked up and forced a smile. "You look pretty damn good, Willy. Pretty damn good."

He grinned broadly. "Really? You think I look like a shootist?"

"I don't know," Cassie said, not wanting to tell him the truth—that he was too short and young-looking to be taken for a gunman. That men wouldn't take him seriously and would knock him silly with their fists if Willy tried to prod them out of a saloon. "Willy, you look good. But maybe you should find Liam and get him to stop drinking."

"Hell, Cassie! Now why should I do a fool thing like that! I like Liam and he's my best friend, but he ain't fit for the job anymore. I am."

"You're no good with Liam's gun."

"I been practicin' a little."

"You only bought it from him yesterday! You should leave it with me and stick to your Winchester rifle."

Willy shook his head. "Cassie, what kind of a shootist is it that uses a damn rifle? I'm askin' you."

"Maybe you could take both," Cassie said after a moment. "I seen you shoot the rifle. You should take the rifle."

Willy moved away from the mirror and sat down on the bed. "Come here, girl."

Cassie came over and sat down beside him.

He took her hand almost shyly. "Cassie, do you like me?"

She laughed outright but when he blushed with embarrassment, her laughter died and she squeezed his hand. "Of course I do, Willy."

"How much?"

Cassie frowned. "What do you want me to say?"

Willy reached up and placed his hand over her small breast as if he might feel there a pulse. "I never had a steady woman, Cassie. And I like you . . . a lot."

"Willy, you better . . ."

"Now listen to me, Cassie. If I can keep this job and start getting the kind of money that Liam got, I'll save it. We could have a thousand dollars a year from now and you could stop doin' it with other men."

She thought about that for a moment. "Why?"

"Why!" Willy came to his feet. "Cassie, I don't *like* the idea of you doin' it with every sonofabitch that has two extra dollars."

She did not look at him and her voice was barely a whisper when she said, "It's what I am. It's what I do."

He reached out and took her hand. "If I can prove to Mr. Flannigan and the other saloon owners that I can handle their troublemakers, I . . . I want to marry you, Cassie."

Her head snapped up. "Marry me?"

"Yeah."

Cassie felt her throat constrict and when she tried to speak, she had no voice.

He took her silence as a reservation. "I'd be real good to you, Cassie. We'd have money. Maybe buy a house and someday start a family. I'd make you happy, I swear that I would."

She came to her feet and moved up tight against him the way that he liked. She buried her face against his neck and whispered, "Damn yes I'll marry you, Willy."

Willy threw back his head and howled at the flaking ceiling of their little room. He picked Cassie up and whirled her completely around and even kissed her on the mouth. He set her down gentle, all the time grinning from ear to ear.

"I love you, Cassie, and I'm gonna make you a happy woman and mother. I swear by the Holy Mary, Mother of God, that I will!"

Cassie had been a whore since her mother had died. During that ten years, many men had asked to marry her, but they'd always been drunk and mostly they'd asked when they were on top of her. This was profoundly different. Willy was sober and he wasn't wanting her right now or anything. He was dead serious.

"I'll wait for you tonight right here, Willy." She drew in a long breath and then she made her own great promise. "And no other man for me, Willy—ever."

Willy kissed her again. She wanted to grab and hold on to him but he whirled, flung the door open, and was gone. He raced down the hallway and out into the street and it wasn't until he'd breathlessly walked into the Silver Dollar that he remembered that he'd forgotten his promise to bring his rifle. No matter. The crowd was small, this being a Thursday night before a Friday payday.

"Good evening, Mr. Flannigan!"

"Willy. How are you doing tonight?"

"I'm just fine. Liam told me that I could have his job."

"Well," Flannigan said, "that isn't exactly true."

"What?"

Flannigan was polishing glasses. He liked to keep busy all the time and when he wasn't pouring drinks, he was polishing glasses. Now, he held a glass up to the light and inspected it very closely. "You see, Willy, the hundred dollars a month Liam earned, as you probably know, came from the four of us who run saloons in this town. Now, I'm willing to pay you my twenty-five, but you have to convince the others that they need to pay the same."

"I know 'em all. Liam and I have kept their saloons free of the riffraff and troublemakers."

"Good. But now Liam is gone. It's just you, Willy. And even though I understand that you've become very good with that six-gun. I'm afraid that your ability is yet to be demonstrated."

"I can handle whatever trouble comes."

"Just relax and go easy," Flannigan cautioned. "Liam would drink and then he'd get too pushy. I want you to stay sober and cut our customers a little more slack. Understood?"

"Sure.

"But I'd like to marry Cassie and—"

Flannigan almost dropped his glass. He let out a great guffaw and said, "Marry her! Why in the hell would you want to marry a little half-breed whore!"

"I . . . I . . ." Willy desperately wanted to be man enough to look Flannigan in the eye and tell him that he loved Cassie, but he just could not.

"Jezus, Willy! Have you and Liam been drinking?"

"No, sir!"

"Forget this marryin' business." Flannigan said, taking the call from a freighter who raised his beer glass signaling for a refill. "You just do your job and prove your worth to us and you'll do fine. Maybe someday you can find a respectable woman."

Willy was smarting when he left the Silver Dollar Saloon and headed outside for the next saloon. It was called the Bulldog Bar and it catered to a rougher crowd. The tables were rigged and the whiskey was heavily watered by the owner, Angus MacCleod, a taciturn and tight-fisted Scot.

"Good evening, Mr. MacCleod."

"Hello, Willy. Where is Liam tonight?"

"Liam isn't working for you and the others anymore, sir. I've taken his place."

MacCleod barked a harsh laugh. "Not on my twenty-five dollars a month, you aren't!"

"Well, Mr. MacCleod, I can do the job. I'll keep the peace and . . ."

MacCleod's bushy eyebrows knitted. He was a short but stout man in his early fifties and his fist-busted nose attested to the fact that he had loved to brawl in his younger days. He always rolled his sleeves up and his forearms were thick and heavily corded with muscle. He had the hands of a very big man and every knuckle on them had been broken.

"Willy, you're a good boy. Now go find Liam."

Willy was just about to argue when a pair of men gambling on one of the back tables got into a shouting match. They both stood up and their hands moved to hover over their six-guns.

"You've been dealing from the bottom of the deck all evening!" the larger of the pair shouted.

"You're a bald-faced liar!"

MacCleod started to reach under his bar for a double-barreled shotgun whose mere presence was almost always enough to quell a gunfight. But Willy was already moving across the room.

"You boys are going to have to take your troubles outside. Either that, or sit down and behave," he ordered, trying to sound officious.

The big man looked like a mule skinner and he was already fighting mad. He glanced at Willy and then scoffed. "Shut the hell up or I'll kick your ass clean outta the door!"

"All right," Willy said, knowing that he had to take control right this moment and that MacCleod was watching closely, "you're both finished for the night."

"Is that right?"

"That's right."

The mule skinner looked across the table at his opponent, then his eyes flicked back to Willy. "And you really think I'm going to just walk out of here after this sonofabitch cheated me out of a week's wages!"

Willy felt his armpits begin to leak. He glanced to the other men. "Anyone else among you see that fella dealing from the bottom of the deck?"

To a man, the other players shook their heads. Willy didn't know if he was relieved or not. "Mister, I don't think you've got a case here for cheating."

"What you think, sonny, don't mean a fiddler's damn!"

Willy swallowed, trying to remember how Liam had handled this sort of thing. Usually, Liam had toughened and bluffed his man down but that didn't seen very likely in this case.

"Look," Willy said, trying to sound reasonable, "I'm afraid that you'll have to accept your losses and come back another time and . . ."

"I don't believe that I will!"

Willy felt the hairs on the back of his head rise and even as he was trying to decide if he'd better go for his gun, the mule skinner's hand flashed to his gun. Willy made a stab for Liam's six-gun but he was so panicky that he did not get a solid grip on the butt and when he tried to lift it up, the weapon spilled from his hand.

"Please, mister, don't—"

The mule skinner's Colt bucked in his big fist and Willy felt just like he had when he'd once been kicked in the chest by a draft horse. He felt himself pitching over backward as he heard more gunfire and then he struck the sawdust floor.

"Cassie!" he sobbed, rolling over and spitting blood into the dirty sawdust. "Oh, dammit, Cassie!"

CHAPTER
11

"Cassie? Cassie, open the door. It's Flannigan."

Cassie opened the door but he did not come into her little room. She wondered if she should tell him that she was going to marry Willy and would not be working for the Silver Dollar anymore but decided to wait because he looked sad.

"Are you all right?"

"No, I'm not." He raised a bottle of his own best whiskey and drank while Cassie began to feel an icy ball of dread forming way down deep in her belly. "I got some real bad news. Willy is dead."

Cassie blinked. Just blinked and felt everything inside go hard and cold. "How did it happen?" she asked in a voice she did not recognize.

"There were two men arguing over at Angus MacCleod's Bulldog Bar. One of 'em was a freighter on contract to the Union Pacific. His name is Leroy Haws."

"I know him."

Flannigan expelled whiskey fumes and wearily ran his hand across his eyes. "There ain't much to say. Leroy pulled his gun quicker than Willy and shot him once in the lung."

Cassie's mouth worked but she couldn't make a sound.

"Listen," Flannigan said, "I don't know how much you thought of Willy, but I know he must have cared a lot for you. Angus says Willy was callin' your name to his last breath."

Cassie reached down and took the bottle from Flannigan's hand and helped herself to a long, hard drink. She handed the bottle back and said, "I told Willy to take his rifle. He wasn't any good with a pistol. I told him to take his gawddamn new Winchester rifle."

"I doubt that would have saved him. Haws has a reputation for being damned quick with a gun. Willy isn't the first man that he's killed."

"Where is he?"

"We laid him out under a tarp behind the Silver Dollar. He'll freeze tonight and then we gotta figure out a way to . . ."

"Not Willy. Haws."

Flannigan's eyes narrowed. "Why, he's gone."

Cassie exploded with rage. "Gone? He killed Willy and everyone just lets him go!"

"Easy, now." Flannigan took a long pull on the bottle and extended it to Cassie but her eyes were riveting into his eyes and so he said, "It's like this, Cassie. There were a lot of witnesses and confusion. It happened real damned fast and some of 'em said that Willy went for his gun first."

"I don't believe that. What did Angus MacCleod say?"

"Not much. He told me that he couldn't see who drew first because Willy was standing in his line of sight. But most people don't want to cross Leroy so they just didn't say anything. But later, I talked to a man that said Haws definitely went for his gun first and that Willy dropped his in the sawdust. They all said . . ."

Flannigan's voice trailed off and he took another drink. "Hell, Cassie, it don't matter anymore what anybody said. Willy got killed and Haws is gone."

Flannigan started to turn away but Cassie's hand clamped onto his forearm like a talon and it bit into his flesh as she whispered, "What did they say?"

"Cassie," Flannigan said gently, "it don't matter anymore."

"Tell me!"

Flannigan wished that Cassie would let go of his arm because her fingernails were biting deep into his flesh. "They say that Willy just stood there for a split second after he'd dropped his gun. Then they heard him beg Haws not to shoot."

Cassie released his arm. "Where did Haws go?"

"He had a load of railroad ties that had been cut last week and he'd been contracted to deliver them at the station. Maybe he went there and maybe he just drove down to another saloon."

Cassie took a back step into her room and started to close the door but Flannigan didn't budge. "What are you thinkin'?"

"That you need to leave. Now."

"Listen, Cassie, Willy was a man. He knew what he was doing when he took Liam's gun and strapped it on. I just wish I'd never seen either one of them."

Cassie shoved Flannigan back and slammed the door in his face. She had been wearing a flimsy and revealing silk nightgown that Willy had saved a long time to buy her but now she quickly changed into a pair of men's riding pants, a rough woolen shirt, and a leather jacket that she kept for going on long walks when the white man's world seemed altogether too evil to bear. Tucking her hair under a slouch hat, she knew that she would be taken for just another young railroad construction worker.

For a moment she considered the justice of killing Leroy Haws with Willy's rifle but then she discarded the idea. A fine new Winchester repeating rifle would attract attention and men did not haul them into the saloons. So instead, she went to a drawer and removed a two-shot derringer and a buffalo skinning knife that had belonged to her Cheyenne mother. The knife had a worn elkhorn handle and its blade had been fashioned from a big sterling silver spoon. The blade was strong but her mother had long ago worn it very thin. Now it was not a good or even a particularly attractive knife but it rested in a worn buckskin sheath and it bore the design of her mother's family so it was one of Cassie's most prized possessions.

She slipped the knife into one pocket and the derringer in the other. The two opposing weapons were symbolic to her of the two warring cultures of her blood. The derringer was far the more deadly, but it had never been a useful or graceful thing like the knife. The derringer was designed only to kill other men while her mother's Cheyenne skinning knife had long helped to feed her Indian family.

Cassie collected her life's savings, which was almost forty dollars. She paused once again beside Willy's rifle and it seemed to draw her to its cold and deadly strength. Succumbing, she took up the rifle, liking the idea of killing Leroy Haws with Willy's favorite weapon. But then, resisting the impulse, she set it down again.

"No," she said to herself. "It would get me killed first."

When Cassie reached the door, she studied the bed where Willy had last lain with her and then, without conscious thought and before she turned and left the room, she whispered, "No other man for me, Willy— ever."

She hurried outside and pulled her hat low over her face. It was very cold and the wind was skimming wispy clouds across a shivering half-moon. There were stars yet in the eastern sky, but they were dying with the approach of dawn. Cassie passed up the street with her head down and her feet moving fast. When she reached the Silver Dollar Saloon, habit made her turn to enter but then she stepped out into the street and studied the tracks. She found one set of irons that had sunk especially deep in the frozen mud, which indicated a heavy load. Cassie followed those deep tracks straight to the train supply yard knowing that it was Leroy Haws's wagonload of railroad ties.

Through a grimy window, Cassie saw two men crowding a potbellied stove inside the supply office. She recognized Haws by his wide shoulders and did not break stride as she crossed the train yard and put her hand on the doorknob. Turning it, she stepped inside, both hands slipping into her coat pockets.

The two men turned to see who had joined them and Cassie kept her face tilted downward so that it was hidden from view. At the same time, she clenched both her mother's knife and the ugly, killing little derringer.

"Say," the night foreman said, "if you want to crowd in here beside the fire and—"

"You killed Willy," Cassie said, looking right into Leroy Haws's bloodshot eyes, "and now I'm going to kill you."

Cassie lunged at the big man. He tried to jump aside but tripped over a pile of firewood and spilled onto his back clawing for his gun. Cassie threw herself on him and drove the knife at the man's throat. Haws cried out in shock and managed to block her thrust with his forearm. Cassie felt him grab her wrist and twist it so hard that bones snapped. Fighting not to lose consciousness, her right hand squeezed the derringer and she struggled to pull it free.

Haws drew the knife down across her throat and Cassie's hat tumbled from her head. His face lit up with shock and recognition. The knife stopped moving toward her throat and Haws exclaimed, "Why, you're that half-breed whore!"

Cassie tore the derringer from her pocket and jammed it tight between them. She pulled the trigger. A muffled explosion was followed by the sharp odor of burning leather and flesh as Haws's mouth flew open. His surprise corroded into horror and he began to blink rapidly as Cassie gave him a cold, killing smile. Pure pleasure coursed through her veins as she slowly pulled the trigger a second time and felt his big body buck and then stiffen.

"You gawddamn dead sonofabitch," she said a moment before his eyes glazed with death and his lungs emptied.

Cassie would have shot him more times if she had been holding a six-gun except that the supply yard man hit her with something hard and heavy right behind the ear.

Liam was sober. He stood bathed in a pale lamplight beside Willy's body. The body was already stiff and lay stretched out on a ripped and faded old faro table that had been discarded in the alleyway behind the Silver Dollar Saloon.

"He's going to freeze solid out here tonight but I don't know what the deuce else to do with his body for the time being," Flannigan explained. "I guess tomorrow morning we'll get some men from the Union Pacific to dig his grave, but the ground is frozen like rock."

"And you say that Leroy Haws got the drop on him but pulled the trigger anyway?"

"That's what a few of the boys are saying in private. But some of Leroy's friends that was in the Bulldog said that it was a fair fight."

"Willy couldn't use a six-gun worth spit."

Flannigan raised the lantern and stared at Liam. "Goddammit, you told me you'd been teaching him how to use a six-gun! You said he was good."

"I lied." Liam cleared his throat. "Willy really wanted the job and I knew I had to say something or you wouldn't have given him a chance."

Flannigan cursed long and loud. Finally, he said, "Well, I gave him a chance and look what happened! He got killed."

"Sounds to me like he got murdered. Where is my gun?"

"He was wearing your gun?"

"Yeah. Where is it?"

"It's under the bar along with everything else that we found on Willy. He had some money and I should have given it to Cassie but I'll do that tomorrow."

"Where did Haws go?"

"I don't know. But I'm sure that he's around. I'd check first at the train yard to see if he delivered his load of railroad ties. Ought to be someone there, but you might have to wake them."

"Yeah."

Liam was freezing and shaking so badly that his teeth rattled. He went inside the saloon and ducked behind the bar. Flannigan came back inside and watched as Liam strapped on the six-gun.

"If you hadn't lied to me about Willy getting good with a gun I'd never have hired him."

"Yeah."

"You better just let this pass and don't bite into more trouble," Flannigan warned. "Leroy Haws is thicker than fleas on a dog with every mule skinner working for the railroad and you know how tough and mean them bastards can be when one of their own is crossed."

"Well," Liam said before he marched back out into the freezing predawn, "then it's mule skinners against scouts and Indian fighters. And I was you, Jim, I'd bet on the latter."

CHAPTER
▬▬▬▬ 12 ▬▬▬▬

Liam had strapped his gun back on determined to find and kill Leroy Haws, a man with a hard reputation. He no sooner reached the saloon door, however, when a man burst into the Silver Dollar and yelled, "Flannigan's half-breed whore shot Leroy Haws to death at the Union Pacific's supply yard!"

Liam spun around and grabbed the man. "Where is Cassie?"

"Knocked out cold on the floor of my office! That half-breed woulda come at me next but I split her head open with a hunk of firewood!"

Flannigan came hurrying around his bar. "Liam, when the mule-skinnin' crowd gets word of this, they'll string her up at daybreak—woman or no woman."

"I know," Liam called, striding for the door. Outside, he turned and headed just as fast as his bad hip allowed toward the supply yard. He knew that Flannigan wouldn't help him to save Cassie; it would kill his saloon business to take the side of a whore against the mule skinners.

Apparently, the night foreman had already told several people about the shooting because there were three or four ahead of Liam moving toward the supply yard.

By pushing himself into a painful run, Liam managed to overtake the men and was the first to arrive at the little office where Leroy Haws lay in a pool of his own blood. Cassie was crumpled up beside the stove and when Liam tried to rouse her, she didn't respond.

"They said the half-breed girl used a knife on Haws," one of the men said, his eyes radiating raw hatred as he stared at Cassie.

"No she didn't," Liam snapped, prying the derringer out of Cassie's fist. "This is what she used. And look! It's damn clear that Haws was going to cut her throat."

Cassie had been slashed across the throat and was still bleeding although the wound was neither deep nor life-threatening. Liam removed his own bandanna and wrapped it tight around the girl's neck. He shoved her derringer into his pocket and then picked up the old handmade skinning knife with its elk handle.

"I never seen Haws carry a knife like that," a man said. "He most generally packs a big old Bowie knife."

Liam lifted up the man's blood-soaked jacket and everyone saw where the two bullets had entered his gut. They could also see that the mule skinner was carrying his own gun and Bowie knife.

"This must be Cassie's skinning knife," Liam said.

"Let's hang her, by gawd!"

Liam looked up at the man. "No. It was self-defense."

"The hell you say! Liam, this breed girl just come up and shot Leroy to death! Ain't nobody going to let her get away with that! We got to set an example or it won't be safe to be with any of the whores!"

"Haws murdered Willy," Liam said, scooping Cassie up and heaving her over his left shoulder. "And this girl just evened the score."

"Gawddammit!" another mule skinner cursed. "It don't work like that!"

Liam could see more men coming down the street and knew that Cassie's chances were rapidly fading. He kept his gunhand close to the butt of his Colt. His heart was pounding and so was his head when he mustered up his best bluff and growled, "You boys step aside."

"Haws was one of us," a mule skinner said, blocking the office door, hand moving toward his gun. "Haws wasn't much, but we can't let that breed get away with killing him."

"Sure you can," Liam said, drawing his Colt and firing in one swift motion.

His bullet struck the man's holstered gun and nearly ripped it apart. The mule skinner bellowed and jumped aside. Liam hobbled through the door and wondered what in the hell he was going to do now. His own Sioux pony was in a corral up the street and there wasn't any chance of reaching the animal before the swelling crowd became bold enough to take Cassie away from him. And if it came right down to his life or that of the breed girl, Liam knew that he was going to hand her over to the mule skinners.

Even realizing that, there was a perverse stubbornness in him that made him want to save Cassie. She was tough and courageous enough to kill Haws. To Liam, that counted for something.

"You ain't takin' that whore!" another man shouted. "She shot one of us and by gawd she'll be hanged!"

Liam's eyes came to rest on Haws's supply wagon still hitched and loaded with the fresh-cut railroad ties. "I'm delivering those ties to Cheyenne," he said, knowing it made no sense at all but unable to think of anything better.

"You're crazy!"

"Maybe," Liam said, tossing Cassie up into the wagonbox and jumping up to the driver's seat. "But I got a job to do."

A big, bearded mule skinner grabbed for the lead mule's bit. Liam's second bullet spun his hat away and the man backpedaled, his hands flying into the air. "Don't kill me!"

Liam swallowed dryly. He was afraid if he tried to speak, the crowd would see his fear. He cleared his throat and managed to croak, "Next man tries to stop me gets the same bellyful of lead that Haws got. Now stand back!"

"You do this and you won't live to see spring!" a mule skinner called from the gathering crowd. "One of us will bushwhack you, you breed-lovin' sonofabitch!"

"Yaw!" Liam shouted, snapping the lines hard against the mules and sending the wagon jolting forward. "Yaw, mules!"

The crowd was cursing and swearing as he left North Platte. Their threats followed Liam all the way down the street as he forced the weary mules into a trot and followed the rails westward.

About a mile out of town, Liam turned and studied the girl. He wondered if she would bleed to death or if the night foreman had struck her over the head so hard that her brains were scrambled eggs. Jezus, he thought, wouldn't that be in keeping with the string of bad luck that he'd been suffering.

Soon after dawn, Cassie regained consciousness but during that first morning was in such pain that she could do little more than hunch forward on her seat and cradle her head in her hands. Finally, she managed to say, "Where are we goin'?"

"We're followin' the tracks to Cheyenne," Liam said. "After that, you go your way, I'll go mine."

"I got nowhere to go," Cassie whispered, her face pale and her eyes dull with misery.

Liam glanced sideways at the girl. She wasn't nearly as pretty as Crystal had been, but he suspected that she was tougher. "You have to go, Cassie. If you don't, some mule skinner is going to open you up like a sardine can. It wasn't easy to get you this far."

"You had to fight?"

Liam started to say yes, but she was staring right into his eyes and he didn't think he could pull off the lie so he muttered, "No, but I sure had to do some fast talking. They'd have hanged you even before you woke up."

"Might have been for the best."

Liam pulled the team to a halt. "You can always climb down and go back. I'm sure that they'd oblige your wishes."

Cassie stared straight ahead as if frozen. She didn't even blink. Finally, Liam said, "Well?"

"Keep driving."

Liam slapped the lines against the mules and the wagon rolled on. After a few miles of silence, he glanced sideways at her. "You got any Indians that you can run off to live with?"

"I haven't lived with my people for a long, long time. I don't think they'd want me back now."

"Well, maybe you had better get down on your knees and beg for them to take you back. 'Cause, girl, you won't last no time at all on this line. Not after what you did in North Platte."

Cassie thought about that for maybe three miles and then she said, "I sure wish I had Willy's rifle."

"And if you did, what difference would that make?"

"A bunch."

"Well," Liam said, reaching under the seat to drag Haws's rifle out. "Here's an old Sharps. It's a single shot, but it looks to be in good condition. Loaded and everything."

"Don't you want it?"

"Nope. There's a brand-new Winchester repeater waiting for me in Cheyenne. I mean to become a scout and buffalo hunter for the Union Pacific Railroad again."

"Crystal told me that you was fired."

"I wasn't fired!" Liam exclaimed. "Why, I could have stayed. It was just that I decided a man shouldn't turn down big, easy money. And then, I had Crystal."

"She said you were always drunk and that someone was probably going to shoot you."

Liam bristled. "Shoot me? Ha!"

"And I saw how you gambled. I'll bet you don't even have any money saved."

"I do so!"

"Let me see it then."

"Go to hell," Liam growled. "I save your neck and what do I get but you talkin' down to me. I ought to just stop this wagon and chase you off for the Sioux to find. They'd have a good time with you."

"Maybe the Cheyenne would find me first," Cassie said. "This is their hunting ground too."

"Maybe," Liam conceded because Joshua had told

him that the Cheyenne and the Sioux both hunted the buffalo in this country. "But there's one thing I know for damn sure."

"What's that?"

"You're going to have to go find your own people. Otherwise, the mule skinners will peel your hide."

Cassie picked up the big Sharps rifle. It was very heavy and she had no idea if she could hit anything with such a cumbersome weapon. She'd already made the sad discovery that her two-shot derringer was missing although her mother's buffalo-skinning knife had been returned to her coat pocket.

"When we get to Cheyenne," Cassie said, "I'll decide what to do."

"Maybe you ought to decide before that," Liam advised. "There's a damn good chance that news of what you done to Haws will reach Cheyenne long before we do."

Cassie supposed this was quite likely. "Liam, what's to become of you?"

"What do you mean?"

"Won't someone try and shoot you too?"

"They might try," Liam said grimly, "but folks know that I'm good with a six-gun."

"Then one of 'em will backshoot you."

Liam had already reached the same troubling conclusion. "Maybe I'll ride out with Joshua Hood first thing until this all cools down."

Cassie thought carefully about that. "Would you ride north, or south?"

"Damned if I know. What difference would it make?"

"If you decided to ride north, I'd go along and try to find my people."

Despite his dark mood, Liam barked a laugh. "Sure, and then they'd probably scalp and skewer the both of us."

But Cassie shook her head and drew her mother's skinning knife from her coat pocket. "I still can speak the language. I lived with Running Elk and my Cheyenne name was Antelope Woman. If I could find Running Elk and his people, they'd probably take us in as their friends."

"That's pure speculation on your part and I damn sure ain't about to bet my scalp on it."

"Like me, you just might have no other choice but the Cheyenne. They're bad enemies but awful good friends."

Liam opened his mouth to tell her that she was making crazy talk, but decided against it. Cassie might have no other place to run, but a Cheyenne village sure didn't fit into his own ambitious plans.

In the days that followed, three supply trains passed Liam as he drove the wagonful of railroad ties westward. News of what he had done had flashed up and down the tracks and the response that he received from the passing trains was mixed. Most of the trainmen and repair crews had known Leroy Haws and had feared him and gone out of their way to avoid him. However, there were plenty of Indian haters that judged Cassie a murderess even if she had acted strictly in self-defense. These men yelled and threatened as their construction trains passed carrying supplies westward to the end-of-line. Several of them actually drew their revolvers and tried to shoot Cassie.

"Damnation!" Liam swore as he whipped the mules

away from the tracks. "Cassie, you won't last a day in Cheyenne!"

Cassie agreed. At each of the train stations they came to, she felt the hard, accusing stares. She overheard the angry threats that Liam was forced to endure and she came to understand exactly what her life had cost this man. But it was a total mystery *why* he had intervened in her behalf.

"Liam, would you tell me one thing?"

"Dunno. Ask me."

"Why'd you save me from hanging?"

"Because I admired your courage."

"And that was all?"

"Yep. Now, can I ask you a question?"

"Okay."

"Why'd you really kill Haws?"

"Because he killed Willy!"

Liam shook his head. "I sure have trouble believing that. You ain't no lovesick virgin. Willy was a good kid, but he wasn't nothing that special."

"He asked me to marry him," Cassie whispered. "He said he loved me."

A smile twisted the corners of Liam's mouth upward. "And you believed him?"

"I did and I still do!"

The wagon rolled on for nearly an hour and then Liam said, "Look, Cassie, I'm sorry. Maybe Willy really would have married you. I dunno. He was . . . well, he was different. And if it means anything, I liked him too and felt real bad that I got him to take my job. I shouldn't have lied to Flannigan about him being good with a six-gun."

"We both made mistakes," Cassie said finally. "It's done."

"But it *ain't* done," Liam argued. "We'll be in Cheyenne in a day or two and there will be more trouble."

"Then let's unhitch this wagon, get on those mules, and go find my people," Cassie said urgently even as Liam began to shake his head. "Why not! What have we got to lose? Joshua Hood doesn't want you anymore. I've heard you admit it every time you get drunk."

"Shut up."

"Well, it's the truth! And there's nothing but trouble waiting for us in Cheyenne."

"I ain't about to take my chances with the Cheyenne Indians. Hell, Cassie, you're just blowin' smoke. You don't have any people anymore. To us, you're a breed. To the Cheyenne you're probably not much better."

"You're wrong," Cassie insisted, grabbing Liam's hand and squeezing it hard. "My people will take care of us."

Liam yanked his hand away and glared at her. "I'm sorry I ever got into this mess, Cassie. I don't know why I did it except that I figured I owed Willy. Saving you was all I could think of to make things right."

Cassie recoiled. "Liam, stop the wagon!"

"What!"

"Stop it!"

Liam pulled in the mules and watched as Cassie jumped down from the wagon seat and reached for the Sharps rifle as well as a pouch with powder, balls and primers.

"Cassie, get back up here!"

"Good-bye, Liam."

Liam looked all around them. Except for the new tracks that stretched into the western horizon, there was nothing but flat, dead prairie grass and a sky of faded blue denim. "Dammit, girl, you wouldn't last any time at all out here by yourself. You think you're still Indian, but you're not. You can't make it out here on your own."

But Cassie wasn't listening. She drew her mother's knife and cut one of the older mules from its traces, then she quickly fashioned a pair of reins. "Good-bye, Liam."

He felt a sudden and powerful sense of loss. It took him hard and by surprise. "Cassie, are you really going to do it?"

"I am. And you should come with me. The white man's life will be the death of you, Liam. If they don't bushwhack you, you'll drink yourself to death."

"Not a chance. I think that blow on the head made you crazy."

"I been crazy working all this time for Jim Flannigan. But no more."

Cassie studied the vast, empty prairie and Liam saw her take a deep gulp of cold, fresh air. "Finally being away from the end-of-track and the saloons makes me realize that now. The only good thing that ever happened to me then was Willy."

"It looks like I stuck my neck out and made a heap of enemies for nothing. I should have let that crowd string you up back in North Platte. I bought myself a passel of grief for nothing."

"Tell them you left Antelope Woman out here to die," she said, leading the mule over to the tracks and hopping onto its back.

Liam guessed that was the best advice that he'd heard in a good long while. And so, without so much as a fare-thee-well, he whipped his mules and continued on toward Cheyenne listening to Cassie's mule bray in its sudden and awful lonesomeness.

CHAPTER
13

Damn this endless winter, Liam thought, as he sat drinking at a back table in Megan's tent saloon. It was now the first week of March and they had just had another heavy snowstorm. The Casement brothers and other Union Pacific officials were crazy to resume construction over the Laramie Mountains. Every day word reached the Union Pacific that the Central Pacific was still bogged down trying to tunnel under Donner Pass in the high Sierras and even this news did little to improve anyone's mood. Most people thought that the Central Pacific Railroad and its thousands of Chinese laborers were doomed to failure. The Celestials would never beat the towering, snowbound Sierras.

But damn this endless Wyoming winter! Liam's muddy boots rested on another chair and he was forced to grunt as he reached for his glass of whiskey, resigned to nursing it through another long, bitterly cold afternoon. There was a foot of fresh snow on the ground and the construction workers were broke and restless. Because of that, lawlessness was rampant in Cheyenne. The situation had become so bad that there was talk of forming a vigilante committee, although no one seemed ready to step forward and lead the movement. It was also rumored that the United States Army under the command of Colonel J. D. Stevenson of nearby Fort Russell was about to take control of Cheyenne until a sheriff could be found who could stop the rash of thefts, muggings, and murders.

Liam didn't care. He was not getting along with Megan or Aileen, both of whom made it clear that they were disgusted with his heavy drinking and the fact that he had taken up housekeeping with Rachel.

To hell with them all. He'd spoken to Joshua Hood on at least three occasions and the Union Pacific's chief scout and hunter had shown no interest in hiring him again because this bitter cold had caused Liam's bad hip to give him fits. Joshua's own wounds had finally healed but the man was surly and the only time he came around was to pay court to Megan.

"Liam," Rachel said, coming over to his table looking all excited, "I just heard that there was some work to be had over at the mercantile! I spoke to Mr. Hackett about you and . . ."

"I ain't interested in being no damned clerk!" Liam said in a harsh voice. "Now stop trying to get me a job. I'll find something to my own liking come spring."

Rachel tried but failed to dredge up a smile. "It's just that you don't seem very happy. And I'm sure that . . ."

Liam emptied the dregs of his whiskey bottle. "Rachel, stop flapping your mouth and bring me another bottle."

"But Megan said . . ."

"Have her take it out of your wages," Liam ordered. "I told you that I'm keeping track and I'll repay you when I get work this spring."

"Well, if you went to see Mr. Hackett . . ."

"Rachel," Liam said, grabbing her wrist and twisting it just enough that Rachel's mouth flew open, "shut up and bring me the bottle."

Rachel nodded and the tears in her eyes told Liam that he'd hurt her without really meaning to. He was about to apologize when a voice behind him said, "That's no way to treat a pretty young lady, mister."

Liam's attention snapped around to fix on a man about his own age dressed in a very expensive leather jacket and tailored pants. He had sandy hair, blue eyes, and the most perfect white teeth that Liam had ever seen. Everything about him exuded confidence and money. He had the same polished look about him that Liam so disliked in Glenn Gilchrist and Liam judged him to be of the same Ivy League educated and monied breed. The man was flanked by two big and tough-looking buckskinners who were glaring at Liam with unconcealed dislike.

"Who the hell are you?" Liam growled.

"My name is Peter Arlington the Third and these are my new hunting friends, Ennis and Emory Malloy."

The Malloy brothers were both well over six feet tall and they were packing Army Colts and big knives. They could not have been more different from the easterner either in their appearance or manner.

Liam dismissed the three intruders and looked to Rachel who was staring at the handsome young eastern snob. "Rachel?"

She pulled her eyes back to him.

"Get me that fresh bottle or I'll knock you to the floor."

Now he had her complete attention. Rachel dipped her chin and started to leave but Arlington reached out and stopped her. "Why don't you let me buy this . . . this man the whiskey he seems to so desperately require."

Liam dropped his boots to the sawdust floor and started to rise but his feet had fallen asleep and even if he had been completely sober, he would not have been able to stand because Ennis and Emory crowded him back into his chair. Liam's first urge was to go for his six-gun and shoot the big bastards but wiser judgment told him this was not the place or the time to fight. Better, much better, to wait until he had the odds tipped in his favor against these men.

"So, you're buying?"

"That's right." Peter turned to call out. "Miss, would you bring your best?"

Rachel smiled nervously and hurried to the bar. Arlington smiled pleasantly. "Since I'm buying, will you allow us to share your table?"

"Sure," Liam answered with grudging admiration for the man's brass. "As long as you're buying the best that my sister has to sell, you can sit with me as long as you want. But that don't mean that I have to be sociable."

"Suit yourself," Arlington said, nodding to his two bodyguards. "I've heard about you, Liam."

"Oh, yeah?"

"That's right. Back in North Platte I heard a lot about you and a Cheyenne girl that they called a 'breed.' Curious and not very flattering term, that."

"Her Indian name was Antelope Woman."

"Very pretty. What happened to her?"

Liam was not interested in talking about his mistakes or about a woman who had probably been scalped.

"Are you a reporter for some eastern newspaper?"

Arlington chuckled and withdrew a very good Cuban cigar from inside his leather coat's inside pocket. "You're very perceptive, Mr. O'Connell. As a matter of fact, I am the son of a rather prominent Boston publisher and I am here to seek stories as well as to shoot trophy buffalo and other game."

"I see." Liam's eyes flicked to the Malloy brothers. "And that's why you've hired these two?"

"Yes. And also for their company."

Liam understood that this was Arlington's offhanded way of saying that the two huge brothers were his buffer against the common frontier riffraff.

Rachel arrived with a fresh bottle of Old Kentucky, Megan's best. She had three glasses and Liam noted with irritation that the one she gave to the eastern dude was polished to a glittering shine. Rachel had never polished Liam's glass and now she seemed inclined to hover about their table.

Liam curbed an impulse to order the girl to go on about her business. Instead, he watched as Arlington filled their glasses, then raised his own in a toast. "To frontier adventure and to the thrill of the hunt."

"Yeah," Liam gritted, tossing his glass down and noticing how Arlington's eyes fell upon Rachel, causing her cheeks to color with a blush.

Ennis refilled their glasses and Arlington said, "I am collecting exciting sagas about the great American West and you, Liam, are emerging as one of the most interesting. Your remarkable escape from that derailed train while saving the life of your sister and niece are exceptionally worthy of print."

Liam sat up a little straighter in his chair. "Do you think so?"

"Of course!"

Liam tossed his whiskey down neat, reached for the Old Kentucky, and poured himself a refill. "And how much would this story be worth to your daddy's Boston newspaper?"

Arlington chuckled. "You're certainly an opportunist, aren't you, Mr. O'Connell."

"Money is tough to come by out west. How much?"

"Well, I would think that the narrative would be worth . . . oh, fifty dollars."

"A hundred," Liam demanded without a moment of reflection. "I'm a real-life frontier hero, Mr. Arlington. And I've plenty of other adventures that would damn sure curl your readers' hair."

"Such as?"

Liam's mind struggled for a moment before he shrugged indolently and said, "I guess you'd probably like to know something about Antelope Woman and me. How I saved her from being lynched in North Platte and how I escorted her north to find her Cheyenne people. When I found 'em, I showed no fear and made a friendship with 'em."

"You actually rode into a Cheyenne village?"

"That's right," Liam said without batting an eyelash.

"But didn't you have a fight with the Indians only a month or two before during which time you proved to be a remarkably steady and accurate shootist?"

"I did," Liam said, almost laughing. "But they were Sioux and I was with Joshua Hood. But that's yet another story that you'll want to do for your father's newspaper."

"I'm sure that it is!" Arlington now seemed genuinely in danger of losing the cool, aristocratic manner that Liam found so galling.

Liam could not help but gloat at the two men dressed in buckskins when he said, "How many Indian fights have you boys been in so far?"

The Malloy brothers exchanged furtive glances. Ennis studied his big hands and muttered to no one in particular, "We figure the smart thing is to avoid them."

"Sure you do," Liam replied with unconcealed contempt. "I'll bet you boys run like rabbits at the first puff of dust or smoke you see on the far horizon."

Emory paled and started to rise but now Liam found the odds to his liking. His hand snaked down to his holster and he yanked out his Army Colt, cocked it, and said in an almost casual voice that made him seem even more deadly, "I'll kill you and your dumb brother if you aren't both out of this tent by the time that I count to five."

The Malloy brothers were seized with indecision. They glanced at Peter Arlington and when he did nothing in their behalf, they looked to each other for help.

"One. Two. Three . . ."

The brothers both jumped up at the same instant, knocking their chairs over backward. Then they turned and sprinted past Rachel and out the door.

Liam laid the hammer of his Colt down and a loud belly laugh formed in the pit of his stomach. He laughed until there were tears in his eyes. "Where did you find that pair of worthless bastards!"

Arlington poured them both drinks and said quietly, "Do you really think that humiliating men or making enemies like that is a terribly smart thing to do?"

Liam's grin froze on his face and then melted into a frown. "I don't go out of my way to make enemies."

"There are plenty of mule skinners over in North Platte who differ with you, Liam."

"To hell with 'em!"

"And you really have no fear of being shot in ambush?"

Liam sighed. "I've no wish to die, but I'm not afraid of it, either."

"A man totally without fear." Arlington shook his head in wonder. "You're the very first I've ever met."

"I'm a fatalist."

"Mr. Joshua Hood says that you used to work for him as a scout, buffalo hunter, and Indian fighter. He says that when he first hired you in Omaha, you were as green as grass."

Liam's hands choked the arms of his chair. "I'll admit that I was inexperienced," he said, choosing his words carefully. "But some men are just meant to be on the frontier and I discovered that I was one of them."

Arlington removed a pad and pencil from his coat pocket. "I'd like to use that quote as a lead to the first article I write on you and send to my father. Would you mind?"

"Not if you pay me a hundred dollars and keep the money and the whiskey flowing."

"Fine." Arlington dug out his wallet and without batting an eyelid tossed the cash on the table. "Now, let's start with a little of your background and . . . by the way, would you like to be my hunting guide when the weather clears? I'm really determined to kill a trophy buffalo, antelope, and grizzly bear. I'll have them packed in salt and sent back to a taxidermist for mounting. It will very much impress my father."

"Sure," Liam said with a wide grin. "Can you handle a big -bore rifle?"

"I'm a marksman."

"And ride a horse?"

"I'm expert."

"We'll see about that," Liam said smugly. "Rachel, bring over some of them pickled eggs and pigs feet. And another bottle of Old Kentucky! We're going to celebrate tonight."

"The three of us?"

Liam was already feeling giddy from the sudden good fortune and whiskey he'd consumed. He also felt magnanimous and a little ashamed of himself for treating Rachel so callously when he'd twisted her arm. "Sure, why not? There's no saloon business to speak of—isn't that right, Henry!"

Megan's gambling partner, Henry Harrison Armbruster, was sitting alone at the far end of the room, absently shuffling cards. He had been watching them and now he called out, "Does your fine new friend wish to play a little poker or faro?"

"Sorry," Arlington said. "But gambling is one habit that I have not yet acquired."

"I can take care of that grave character defect," Henry Harrison said with a disarming grin.

"Perhaps some other time," Arlington said good naturedly. "Would you like to share our company?"

Henry Harrison started to rise but then Liam's words changed his mind. "Henry doesn't 'celebrate' much of anything, Mr. Arlington. For example, he won't drink whiskey or any other hard spirits because he says it 'clouds his mind.' As far as I can tell, Henry Harrison lives only to fleece those who stumble into his tidy little web."

Megan's professional gambler paled. Henry's eyes blazed but he said nothing as he sat back down in his chair, picked up his cards, and resumed shuffling his deck.

"Liam, you shouldn't say such things about Mr. Harrison!" Rachel scolded. "If Megan were here, she'd give you a real tongue lashing."

"But she isn't here so shut up and pour while I tell Mr. Arlington about the time that I saved Joshua Hood and his men from almost certain annihilation."

"I'd rather have the other story first," Arlington said. "The one about how you saved that Cheyenne girl and took her to her people. You must have cared a great deal about her to have taken such a great personal risk."

Liam glanced at Rachel. He knew how she hated the thought of him with another woman. Especially a half-breed girl that had shot a white man to death.

"Antelope Woman took a shine to me, all right," he conceded. "And I'll have to admit that she was damned handsome."

"Excuse me!" Rachel said angrily. "But I think that I'd better get back to work."

Arlington raised his eyebrows. "Oh, I am sorry! I wasn't thinking and . . ."

"Never mind," Rachel said with a trembling voice. "Go ahead and let Liam tell you all about himself and his filthy conquests."

And with that, Rachel stormed out of the saloon tent.

There was a long, awkward silence until Arlington finally broke it by saying, "I'm afraid that I've gotten you in trouble with that pretty young lady."

"To hell with her too," Liam said, downing his drink. "She don't own me and I don't much care what she thinks."

"Is that right?"

"Yeah."

"Then you wouldn't mind if I . . ."

"If you what?" Liam demanded.

"If I confess that the woman greatly attracts me and that I'd like to attract her."

Liam took a deep breath. What he wanted to do was shove his fist down this rich man's throat. Bust his handsome and smug face up so that Peter Arlington III would never catch another woman's eye. But there was two hundred dollars on the table and a lot more to come if he played this game right.

"You take whatever you can get from Rachel," he heard himself say. "I don't lay no claim on her and she damn sure don't have one on me."

Arlington beamed. "That's excellent news! But now, let's talk about that Cheyenne woman that you saved from a lynch mob and delivered to her people."

"She fell in love with me."

"Of course she did! You saved her life."

"Yeah."

"Go on," Arlington urged, pencil poised over paper.

Liam expelled a deep breath and then he began to talk about himself, something almost as enjoyable as making love or drinking Old Kentucky whiskey.

CHAPTER
14

Assistant Chief Surveyor Glenn Gilchrist toyed with his coffee cup and studied Peter Arlington. "So you'd like to write some articles about the Union Pacific Railroad?"

"Absolutely. And I want our eastern readers to get a real sense of the great courage and sacrifice that is taking place out here. A transcontinental railroad linking east to west is an epic undertaking. A monumental drama unfolding across the great stage of America's last frontier."

"You are given to superlatives."

Arlington blushed. "Perhaps it comes with my background. I am not interested in the mundane. To that end, I assume that you've already heard that I'm writing the exciting adventures of Liam O'Connell."

"Certainly," Glenn said with a wry smile. "I think everyone in Cheyenne has heard Liam's accounts more often than they care to remember."

Arlington puffed contentedly on his Cuban cigar. "It's true that modesty is not one of Liam's great attributes. But he is a very brave and resourceful man."

"Agreed."

"And I'm sure you heard about how he saved that Cheyenne girl from being lynched."

"Yes, several times."

"Well," Arlington said, "the man is quite extraordinary. When I first contacted your Union Pacific headquarters in Omaha, they told me that Joshua Hood was the man that had all the exciting stories to tell. But I've tried to engage Hood and I find the man cold and entirely uncooperative. He seems distant . . . almost aloof. I can't get anything out of him and I've given up trying."

"Joshua isn't much for tooting his own horn," Glenn admitted, "but he's the genuine article. He actually lived with the Sioux and understands Indians far better than any white man I've ever known."

"Liam also lived with the Cheyenne after he saved Antelope Woman."

"Is that what he told you?"

Arlington blinked. "Well, isn't it true?"

Glenn had no wish to get embroiled in dispelling Liam's fables. After all, the man was Megan's brother and the sledding with Megan was already plenty difficult enough without getting Liam upset.

"If Liam says he lived with the Cheyenne, then I guess he has," Glenn hedged. "I'm not trying to diminish his reputation, but Joshua Hood is the Union Pacific Railroad's true expert on the Plains Indians. And, if the truth is to be known, he's pretty sympathetic to their cause."

"Sympathetic?"

"Sure. Joshua understands that the transcontinental railroad will destroy the migration of the buffalo herds and attract a flood tide of hunters. I agree and predict the greatest slaughter of a wild species in the history of the world."

"Oh, come now," Arlington exclaimed. "I've told you that I'm interested in a trophy. But don't ask me to seriously believe that I'm going to be a part of exterminating some . . . some unique facet of the great American West."

"By themselves, your buffalo kills won't amount to anything. But hides are already worth a lot of money and the value is rising. Tens of thousands of buffalo will be slaughtered for nothing but their hides. They will be exterminated and the Plains Indian will starve to death, if they aren't all shot along with the buffalo."

Arlington's brow knitted. "You paint a very dark picture of things considering that you work for the instrument of the destruction you describe."

"No one can stop progress. The rails are bound to link the Pacific to the Atlantic coast. And I'm proud to be a part of that. However, I can't delude myself by turning my head to the blight that this will inflict on the Sioux and the Cheyenne."

Arlington looked away, his expression troubled. Outside, the snow was melting and the day was warm, the sky indigo blue. "Has construction resumed in the Laramie Mountains?"

"Yes. In fact, we've been laying track for almost three weeks. In another week, half of Cheyenne will be packing up and leapfrogging over to Laramie."

"I see. How much track does the Union Pacific hope to actually slam down this year?"

"Durant and Dodge have set the ambitious but realistic goal of reaching the Utah Territory before year's end."

Arlington gaped with astonishment. "Why it must

be a thousand miles between the Utah Territory and Omaha!"

"I'm surprised you'd know that," Glenn said. "Yes, it will be a thousand miles. After the Laramie Mountains, we've got pretty smooth sailing. The going ought to be flat and fast all the way to Utah."

"And you want to capitalize."

"Exactly! We've only got one more mountain range to tackle before we drop down into the Great Salt Lake basin and race across Nevada."

"Wow," Arlington said, shaking his head. "Those really are ambitious plans."

"But very attainable. You see, the United States Congress never set a place for the rails to join so we figure that the more track we lay, the more we'll own. As far as we're concerned, we'd like nothing better than to meet the Central Pacific Railroad in Reno after they've done the impossible job of breaching the Sierras."

"But what about the Indians? Couldn't they put a big crimp in your ambitious construction plans?"

"Of course. But we don't anticipate as much trouble from the Cheyenne as we've already had with the Sioux. Furthermore, we've gone to the precaution of heavily arming all our construction crews—the surveyors, bridge builders, road graders—everyone. The Army hasn't been much help—they're just too short-handed—so we've taken full responsibility for our own people."

"Interesting. What about the problem of wood for fuel and railroad ties?"

"You know a lot more about the railroad than I'd expect from a Bostonian."

Arlington laughed. "Don't forget, we've got our own railroads and besides, my father taught me that it pays to do a little background research. That's why I spent a week in Omaha interviewing your officials."

"I see. Well, we do have a big problem with wood," Glenn admitted. "These plains are almost treeless except along the Platte and the other rivers. Now, there's plenty of timber in the Black Hills to the north of us and these Laramie Mountains are heavily forested, but the deeper we go into Wyoming, the more difficult it will become to feed locomotives and find good railroad ties."

"Ties have always been a problem for you, haven't they?"

"Yes. The riverside cottonwood is much too soft. It won't stand up to the tremendous weight and the ties we've used from them are already showing signs of rot. We've burnetized the rails with a zinc chloride process that helps to preserve them, but even that isn't going to give soft cottonwood or pine more than a few years of extra life."

"So what is the answer?"

"I don't know," Glenn confessed. "I suppose that we just push on as hard and fast as possible and once the rails are down and the trains are running, we can haul in good hardwood ties for replacements."

"Same with fuel?"

"We're hopeful that we can find a coal deposit in Wyoming that will satisfy our locomotives' needs. Joshua Hood has an area in mind that shows great promise."

"Is that right?" Arlington looked very interested.

"Yes. And it will be easy to convert the locomotives from wood to coal burning. Very easy. Finding a big coal deposit near our tracks is a huge Union Pacific priority and I'm going to be working on that myself."

"Running around scouting for coal deposits sounds like a good way to get yourself scalped."

"There is a danger," Glenn admitted, "but we've got to have coal. It's costing a fortune to run the locomotives with wood and the costs will soar even higher as we move westward."

"I was wondering what your plans are about the Wasatch Mountains of western Utah. I hear that they are quite formidable."

"They are," Glenn agreed. "I haven't seen them yet, but I'm told that we're going to have to do some major cutting into mountains, filling in, and even tunneling. But we'll be worrying about that a year from now. Until then . . . well, we're just going to go full steam ahead."

Peter Arlington had been taking notes and he wanted to talk longer but Glenn had received a note from Aileen asking if he might drop by to visit her at the women's boardinghouse where she was recuperating. Aileen had been recovering from her injuries all winter and was still quite weak and dependent on Dr. Wiseman. She was, as Megan herself confessed, not a strong woman.

"I have to leave for another appointment," Glenn said. "I want to thank you for asking me to dinner."

"My pleasure." Arlington stood up, punched his expensive, half-smoked cigar out, and extended his hand. "I'd like to write a few of *your* adventures, Glenn."

"I'm afraid that I've not a great deal to relate."

"Nonsense! You ventured out alone to find the Sioux and strike a new peace treaty. That took enormous courage."

"More like stupidity," Glenn confessed. "I almost lost my life. I was shot with arrows and would have died if Joshua and his scouts hadn't risked their lives to save me. Even as it is, I should have lost my hand."

"Well, I'm just glad you didn't. And I hope we can do this again very soon."

"Me too," Glenn said before he winked and added, "especially if you're buying."

"I'm not buying, my father's newspaper is," Arlington said good-naturedly. "Coming from an eastern background of wealth like myself, you must share my appreciation of how fortunate we are to have money so that we can seize this western adventure."

Glenn's smile slipped. "It's an adventure, but I've received no money from my family. Not since I left home and chose to join this race across the frontier despite my father's strenuous objections."

"Oh," Arlington said, looking a little chagrined. "Well, if you need a little loan sometime, I could . . ."

"No thank you," Glenn said, trying to conceal his displeasure. "I'm just fine."

"Well," Arlington said, "actually, it would only be right to pay you for this interview."

"You paid me with lunch. That's enough."

"I hope I didn't offend you," Arlington said, looking at him closely as he slapped a more than generous amount of money down on their table.

"No offense taken."

"Good!"

Glenn left the man knowing that he really had been offended by the offer of money. Perhaps he shouldn't have been, but he was and it rankled that Peter Arlington would even suggest that he take money. Pushing that out of his mind, Glenn hurried off to see Aileen.

When the landlady ushered him into the boarding-house and he knocked at her room, she called out sweetly, "Come in, Mr. Gilchrist!"

Glenn went inside and was immediately assailed by medicinal odors more common to a hospital than a hotel. Despite them, he was pleased to see that Aileen was looking very chipper and her color was excellent.

"Miss O'Connell, you look very well today," he said, extending his hand as he approached her bedside.

She blushed prettily and said, "Pull up a chair. We have some very important matters to discuss—or perhaps I should say plot."

"What does that mean?"

Aileen waited until he was seated beside her and then she reached out and took his hand. "The matter concerns you, and me, and Thaddeus and Megan."

Glenn steeled himself. "I'm afraid that I don't understand."

Aileen squeezed and then released his hand. She was dressed in a pink silk wrapper and she looked lovely. Glenn was not accustomed to visiting a woman in her bed and he glanced back over his shoulder to make sure that the door was wide open and that the landlady was bumping around in the hallway so that every propriety was being observed.

"Well, Glenn, it's no secret that you have proposed marriage to my sister on more than one occasion."

"And been rejected."

"Yes." Aileen frowned. "Have you wondered why?"

"Your sister has this fear of ever again becoming dependent on a man. Her late husband, I understand, was very irresponsible."

"As was mine. Their deaths in that Missouri River flood were a terrible shock and hardship. But thanks to your intervention and the generosity of the Union Pacific Railroad, we managed to survive."

Glenn knew that they had done much better than that. Megan had openly threatened Thomas Durant and the other top officials of the Union Pacific that she would bring a lawsuit and create a huge amount of bad publicity if they did not compensate her and her sister for the loss of not only their households and husbands, but also for all the Irish families who had suffered grave losses due to that devastating spring flood. Glenn recalled that Aileen had received $5,000 and Megan $3,000, which she had used to buy her tent and saloon supplies, thus gaining financial independence and the opportunity to reach the storied California.

"Anyway," Aileen was saying, "I have a confession to make but it is one that you must promise to keep a secret."

"I promise."

"I've fallen wildly in love with dear Thaddeus."

Aileen breathlessly stared at him until Glenn blurted, "Well that's wonderful! Dr. Wiseman is a fine man. An extraordinary doctor. I owe him my life."

"So do I! And he loves me too!"

Glenn's spirits soared. "Really?"

"Yes! We have been together so much that it just . . . well, it happened. And he loves Jenny as if he were her real father."

"I'm so happy for you!" And Glenn was, but also for himself because he had been sure that the doctor had fallen for Megan and that his affections were being returned. "What a delight and a surprise! Are you engaged to be married?"

"We haven't talked about that yet," Aileen gushed. "In fact, only Jenny knows of our love and devotion. It was she that told dear Thaddeus that she wished she had him for her father. When Jenny said that, you should have seen that dear, dear man's face. Thaddeus actually cried."

"He did?"

"Yes," Aileen whispered, her own voice thick with emotion. "And that's when I told him that I also loved him. Well, after that, he said he loved us too and . . . what else can I say!"

"Nothing," Glenn replied. "Absolutely nothing. I could not be happier for you and Thaddeus."

"I'm going to try and become his assistant when my health allows," Aileen said, her eyes filling with excitement. "If Megan could do it, so can I!"

"Of course you can!"

Aileen swooned. "I have never, ever been so happy in my entire life, Glenn. And I wanted to make *you* happy as well. That's why I asked you to come and visit."

"You knew that I thought . . ."

"Of course," Aileen said, saving him from further embarrassment. "I knew that there was some small spark of attraction between Thaddeus and my lovely sister. And losing my own heart was the furthest from my mind. But when Jenny told him that she loved him . . ."

Tears welled up in Aileen's eyes and Glenn squeezed her hand. "I am overjoyed for you."

"Good!" Aileen sniffled. "You have a wonderful and kind heart, Glenn. I knew that when you helped us get that generous Union Pacific settlement and risked losing your own company job. I have no use for Joshua Hood and he would be a disaster if Megan was foolish enough to marry him. You're the only one that can bring real happiness to Megan. And now, I say that you should redouble your efforts to win her heart and her hand in marriage."

"I will!"

"Perhaps . . ." Aileen blushed and could not go on.

"Perhaps what?"

"Well, perhaps we could even get married in a double ceremony."

Glenn drew in a deep breath, oblivious to the medicinal odors that had nearly overwhelmed his senses a few minutes ago. "I will promise you that I will do everything in my power to make that dream a reality. Maybe we can even live happily together in some lush California valley—the kind that Megan has always pictured."

"I'll do everything I can to help you win Megan," Aileen promised.

"Have you already told her about you and Thaddeus?"

Aileen's expression clouded. "No. He asked me not to. Thaddeus wants to tell Megan himself."

"I see."

Glenn did not really hear much of anything else that Aileen said after that. He was in a daze and his heart was filled with hope. He realized that he had all but given up the chance of winning Megan. But now that Thaddeus was going to marry dear, sweet, delicate Aileen, there was an abundance of hope.

"This time, I'll not fail to win Megan's love," he told himself as he went to see her again. "And before we reach the Utah Territory this winter, she will be mine!"

CHAPTER
15

When Megan opened her door and beheld Thaddeus standing in the hallway with his hat clutched in his hands, her spirits soared. "What a nice surprise! Please come in!"

Thaddeus managed a smile, then lumbered into Megan's room. His expression was so somber that Megan's own smile quickly faded. "Is something wrong? Is Aileen . . ."

"No, she's fine," Thaddeus blurted.

"Then another patient. I guess you're still very worried about that man they brought in a few days ago with a crushed chest that . . ."

"He'll be fine too," Thaddeus said quietly. "Megan, the reason I'm here is to tell you that I have decided to ask your sister to marry me."

Megan staggered. She felt as if she had been struck between the eyes with a blunt and very heavy instrument. "I . . . I don't understand. I thought we . . ."

He took her hand in his own great paws and led her over to a chair. "Please sit down while I explain."

Megan wasn't sure that any explanation was possible. Without actually admitting it until this very moment, she had come to believe that when this transcontinental railroad was finished, she and Thaddeus would be wed. She had assumed they had an understanding.

"Megan, I want to begin by saying that I love you very much."

She drew back as if scalded. "How can you say in one breath that you are going to marry my sister and in the next breath that you love me!"

"Aileen needs me," he stammered awkwardly, "and I do care very much for her."

Megan struggled for the control that she felt slipping away. "Thaddeus, you may care for Aileen but you *love* me!"

"Yes, but your sister needs me and so does Jenny. I have won their hearts, Megan. That little girl should have a loving father and Aileen isn't strong. You are!"

Megan pulled her hands away and came to her feet. This entire conversation seemed unreal. "So, because I am strong and my sister is weak, you choose her?"

He looked devastated and she didn't give a damn. "And because of Jenny too. The child needs a father. Jenny never really knew her real father, and from what little I know, that might have been a blessing. But now . . . now she sees me as her father and I am captivated by her charm, wit, and lovely innocence."

"You're not marrying Jenny!"

Megan's hands knotted, knuckles pinched white. "Thaddeus," she said, forcing herself to be calm. "I know that Aileen needs a good and a strong husband to support her. And I also adore Jenny. But you shouldn't marry someone out of a sense of duty!"

"And why not? Duty. Honor. Sacrifice. Those are the ideals and qualities that have guided my every decision since boyhood. They're the reason I am what I am. Why I'm a doctor!"

Megan could feel tears starting to burn her eyes. She turned away quickly and marched across her room to another chair because she did not trust her legs to keep her erect. She stared at Dr. Thaddeus Wiseman for a moment and said, "Don't you think it rather cruel that I am being hurt because I am strong?"

"Megan," he whispered, coming over to kneel before her. "I am sorry. But you will forget me and I know that Glenn or Joshua or some other man will claim your heart. You are a woman who can persevere and triumph. But Aileen would be lost and broken if she married another failure and Jenny needs me to help mold her values. To give her a healthy chance at life!"

Megan felt her tears slide down her cheeks. This big gentle man was right—but also terribly wrong. Everything he said was entirely logical without any consideration for the heart. When Thaddeus reached into his coat pocket for a handkerchief, Megan jumped up and pushed past him. She found her own silk handkerchief and dried her cheeks. "Thaddeus," she said, "you are absolutely right. You should marry Aileen at once because she does need you and I certainly do not."

"I don't think I believe you mean that, Megan."

She raised her head, eyes wet and angry. "Does it matter what I believe! You've weighed everything out and made an intelligent, logical decision. That's the kind of a man that you must be in order to practice frontier medicine. I'll bet you had to close off your heart during the Civil War when so many soldiers were dying and you had to make those terrible decisions on whose leg to amputate and who would be wasting your time and—"

"Megan, stop it!"

"Get out," Megan choked. "Go away!"

He groaned, taking a step toward her until she retreated with her fists clenched between them. "Megan, what have I done!"

Megan roughly wiped her forearm across her eyes. "Thaddeus, you've shown me that the heart must always take a second seat to the coldness of the mind."

He sobbed and then he was gone.

Megan was not normally a drinker but this afternoon she made an exception. Never mind that. Rachel, Victor, Henry Harrison, and her steady customers would all wonder what had happened to her and why she was not at her saloon. They might think her sick, become alarmed, and come to investigate. Megan would feign a headache and then she'd create a hangover big enough to override her broken heart.

She was into her second glass of whiskey when there was a soft tap at her door. Her heart skipped a beat and she whispered, "Thaddeus?"

"Megan?"

She recognized Glenn's voice. "Go away!"

"Megan? Is something wrong?"

"No, I just . . . I don't feel well."

"Then I'll find Dr. Wiseman."

"No!" She lowered her voice and mumbled. "For God's sake, no."

"Megan, open this door or I'm going to knock it down. I'm not leaving until I see you."

Megan knew that Glenn wasn't bluffing. Straightening her dress she brushed her hand across her thick mane of auburn-colored hair. She caught a glance of herself in the mirror and was thinking just clearly enough to hide her bottle and glass behind her nightstand. Satisfied that all was in order, Megan walked very carefully over to the door and unlocked it. She thought she probably looked just fine.

The instant that Glenn saw her, his eyes widened and he said, "You're not sick, you've been drinking!"

"I have not!"

"Yes you have," Glenn said, closing the door behind him and taking Megan's arm. "I can smell the whiskey all over you."

"Well, what do you expect from a woman who runs a miserable tent saloon in a hell-on-wheels rail town!"

"Megan, dear Megan," he said, leading her over to her bed and setting her down as if she were a fragile China doll. "Is this about Thaddeus and Aileen?"

Megan started to shake her head but suddenly she was falling apart and crying as if her heart were broken. Glenn gathered her into his arms and held her close. "I know how much it hurts when the one you love chooses someone else. For a long time now—I guess since your sister arrived and you left with Thaddeus, I knew that he'd won your love and that I had somehow lost it."

Megan shook her head but couldn't speak.

"It's all right," he said, stroking her hair. "Thaddeus once told me that a broken bone mends stronger. Maybe it's the same with a broken heart. I hope so. And I won't give up trying to win your love, Megan. Every day I'll say a prayer that you'll come to love me and want to spend your life with me. I'll never give up hope. Never."

When she had cried herself out, he put her to bed. "I feel awful," she moaned. "I think I'm going to get sick."

"How much did you drink?"

"Way too much." Her eyes were so heavy she closed them. "Sleep would be a blessing, dear Glenn. A blessing."

Megan didn't hear his soft reply or the sound of her door closing as he tiptoed out of her room. Glenn had nothing more to say because he had said it all. He loved Megan and believed he always would.

In the first weeks of spring, the Wyoming winter finally broke its determined grip and the days grew warm enough to melt even the Laramie Mountains' snow. At last, General Dodge, Sam Reed, and the Casement brothers had what they'd longed for since leaving Omaha—flat, clear terrain that they could really begin to lay track across in a hurry.

And lay track they did! One brilliant and warm April day Glenn watched as the Union Pacific construction crews laid three miles of track in what Peter Arlington described as a "ballet of muscle and steel." Teams of five "rust eaters," as they liked to call themselves, would grab a quarter-ton rail from the lead construction car and race forward to slap it down on the freshly laid burnetized ties. The men with hammers that never missed a beat would rise and fall as regularly as a metronome. Thirty spikes to the rail, three blows to the spike even as the rail's twin was being slammed into place. Everyone knew that it took four hundred rails to span a mile of track and that not a moment was to be wasted.

The teams of rust eaters competed against each other. No one wanted to fall behind and so they raced while the Casement brothers and Sam Reed shouted orders and encouragement. The usual crowd of onlookers cheered as the lusty men worked like demons and yelled good-natured insults back and forth at each other, goading themselves to maintain the feverish pace.

Glenn shared the sense of pride that everyone felt as the days began to stretch into weeks and the tracks raced deeper into Wyoming. The afternoons grew balmy, then warm, but the crews stayed alert, ever ready to defend themselves. Seventy miles to the west, a crew of bridge builders was attacked by Cheyenne and two Irish were shot before the Indians were driven off by the sharp-shooting ex-Civil War veterans. And farther out, the survey crews worked with a transom in one hand and a Winchester clenched in the other.

Glenn was sent to help survey the bridge that would span the North Platte River. He and the Union Pacific's chief engineer both agreed that the bridge would not be a great obstacle and that work could begin immediately. At the end of a month, Joshua Hood and his scouts arrived at the surveyor's camp. Joshua looked grim and was in no mood for small talk.

"The Cheyenne haven't even begun to fight yet. There is going to be a lot more bloodshed by the time the tracks are laid across this sea of buffalo grass."

"Well," Glenn said, "let's just hope that it's not too bad."

"Dodge wants you back and sent me as an escort," Joshua announced. "I guess he needs a report. And he also made it clear that we are expected to find a coal field."

"Can we?"

"Sure. It'll take a few extra days but I know that management wants to get a bead on the coal. But I ought to warn you that there's a real good chance we might come across some Cheyenne and have ourselves quite a battle."

Glenn felt a shiver of dread worm up and down his spine. He recalled how terrified he'd been when he'd nearly been killed by the Sioux and how lucky he'd been to escape with his life. The idea of riding off with only a handful of men into hostile territory was less than appealing no matter how necessary.

"I'll have my rifle and pistol at the ready," Glenn said. "I intend to see Megan again."

Joshua chuckled.

"What do you find so amusing?"

"Well," Joshua said, "I understand that the doctor decided to marry Aileen instead of Megan."

When Glenn chose not to comment, Joshua continued, "So that lets you and me back in the race. Now, if we was to get jumped by a huge war party of Cheyenne and killed . . . well, I was trying to imagine who Megan would turn to next."

Glenn did not share Joshua's perverse amusement.

"Maybe she would turn to that fancy Bostonian, Peter Arlington. He's got the look of a man who can turn a girl's head. But then, I hear he's sparkin' Rachel. Wonder how that is sitting with Liam?"

"Liam won't like it," Glenn said tightly. "And I told Peter to watch out for him because Liam is green with jealousy no matter what he says to the contrary."

"Liam is dangerous, all right. Maybe I should have overlooked that bad hip and let him come back with my boys, but after a day's ride, he's in agony. Too proud and tough to admit it, of course. Anyway, I was hoping that Liam might find something else to do besides fighting Indians and hunting buffalo."

"He has."

"What?"

"Liam discovered that he can make a lot of money on the basis of his notoriety."

"His what?"

"His reputation," Glenn explained. "Peter Arlington is paying him for his stories, some of them involving you."

"Well I'll be damned!"

"And I hear that Liam has also agreed to take Arlington out on a buffalo hunt for a trophy-sized specimen."

"Liam is likely to get both himself and that rich fella scalped."

"I know, and his sister is having fits. But Liam has a strong stubborn streak. I've noticed that whenever you tell Liam to do one thing, he'll just naturally want to do the other."

"I noticed the same thing," Joshua said. "So when is this buffalo hunt supposed to begin?"

Glenn shrugged. "The last time I saw Arlington, he said that he and Liam were outfitting themselves for the hunt. I hear that they're taking along the Malloy brothers for added protection."

At the mention of the brothers, Joshua snorted. "They're just glorified mule skinners. They don't know a damn thing about Indians or buffalo."

Glenn had reached the same conclusion after asking around and finding that no one held Ennis and Emory

Malloy in high regard. "Then it's up to Liam."

"He don't know anything about Indians either!"

"He helped that half-breed girl and he rode with your scouts last year. He must have learned something."

"What he learned from that breed girl might not be worth repeating," Joshua said quietly. "And as for the fighting, well, I admit he's damned good. He shoots straight and fast with a gun or a rifle. And he don't crack under fire. But if he runs into a big bunch of Indians, he can't carry enough bullets or rosary prayer beads to save his scalp."

"Would you talk to Arlington when we get back to the end of the track? I tried but he's dead set on killing a trophy animal so that he can preserve it and have the damned thing put up on the wall of his father's newspaper office."

"I'll talk to him," Joshua allowed, "but he won't listen. You see, I didn't exactly cozy up to him in Cheyenne."

"That's what he said. Why were you so standoffish?"

"I dunno," Joshua said. "I guess after you, I'd had my fill of rich college boys that come west for no better reason than to have a good time."

Glenn snorted. He and Joshua had ridden and fought together and they respected each other but had little in common save their interest in Megan O'Connell.

"Well, let's find some coal," Glenn said before turning on his heels and striding away.

"You better bring plenty of ammunition!" Joshua called.

Glenn stopped. "I thought you had lived with the Cheyenne and they were your friends."

"Used to be," Joshua said. "But that was before I joined the company of the Iron Horse. Now, they consider me just another white hunter out to put them in their graves."

Glenn opened his mouth to speak, then changed his mind. He usually took Joshua Hood with a grain of salt. Only this time he realized that he would have to take the man very seriously.

CHAPTER
16

A dozen scouts and mule skinners left the surveyor's camp heavily armed and slowed considerably by four wagons that Joshua was required to fill with buffalo meat in order to help feed the ravenous end-of-line construction crews. Glenn felt exhilarated to be back in the saddle and riding side by side with these buckskin-clad frontiersmen. That long, beautiful morning there was not a cloud in the sky and the air was fresh and unbelievably clear. In every direction he turned, Glenn could see at least a hundred miles.

"Where are these coal deposits?" Glenn asked when they stopped to rest the horses about noon.

"They're to the southwest," Joshua announced.

All Glenn saw was sagebrush and red rocks that flowed endlessly toward a distant line of black mountains that formed the base of the Continental Divide.

Joshua eased up in his stirrups and pointed. "Do you see them far mountains yonder?"

"Sure."

"They're made of coal."

Glenn stared. He was not a geologist but he doubted that any mountains could be made of pure coal. "Have you actually been there?"

"Yep," Joshua admitted, "when I lived with the Cheyenne we used to hunt buffalo and even wild horses out in that big basin. We used to drive them up against those black mountains and trap them in the canyons."

"I see." Glenn pulled his hat down close on his brow and squinted into the vast and empty distance. And despite his eagerness to see how much coal might really be hidden in those mountains, he could not help but think of the Indians. "It's a long, long way out there. If we were attacked by the Cheyenne, there's no place to make a stand."

"That's right. But at least we wouldn't be caught by surprise. We'd see a war party a long time coming."

Glenn did not find this assessment very reassuring. He twisted around in his saddle and regarded the Union Pacific's lumbering meat wagons. "Maybe we should leave these wagons. I don't see any buffalo to hunt way out there."

"I'll admit that it looks empty as air, but it ain't. There's canyons and valleys where we'll find buffalo that wintered in the foothills of them black mountains."

Glenn knew that if Joshua said they'd find buffalo, then they'd find buffalo. But the idea of traveling across that huge sage-covered basin without cover of any sort save a few scrubby piñon and juniper pines was not to his liking.

"How far to those mountains?"

"Forty, maybe fifty miles. If we push, we'll camp in the foothills tomorrow night."

"Is there any water after we leave the Platte?"

"You bet. At this time of year, all the springs are full and there are creeks running down through those coal deposits."

Joshua chuckled. "What's the matter, college boy? You afraid to leave the U.P. line and sally out where the buffalo roam?"

Glenn flushed with anger. "I don't believe you are any more ready to be scalped than I am. Let's find General Dodge and Mr. Durant that coal that they are so anxious about."

Even though Joshua acted as if he did not have a care in the world and that this was just another lark, he gave instructions to the mule skinners that in the event of an Indian attack, they were to circle up the wagons and dig in for a fight. Joshua also sent scouts both ahead and off to their flanks. These riders stayed about two miles out and were careful to stay in plain sight.

That night they camped at a grassy spring and ate buffalo jerky and sourdough bread that they had brought from the end-of-track in a big burlap sack. There wasn't much conversation and a pair of guards were posted and ordered to keep moving in opposite perimeters about a hundred yards from camp. Glenn noticed how the meat wagons were tightly circled and the livestock picketed inside the protective ring after they had been allowed to graze during the twilight hours.

They bedded down on grass just above the spring without the benefit of a campfire. Within minutes, most of the scouts and freighters were snoring.

"I suppose," Joshua whispered just as Glenn was about to drift off to sleep, "now that saintly doctor has decided to marry Aileen, you think that leaves you in the driver's seat to marry Megan."

Glenn's eyes snapped open. "I don't take anything for granted when it comes to women. I've never understood them and I doubt I ever will."

Joshua must not have been expecting this admission because he was quiet for several minutes, then said, "I never could figure out what Megan saw in Dr. Thaddeus. Sure, he's a good man. But he can't ride, nor shoot, and I'd guess that he's pretty damn worthless except for patching folks."

Glenn smiled to himself as he gazed up at the starry heavens. It was just like the uncomplicated Joshua Hood to judge all men by his own frontier standards. That being the case, Glenn knew that he would not rate much higher than the doctor.

"Did you propose marriage again?" Joshua finally asked.

Glenn rolled his head sideways and tried to read Joshua's expression but the light was too poor. "No," he said, "but I did tell her that I meant to win her heart."

"So do I," Joshua said. "I figure if I had money and bought a big ranch and built a fancy house for her in California, she'd be certain to choose me over you."

"Maybe so, but I doubt it. Besides, I can't picture you as a rancher."

"I got to do something after the Indians are all killed or driven onto the reservations and the buffalo are gone. It's already happening."

"I know."

Joshua stood and stretched. He peered into the darkness and Glenn wondered if Joshua could actually see moving guards. Finally, Joshua lay back down and said, "After this railroad is finished, what are you going to do?"

"Marry Megan and raise a family."

"Hell," Joshua said, "Megan probably won't marry either one of us."

"That's possible."

Joshua didn't have a reply and in a few minutes he was snoring.

They broke camp at daybreak and hitched up the meat wagons. Chewing a breakfast of buffalo jerky and more bread, they saddled their horses and rode on toward the dark hills, the air chill and invigorating.

Not a minute passed that morning that Glenn did not turn his head and scan the horizon for Indians. He could feel the tension mount when Joshua's scouting and hunting party came upon the tracks of many ponies. So many ponies that the basin's damp earth was churned by their passing.

Joshua dismounted as did most of the other scouts. They squatted on their heels and said nothing until Glenn was about to burst with curiosity and then one of the scouts said, "About a hundred wild horses."

All of the scouts and hunters looked to Joshua who arose to step carefully into the swath of horse tracks before squatting back down on his heels. "Not this one," he said, finger tracing an outline. "It's mounted. I think we'll find others."

Glenn was fascinated as he stared at the print that Joshua had selected from all the others. Glenn couldn't see what set it apart except that it was a little deeper and that meant either the pony was exceptionally large or else it was carrying a rider. The buckskinners all joined their leader and soon they were picking out other mounted ponies.

"This bunch passed yesterday, probably about now."

"What do you want to do, Mr. Hood?" a scout asked. "We sure as hell don't want to get caught by a big Cheyenne war party out here in this open basin."

"Then we'd best push on," Joshua announced. "There's some canyons in those foothills and I expect more than a few buffalo."

No one seemed very happy with this decision but knew better than to object. So the men remounted their horses and Joshua gave the word that the mule skinners were to push their mules and keep them moving at a trot.

All afternoon they kept up a hard pace, the mules especially having trouble because the wagon wheels sliced into the soft spring earth like plowshares. Sometimes the wagon wheels got tangled in the heavy brush and then they'd be roped by the horsemen and dragged over their obstacles. They kept rolling ever higher into the foothills.

By four o'clock that afternoon they were finally hidden by ridges and moving up into a grassy canyon that hadn't even been visible from the basin they'd just crossed. And now Glenn could see that the surrounding hills were riddled with deposits of crumbling black coal. In many places where a bluff had broken off due to weathering, there was a landslide of the stuff. Glenn hoped that this coal was of good enough quality to serve the needs of the Union Pacific's ravenous locomotives.

"We'll find buffalo here if they hold to their old patterns," Joshua promised less than an hour before they saw a herd of about five hundred of the massive, shaggy beasts.

Glenn's heart beat faster. These were not the first buffalo he'd seen since joining the railroad, but they were the largest single herd and he had the impression that they had rarely been hunted for they did not seem especially alarmed when Joshua ordered his men to prepare for the hunt.

"This trip we'll shoot forty," he told his hunters. "That'll fill the meat wagons and give us plenty to eat besides."

"Can we keep the hides?" a bearded buckskinner asked.

"If you want to skin 'em out after dark, you can," Joshua announced to his hunters. "Because first thing tomorrow morning, we're heading back to the rail line."

The hunter grinned through missing teeth. "Hides are bringing a dollar."

To Glenn, it didn't seem worth the mess and trouble to skin one of the great, shaggy beasts and lug the extremely heavy, stinking hides all the way back to the railhead just to sell for a dollar. But the hunters thought differently and since a man could buy a cheap bottle of whiskey for a dollar in one of the tent saloons, it was considered more than worth the effort.

Glenn was surprised to hear Joshua say that they would make the kill immediately because the sun was already beginning to dive into the coal-rich hilltops. But he kept quiet and watched as the hunters checked their weapons and then prepared to stalk the herd on foot.

"You comin', college boy?"

"Sure," Glenn said, surprised that he had been invited because he'd expected to remain with the mule skinners and their meat wagons.

Joshua and the hunters had all been armed by the Union Pacific with the new .44-caliber rimfire Winchesters but now they went to the wagons and replaced those relatively light repeating weapons with their old and trusted single-shot Sharps buffalo rifles. These ranged in a variety of calibers, most being .45 and .52 breechloaders that Glenn had heard hunters boast could drop a bull at a thousand yards. Including Joshua, there were eight hunters and they fanned out and began to approach the herd from downwind.

"How come they don't run?" Glenn blurted as they drew nearer and nearer.

"Shhh! They can't see worth spit but they can hear and smell. Just keep your mouth shut and your eyes open."

Stung by Joshua's sharp reprimand, Glenn moved a little away from Joshua and behind the advancing line of hunters. Using a hand signal, Joshua dropped to a prone position. He eased the big rifle out in front of him and then placed five linen-wrapped cartridges side by side before he turned to motion Glenn over.

"The leader of a buffalo herd," he whispered, "is almost always a cow. Unless you pick her out and kill her first she'll get 'em to runnin'."

"How do you know which is the right cow?"

"That's the only tricky part," Joshua said and pointed a blunt finger with a tight smile as he studied the herd.

Long minutes passed and then Joshua said, "That one."

Before Glenn even had time to be sure which one that Joshua had chosen, the hunter drew a bead on the cow and slowly squeezed his trigger.

The heavy Sharps bellowed like a cannon, and through the cloud of billowing smoke, Glenn saw a cow throw up her head, roll her eyes, then buckle in the front knees and collapse, mouth spewing bloody saliva.

Glenn was astonished to see the lack of reaction from the other buffalo. They began to stomp and throw their heads about, but otherwise they simply milled about in bewildered confusion as Joshua quickly inserted another linen cartridge into the buffalo rifle.

With a grin, he turned to Glenn and said, "Told ya they'd get confused and not stampede if I shot the right cow."

Glenn was staring at the dying cow and the calf that had rushed to her side and began to bawl. He looked up just in time to see Joshua signal to another of the hunters to take his turn if he'd picked out the new leader. The hunter nodded, picked one particularly agitated cow out of hundreds, and shot her cleanly through the lungs.

Glenn soon lost track of time and reality. It was clear that Joshua and his hunters had done this many times. But to Glenn, it was a shock to see the deliberate way that the hunters selected each replacement leader and killed her, then waited to see what cow would be next while the entire herd milled about in growing confusion and anxiety.

"They're about to stampede," Joshua said when perhaps a dozen of the cows were in various stages of death. And with that, Joshua laid his sights on a bull and shot the huge bellowing beast through the heart.

Glenn swore he could feel the earth tremble when that woolly giant landed and its hooves began to beat at the sky and its horns gouged up hunks of grass. Killing the bull had been a signal and the other hunters began to fire rapidly. Glenn doubted if any of them missed as a cow suddenly bolted away and the rest of the herd began to follow.

The last three bulls were dropped as they began to run after the herd and one of them turned back to face the line of hunters that he could not even see. A volley of rifle shots drove the bull back on his haunches and Glenn looked away as the last bullet struck the beast in the face.

"What's the matter," Joshua asked. "The sight of the kill too much for your delicate nature?"

"Go to hell," Glenn snapped, striding back to the meat wagons. The mule skinners were already climbing into their wagons and starting forward as the dying sun flared across the coal hills and the night shadows raced east to cover the valley of death.

CHAPTER 17

"Let's get rolling!" Joshua shouted across the field early the next morning as the last wagons were being loaded with the quartered buffalo carcasses and their hides.

Glenn was as eager as Joshua to get moving. He'd stayed up late that night helping with the butchering of the forty buffalo and there had been little time for sleep. Now, gritty-eyed and with his clothes stiff with dried blood and congealed fat, all he wanted to do was to leave this valley and return to the relative safety and comfort of the Union Pacific Railroad's construction crews. He yearned for a shave, hot bath, clean clothing, food, and the chance to see Megan again.

"I'd better bring back some coal samples," Glenn said, untying his saddlebags. "They'll want to judge the quality of these deposits."

"You should have collected your damn samples before now," Joshua growled.

"I'll be back before you leave," Glenn said, mounting his horse and galloping about a quarter of a mile up to the face of a crumbling black hill where he dismounted.

Glenn wasted no time in stuffing his saddlebags with small chunks of coal. It looked very pure and of high quality, but Glenn was not prepared to jump to any conclusions. He'd leave that to the geologist hired by the Union Pacific and then he'd let them figure out what conversions might have to be made to the locomotives. Dodge had told him that the locomotive stacks would have to be modified for coal but otherwise very few engine modifications were necessary.

"If this is high grade," Glenn said to himself as he buckled the straps to his saddlebags and tied them to his saddle, "it will supply the Union Pacific's locomotives for at least a hundred years."

Glenn galloped back down to the camp just as the mule skinners jumped up on their wagon seats. One by one they cracked their whips and maneuvered their now heavily laden wagons into traveling formation. Glenn figured that their return to the U.P. line would be slow because of the tons of meat and hides that they were transporting. At least now, however, they would be dropping out of these foothills toward the vast sage-covered basin about to be severed by the Union Pacific's new rails.

As they rolled out of the huge, grass-covered canyon, Glenn looked back to see a swarm of vultures circling low in the sky. Glancing over at Joshua with more than a little alarm, he said, "Aren't you afraid that they'll attract the attention of the Cheyenne?"

"You're learnin', college boy," Joshua replied.

Glenn's eyes were pulled to the carrion they'd left behind. He wondered if the buffalo herd that had escaped would return to this place or if the smell and sight of death would spook them away for a long, long while. He would have liked to have asked Joshua but finally decided that the man would probably ridicule

him for asking a pointless question. Besides, the buffalo had proven themselves to be half-blind and plenty
stupid enough to return in a few days. That was why
the great buffalo herds faced almost certain extinction
during the next decade when the transcontinental railroad ushered in a flood tide of emigrants.

It was midmorning when Joshua's point rider suddenly threw his pistol into the air and emptied three
warning bullets at the azure Wyoming sky. Glenn saw
the small puffs of gunpowder, then a moment later
heard the retorts. "What . . ."

"Indians," Joshua said as he reined his horse around
and spurred back toward the meat wagons.

Glenn followed the man as the hunting party's out-
riders came racing in from the point and the flanks.
In moments the wagons were circled just as the first
Oregon Trail emigrant wagon trains had circled when it
appeared that an Indian attack was imminent. The mules
skinners hobbled the animals and everyone dragged out
their Sharps buffalo rifles along with their new repeating
Winchesters.

Their little party numbered thirteen, a fact that Glenn
hoped did not prove to be unlucky. Every man was a
veteran fighter and most were crack shots. Given that
they had the significant advantage over the Cheyenne
because of the Winchester repeaters, Glenn knew that
it would take a huge force of Indians to overrun and
slaughter them. It would be an extremely costly victory
for the Cheyenne.

"Nobody fire unless I tell you to!" Joshua ordered.
"And if this goes bad, your first shot had better be with
the Sharps and it damn sure had better count."

Glenn didn't have a Sharps but he did have a Winchester and a pistol. He waited with his heart drumming in his chest as the Cheyenne war party grew larger and larger on the horizon. Every man was counting the number of Cheyenne and several began to call out their hurried tallies.

"I count seventy-three!"

"Eighty-five!"

"Hell, I'm at a hundred and still counting!"

Glenn realized his throat was parched and the palms of his hands were clammy. He remembered the last time that he had faced Indians and almost been killed and he prayed that he would be spared either death or injury. But as the body of Cheyenne horsemen grew ever larger, his hopes plummeted. Glenn was sure that there were well over a hundred Cheyenne warriors galloping toward them.

Joshua glanced at Glenn and said, "You ready for a hard fight to the death?"

"If necessary," Glenn replied in a voice stretched thin enough to mock his words.

"Maybe when they see we mean to fight and have Winchesters they'll decide to bargain," Joshua offered, not sounding very hopeful.

"Will they just charge, or what?"

"I doubt they've thought it out yet themselves," Joshua replied. "I know these people and they aren't any more interested in dying than ourselves. I expect they'll take a good hard look at us and then decide how best to get whatever it is they want."

"Probably our scalps."

Joshua didn't either agree or disagree with Glenn's comment. He just cradled his buffalo rifle and waited patiently as the Indians drew to within a half mile and then fanned out in a line that was about fifty yards wide.

"There's a hundred and seventeen of them," one of the mule skinners said to no one in particular.

"Shit," another man swore, "every damn one of 'em have rifles."

"Hell, they're just old trade rifles that can't match ours. Probably half of 'em won't shoot straight."

"That's not true," Joshua warned his men. "Those braves won't have repeaters, but you can bet that a few of them have these Sharps and some Hawkens. And they know how to use them."

"Will they wait to attack at night?" Glenn asked, afraid that his question was foolish.

"No," Joshua said, "they don't like to fight in the dark any more than we do. Sundown, sunrise, they like to attack when the sun is in your face and at their backs."

Glenn looked up at the sun, which was directly overhead. If the Indians waited until sundown, it was going to be a long, teeth-grinding afternoon.

"Look!" one of the mule skinners said. "They're comin' out to palaver!"

Everyone saw three Cheyenne detach themselves from the group and ride forward with their rifles resting on their thighs, barrels pointed straight up.

"Joshua, do you recognize any of them?" Glenn asked hopefully.

"Uh-uh. But this is encouraging. Guess I better talk to 'em. You want to ride out with me, college boy?"

Glenn surprised himself by saying, "I wouldn't miss it for the world."

"You sure?"

"Yes," Glenn said, hating himself for his foolish pride. He couldn't bear the idea that Megan might hear that he had declined to ride into danger with the U.P.'s chief scout.

"I want to go too," decided another scout named Audie. "Besides you, Mr. Hood, I'm the only one that has lived with those people. Might be that one of 'em will recognize me."

"All right," Joshua agreed, "let's mount up."

"Do we bring our Winchester repeating rifles?" Glenn asked.

"Damn right we do! I want 'em to know what they'll be facing if they decide to fight."

Glenn told himself that he was insane to be doing this. He silently gave himself a good cussing as he checked his cinch to make sure that his saddle wouldn't roll if he had to beat a hasty retreat back to the circle of meat wagons.

"You finally ready?" Joshua asked.

"I'm ready," Glenn answered as he jammed his boot into his stirrup and threw a leg over his cantle. "Ready as I'll ever be."

"Then let's visit these fighting roosters."

They rode out between the wagons at a walk and Joshua said, "Hold your rifles just like the Indians and try to remember to smile."

"Smile?" Audie managed a nervous laugh. "Mr. Hood, my liver is already shakin' so hard that I'm about to plumb tickle myself to death."

Joshua laughed loud enough to be heard by both his men and the Cheyenne war party but even to Glenn it sounded forced and very hollow. He swore that his heart was beating so loudly that it surely must be heard by the Indians.

"Far enough," Joshua called, raising his left hand while his right held his reins and rifle.

Glenn and Audie followed suit and so did the three Cheyenne. Joshua said to Audie. "I don't recognize a single one of 'em, do you?"

"I wish to God I did."

In rapid sign language coupled with guttural Cheyenne words, Joshua began to carry on a solo conversation. Glenn watched the Indians' faces closely. They were not wearing war paint, but he knew that didn't mean they weren't spoiling for a fight. They were tall, strikingly handsome men with cold, hard eyes and high cheekbones. They wore buckskins and feathers, but no warbonnets. One man carried a quiver of arrows slung by a thong over his shoulder and a bow in one hand and an old Army Colt pistol jammed into a colorfully beaded belt. Their saddles were really just pads with leather loops for stirrups and they controlled their exceptionally fine horses with thick rawhide thongs looped over their mounts' lower jaws. Their horses were all lean, powerfully muscled stallions with fire in their eyes.

Glenn didn't trust himself to glance sideways at Audie. His heart was racing and yet he was fascinated by the three warriors who now began to take turns speaking and making sign. Glenn knew only a few gestures of the universal sign language and one of them was for buffalo, which was both forefingers hooked inward. From what Glenn could tell, the Cheyenne were upset about the meat wagons and what they knew to be a large kill back up in the foothills.

Their voices were angry, their gestures sharp and abrupt. Everything that Glenn could read told him that these Cheyenne were furious about the buffalo kill. Glenn could feel sweat trickle down his spine and he wondered how fast he could drop the barrel of his rifle and use it to good effect. The Indians were all armed with bone-handled knifes and he had heard that they could draw their knives and hurl them in the blink of an eye and rarely miss. If that was the case, Glenn thought that he was probably a dead man.

Through the angry talk, Joshua remained very calm, which was all the more remarkable because Glenn knew the chief scout to be a man with an explosive temper. Joshua kept speaking in a soft voice and making slow and very deliberate sign so that his words and his hands would leave no room for misinterpretation.

Many gestures were made toward the meat wagons and finally Glenn dared to say in a hushed voice, "If they want the meat, give it to them! It's not worth dying for."

"It might be to them," Joshua said. "And it's a matter of honor to our side. We give them too much and they'll expect more the next time."

Glenn wasn't worrying about a "next time" but decided that he had better remain silent. One of the Indians—a tall, proud-looking warrior with a terrible scar across his left cheek—kept glancing up at the buzzards and when they disappeared into the canyon, indicating they were beginning to feed, he pointed his rifle in their direction and spoke rapidly.

"What is he saying?"

"He says that they must go up there and get meat or the kill will be fouled by the buzzards."

"Then we won't have to give them our meat?"

"I have offered them three buffalo. They want twenty."

"Jezus," Glenn whispered, "give it to them!"

"Uh-uh," Joshua said. "But I believe we're about to settle for ten."

Another anxious quarter hour droned on until Joshua said the words "Antelope Woman" and pointed north. The Indians nodded and pointed too.

"She's with them in Running Elk's camp," Joshua said without taking his eyes off the Cheyenne. "They say that she came alone and asked to stay. I know Running Elk. He's a great chief among these people."

Glenn nodded. He had known the half-breed girl but not all that well. It was hard for him to imagine any woman doing such a thing but Glenn was happy to hear that Cassie had not been killed or tortured by the Cheyenne and instead had been accepted back into their villages.

Joshua and the Cheyenne finally reached an agreement of ten buffalo kills that filled one entire wagon. The wagon and its mules, of course, would also be part of the price for they were needed to deliver the meat to the hungry Cheyenne villages. For this, Joshua and his scouting party would be allowed to return to the camp of the Iron Horse with the other three wagons.

Glenn expelled a deep sigh of relief that the scarfaced Indian heard and found amusing enough to give a fleeting smile. Or maybe he was also relieved not to have to face the Winchester repeaters and a hard fight with the experienced and determined U.P. scouts and mule skinners.

"It's done," Joshua said, leaning over his saddle horn.

"Are we going to smoke a peace pipe or anything?" Glenn blurted.

"No. We're just going to leave one wagon and put as much distance between us and them as we can before sundown."

The meeting was over. Glenn nodded to the Indians and each in turn nodded to him and used sign to say farewell. Then they whirled their horses around and galloped back to their war party. There was some yips and whoops that Glenn hoped stemmed from acceptance rather than displeasure at the agreed upon peace terms.

"Dudley!" Joshua called as soon as they had returned to their circle of wagons.

"Yes, sir!"

"Climb down from your wagon and ride with John Pardee. I gave them Indians your wagon, mules, and buffalo meat."

"But, Mr. Hood! These here are my own mules! I contracted the railroad for 'em. I brought 'em all the way from Missouri to Omaha and out here."

"They're old, Dudley. The worst team of the bunch. Now do as I say and I'll see that you get a better pair."

Dudley covered his face and turned away to hide the grief he felt at losing his beloved mules to the Indians. Glenn watched as the man jumped down from the meat wagon and spent a moment with each of the four Missouri mules. He put his face to their graying muzzles and whispered farewells.

"They'll eat 'em," Dudley said a few minutes later to no one in particular. "Them bloody sonsabitches will eat 'em all."

"No they won't," Joshua said. "Apache like mule meat, but not the Sioux or the Cheyenne."

"They don't?"

"No," Joshua said firmly. "So stop acting like a gawddamn fool and get up on Pardee's wagon before we let those Cheyenne use you for target practice."

"Yes, sir," Dudley said. "If you're sure that they won't eat my mules."

"I'm sure," Joshua promised. "Now, let's line the wagons out and make tracks."

"Will they honor the agreement?" Glenn asked.

"They will," Joshua said. "But that don't mean that we won't meet another bunch that'll want to fight more than eat."

Everyone understood. The wagons were pulled out of the circle and into line as the Cheyenne, whooping and yipping, raced over to the abandoned meat wagon. The Indians jumped off their horses and began to hack off big hunks of raw buffalo meat and devour it.

"They act like they're starving," a scout said.

"Well, they were hungry," Joshua said. "It's been a hard winter an' I'll bet their village, wherever it is, could sure use that meat. They'll be riding up to the kill and beating off them buzzards."

"What for?" Glenn asked.

"Because their favorite cuts are the hump fat and the tongue which we left to rot. Same with the intestines."

"They eat those too?" Glenn asked with astonishment.

"You bet they do. Any warrior worth his salt will feed an intestine down his gullet just like a sparrow swallowing a big worm."

Glenn looked back at the Cheyenne who were hacking at the meat. One of the mules began to bray and Dudley broke down and cried like he'd lost his best friends, which maybe he had.

"Let's roll!" Joshua shouted. "We ain't stopping until we reach the end of the track!"

That was fine with Glenn. He would have liked to have known what Joshua and the Cheyenne had said to each other during their long and lively talk but maybe he could find that out later. And he supposed that Liam would be interested to learn that Cassie, now called Antelope Woman, was still alive and had been accepted back by the Cheyenne.

But Glenn knew all that was really insignificant compared to keeping his scalp intact and seeing Megan's lovely face once again.

CHAPTER
18

By the time that Joshua and his hunting party arrived at the end-of-track, they were calling the latest hell-on-wheels town Medicine Bow. The construction crews had been subsisting on beef and beans so when the meat wagons rolled in, there was a good deal of excitement. The crews stopped working for a few minutes to call out to the scouts and hunters. Mostly, they yelled friendly taunts and insults.

"See you boys still got your hair!" a big Irishman bellowed.

"More'n you got!" came the taunting reply.

"Ha, you lucky bastards do nothin' but ride around and shoot buffalo while we're here bustin' our asses and building a railroad."

"Ain't my fault that you work like a slave and are dumber than the buffalo we shoot!"

Glenn was amazed at the Union Pacific's rate of construction progress since he'd last been at the end-of-track. At this rate, he was sure that the rails would indeed reach the Utah Territory before next winter closed the operation down.

"How many you shoot?"

"Forty but we gave the Cheyenne a wagonload in exchange for our scalps."

"Good trade!"

Glenn enjoyed the easy banter and it felt good again to see the smiling faces of men he'd hired and worked with for almost two years. These were rough, unprincipled men quick to fight and curse but also honorable and hardworking. Most of them were bachelors, but a few had left families in search of work and a chance to tame the West. Later, they'd send for their families to join them where the rails met.

As they rode down the street of Medicine Bow, the workers who were taking a breather fell in behind the meat wagons, anxious to inspect the kill. Buffalo meat was always a favorite of the construction crews and this latest kill would last a couple of weeks. There would be rich buffalo stew and roasts along with thick steaks until, at the last, they would be eating buffalo hash.

As they traveled through the crowd of curious onlookers, Glenn was searching for Megan's tent saloon that he finally spotted at the east end of the tent city. However, before he could reach it, a young railroad clerk hurried up and said, "Mr. Gilchrist, General Dodge wants to see you and Mr. Hood right away."

"You mean the general ain't even going to give us enough time for a couple of glasses of whiskey in Megan's Place?" Joshua snorted. "What the hell is the big rush?"

"Word travels fast. We hear you made peace with the Cheyenne, Mr. Hood."

A silence fell over the crews and the hammers stopped ringing because men wanted to hear Joshua say that they no longer had to worry about being attacked.

Joshua scratched himself and said, "I have to tell you the truth—we bought 'em off with meat and a wagon. But that sure don't mean we are at peace."

"Oh," the clerk replied, unable to hide the disappointment in his voice. "Well, we're still glad that you and your scouts made it back alive. Now, if you'll follow me, General Dodge and the Casement brothers are waiting."

General Grenville Dodge had been a Civil War hero who had been severely wounded and tested in many battles. His bravery and leadership were unquestioned among his soldiers but he had also distinguished himself as a bridge and railroad builder for the Union Army. He had once been on intimate terms with no less than President Abraham Lincoln who consulted him as to the best route needed to link the East with the West.

Dodge was not a physically imposing man and would not have stood out at a social gathering. He was neither eloquent or handsome but his dedication and perseverance to achieving his goals were legendary. He was like a bulldog in his single-minded determination to build this railroad. Glenn had learned that the man did not appreciate idle talk, jokes, or banter. Dodge was temperate in his habits and expected those who answered to him to be of a like nature. When you went to see Dodge, you got right down to business and you had better not embellish your accomplishment, overestimate your abilities, or waste time trying to impress the chief engineer or you would be abruptly dismissed.

"Gentlemen," Dodge said when they had been ushered into the Union Pacific's headquarters coach with its polished mahogany furniture and plush green velvet drapes, "I understand that you had an encounter with a big war party of Cheyenne. We'd very much like to hear about it."

"They were Cheyenne," Joshua said.

"Did you know them from the time when you lived among those people," Dan Casement asked.

"No, sir."

Brigadier General John Casement scowled. Like his brother, he wore a full beard and was short of stature but very aggressive and hard driving. "We were hoping that you might have forged us a new peace treaty."

"I'm sorry, sir. All I did was to avoid a fight."

"That's still important," Dan Casement finally said. "Mr. Hood, do you think that we can negotiate a safe crossing into the Utah Territory?"

"I doubt it," Joshua said bluntly.

Dan looked to their chief engineer. Dodge stroked his beard and said, "Which chief did you run across?"

"He was a sub-chief named Bent Wing."

"How large was his party?"

"A little over a hundred. They were almost all armed with single-shot percussion rifles."

"But no Winchester repeaters?"

"No, sir, but they sure had their eyes on ours."

"Were they on the warpath, or just a hunt?"

"General, I think they were just mighty damned hungry. It was plain to me that they wanted our buffalo meat. After they were full, I expect they'd get around to thinking of starting a bad fight."

It was clear from Dodge's expression that this was not the news that he'd hoped to hear. "Did you invite them here to talk peace?"

"I did."

"And they said?"

"They said that they wanted to eat."

"Nothing more?"

"No, sir, they looked pretty hungry." Joshua glanced sideways. "Isn't that right, Glenn?"

"Yes," Glenn said, the memory of how the Cheyenne had ravished Dudley's meat wagon still very vivid.

Dodge looked to the Casement brothers. "I think this is still encouraging news," he decided. "If they had been sworn to fight, I don't think that Mr. Hood and Mr. Gilchrist would be alive to tell us about this encounter."

"That's a good way to look at it," Joshua said, "and probably true. I got a feeling that the Cheyenne are going to be easier to deal with than the Sioux, but they'll still raid."

"Undoubtedly. We lost three men yesterday at Rock Creek," Dodge said, an undercurrent of bitterness in his voice. "A war party of Cheyenne struck a small crew I'd left to repair some line right after daybreak. They killed and scalped all six men and took their horses and mules. I won't send another repair crew unless I get some help from the Army and that doesn't seem to be very damn likely."

"I do have some good news," Glenn offered.

"Let's hear it," Dodge urged.

Glenn had carried his saddlebags into the plush coach and now he unbuckled them. He extracted three lumps of coal and handed them to Dodge and the Casement brothers. "This coal was found about forty miles southwest of Fort Steele."

"It looks good," Dan Casement said, inspecting the lump in his hand very carefully. "As good as we buy and ship out here from the East."

"I think so too," Dodge commented. "How large would you estimate the deposit?"

"There is at least enough to last this railroad a century," Glenn said without hesitation.

"Forty miles," Dodge mused. "Even with heavy armed escorts, it would put our freighters at great risk. I'm afraid that's unavoidable. Firewood is becoming very scarce and we sure can't afford to keep hauling it in from the Laramie Mountains or the Black Hills."

"General Dodge, as we build westward, we may find deposits closer to your proposed line," Joshua said. "Glenn collected this in a canyon where I knew we'd find buffalo."

"I'll send these coal samples back to Omaha where our geologist can give us his opinion as to their quality," Dodge said. "I'm sure that when we receive his report, we'll want to send a heavily escorted train of freight wagons out here along with enough men to protect themselves while they fill the wagons. I'll expect you to escort them and bring us fresh buffalo meat, Mr. Hood."

"Yes, sir."

Joshua shifted impatiently on his feet. He smelled and looked rank in his blood-crusted buckskins and with his hair all tangled and greasy. Glenn knew that he looked and smelled every bit as bad.

"You may be excused, Mr. Hood," Dodge said. "And I'd like you to pass on to your men our appreciation for a job well done. Not only does your buffalo meat add variety to our rations, but this coal field that you have shown Mr. Gilchrist will be enormously beneficial to the Union Pacific and most certainly result in a huge savings."

"Does that mean I'll get a bonus, General?" Joshua asked with a grin.

Dodge actually smiled. "No, but you get to keep your job, Mr. Hood."

"Thank you, sir."

When Joshua was gone, Dodge ordered drinks all around and one of his assistants quickly filled crystal tumblers with good Kentucky whiskey. Dodge raised his glass and said, "To a peace treaty with the Cheyenne."

They all seconded the toast and then Dodge turned to Glenn and said, "Now what was *your* impression of that meeting between the Cheyenne and Mr. Hood?"

"It was just as he described," Glenn answered. "The Indians would have attacked if we had not been carrying our Winchester repeating rifles. I think they, along with Mr. Hood's coolness and ability to speak their language, were the deciding factors for our peaceful outcome."

"Yes," Dodge agreed, "the Indians realize how devastating those rifles can be in the hands of veteran fighters. Did Mr. Hood conduct himself well?"

The question caught Glenn off guard. "Yes, sir! It seemed obvious to me that he was able to calm down the Indians and strike an agreement. I could tell at first that they were damned upset about our killing so many buffalo."

"I imagine so," Dodge said. "They understand that the buffalo is their lifeblood and that we will kill them in great numbers. To try and convince them otherwise is folly."

"These coal deposits will be of huge benefit to the Union Pacific," John Casement said. "In your opinion, Glenn, how does the land run from west of the Platte crossing?"

"Most of the time I was surveying and drafting construction plans for the bridge," Glenn explained, "but on two occasions I did ride west to survey. There is one pretty good grade about twenty miles west of Fort Steele and then it drops down into that desert."

"Did you find any water out there?" Dodge asked.

"Yes, but I can't promise you that the streams and springs will still flow this summer when we cross that desert. It's impossible to tell. That's still pretty high country—well over six thousand feet and even this late in the year there are big patches of snow on the ground."

"We'll be through it by August," John Casement vowed. "The important thing is to get that Platte River bridge up and keep the grading crews working way out ahead of the construction crews."

Dodge nodded in agreement. "You and Mr. Hood did very well. Any complaints from the Platte?"

"No, sir," Glenn said, knowing that Dodge was referring to the bridge-building crew and the surveyors whose lives were always at risk because they were the Union Pacific's vanguard. "They're very concerned about the Cheyenne and never stray far from their new rifles which they treat with more respect than they do their surveying instruments."

Dodge flashed the briefest of smiles. "Mr. Gilchrist, I can see that you are in real need of a bath, a shave, and a fresh change of clothes so we'll let you go for now."

"I do have one other matter to relate," Glenn said.

"I'm sure that you recall that Liam O'Connell brought in a wagonload of railroad ties from North Platte."

"Of course. That was a very explosive situation. I thought our mule skinners were going to lynch the man for saving that Cheyenne half-breed."

"Well," Glenn said, "the woman was accepted back by her people."

Dodge glanced at the Casement brothers and then back to Glenn. "Has that any bearing on our relationships with the Cheyenne?"

"I don't think so, or Joshua would have mentioned it. I just thought that you might want to know. Apparently, her Indian name is Antelope Woman and she is living in Running Elk's village."

"Did you know the girl?"

"I'd seen her a few times when I visited the Silver Dollar Saloon in North Platte. I even exchanged pleasantries with her . . . but nothing else. Cassie always struck me as a cut above most saloon girls."

"She did knife Haws in cold blood," John Casement said with a scowl. "I think it all worked out for the best that the half-breed ran off to live with the Cheyenne. I know that we couldn't possibly have protected her from the mule skinners. The Army wouldn't even have tried."

"Yes, sir." Glenn downed his whiskey and excused himself to get a bath and shave. He had never felt so grubby. Glenn was afraid that Megan wouldn't even recognize him if he didn't clean up before he went over to pay his respects.

And so, it was a good two hours before he walked into Megan's Place wearing a fresh suit and starched collar. His jowls were shaved to a shine, his hair was combed, and his boots were polished.

"Hello, Rachel!" he called, for she was the first person that he saw when he walked into the saloon. "How are you?"

"Mr. Gilchrist! Welcome back to civilization!"

Glenn smiled because he had always liked Megan's friend and assistant manager. Rachel had long had a crush on Liam but now, as Glenn came over and gave her a hug, he saw Peter Arlington sitting at the preferred table with his Cuban cigar and his million-dollar smile.

"Glenn, good to see you again!" Arlington called out. "Come join me for a drink."

Glenn disengaged from Rachel and walked over to shake hands with the polished Bostonian. "How have you been while I've been trying to keep my scalp?"

Arlington laughed. "Well, perhaps you ought to join my hunting party. It would be exciting."

"No thanks," Glenn said. "At least the Union Pacific pays me for risking my neck."

Arlington's smile slipped a little. "I pay very well too," he said, clearly misunderstanding Glenn's words. "You can ask Liam or the Malloy brothers."

"I didn't mean to imply otherwise."

"Of course you didn't," Rachel said, looking at Arlington with concern. "What is the matter with you, Peter? You don't seem yourself today."

"It's nothing," Arlington said brusquely. "Glenn, can I buy you the best whiskey this saloon has to offer?"

"Of course." Glenn looked around. "Where's Megan?"

"She is visiting Aileen and Jenny. Did you know that Aileen's marriage to Dr. Wiseman has been set for the day after tomorrow?"

"I had no idea that it was going to happen so soon."

"Oh, but it is," Rachel said, pausing to look straight into Arlington's eyes. "Isn't it wonderful!"

"I suppose," Arlington said without enthusiasm.

If Rachel was disappointed by his lukewarm reaction, she did not let it show and said to Glenn, "The Reverend Holloway is coming all the way from Cheyenne to perform the ceremony. They'll be married out beside the track and Peter is going to write a big article and there will be a photographer."

"I see."

Rachel placed her hand on Arlington's shoulder. "Megan is so generous. She's hosting the reception and it will be a real wingdinger. I'm green with envy."

Glenn could sense that Rachel really was envious. And it was clear from the way that Peter Arlington was squirming and frowning that Rachel had pressed the wealthy young man from Boston to make it a dual marriage ceremony. This was a shock to Glenn because when he'd last been among these people, Rachel was still acting as if she was in love with Liam. Obviously, she had set her sights a whole lot higher.

"Tell me about your adventure out in the wilderness," Arlington said. "I understand that you had an encounter with the Cheyenne. Enough of them to make things very interesting if they'd decided to fight."

"That's the truth," Glenn admitted, expecting Arlington to take notes for his father's newspaper. "Joshua and our rifles made the difference."

"Could you have defeated them?" Arlington asked without reaching for paper or pen.

"I don't know. I think we could have held them off indefinitely. Our wagons were circled. We had barrels of water and four wagonloads of fresh buffalo meat. We were all heavily armed with the Winchester repeaters, buffalo rifles, and pistols. I believe we could have given a very good account of ourselves and killed a lot of Cheyenne warriors."

"I see."

"Why are you still at end-of-track?" Glenn asked. "I would have thought that you and your employees would have been out stalking that trophy buffalo by now."

Arlington threw up his hands in a gesture of exasperation. "Liam says that it is still a little early in the year for us to go out and the Malloy brothers are having second thoughts about the risks with Indians."

"I see." Glenn shrugged. "Those risks are very real, Peter. I really think that you ought to stay close to the tracks."

"Then how am I supposed to find and kill a real trophy buffalo?"

"Maybe you aren't," Rachel said, leaning in between them. "Maybe you're meant to stay here with me."

Glenn watched as Rachel squeezed Arlington's hand. Arlington's reaction was to pull free and drain his glass of whiskey.

"Why don't you refill my glass and bring the bottle over," Arlington said, avoiding Rachel's eyes. "Glenn looks like a man who needs a drink."

Rachel flushed with anger. "Sure! Anything you say, Mr. Arlington!"

Rachel got up from her chair and huffed away.

"She is really wearing on my nerves," Arlington said quietly. "I have no intention of marrying a saloon keeper."

Glenn bristled at that remark. After all, Megan was a saloon keeper and there was no woman in the world that he placed as high. "There's no disgrace working in a saloon."

"I didn't mean to imply any superiority," Arlington said quickly. "Because, really, I do not. It's just that Rachel is obviously not an educated person like ourselves and comes from a much lower station."

"I see," Glenn managed to reply, wishing that he had not taken a seat at this man's table and instead had gone over to visit Megan and Aileen.

"I expect that I shall be leaving before too much longer, trophy or no trophy."

"What about all the stories that you had intended to write on the Union Pacific?"

"Oh, those. Well, I have written quite a few but I just received a telegraph from my father indicating that they are not generating the kind of excitement that our newspaper had hoped. My father is also now overstocked with my accounts of frontier Indian fights and adventures."

"I see. So what are your plans other than to shoot a few trophy buffalo?"

Arlington drummed his fingers impatiently on the table and glanced toward the bar, obviously irritated that Rachel was taking so long to bring them a fresh bottle.

"My father is urging me to go to California and write stories about your rival—the Central Pacific Railroad."

"I guess that makes sense."

"Of course it does!" Arlington leaned closer. "I'm sure I don't have to tell you that Donner Pass stirs some rather powerful and macabre images."

Glenn knew that he was referring to the ill-fated Donner Party that had suffered so terribly a few years earlier. "Yes," he said, "I'm sure that it does."

"At any rate," Arlington said, "I do want to make at least one serious attempt to bag a trophy buffalo and I think that I shall do so in the very near future."

"Good."

"I do have to admit, however, that I will be ever so glad when this damned wedding is over and that reverend has returned to his congregation in Cheyenne. Maybe then Rachel will stop pestering me to marry her."

"Maybe," Glenn said absently, wishing that Rachel would bring him a drink so that he could down it and escape to find Megan.

CHAPTER
19

Liam's hip was paining him again as it always did just before it rained. And now he stood fidgeting in a new suit of scratchy woolen clothes and a starched collar that was damned near choking off his wind. His stomach was boiling with bile and his head was pounding. Liam was miserable.

"What the hell are we waiting for?" he hissed out of the corner of his mouth to Glenn. "I thought this wedding was supposed to be at noon!"

"It was," Glenn replied in a hushed voice, "but the Reverend Holloway is running late. I don't know the reason."

"Shit," Liam swore under his breath. "I hate waitin' on anybody. Even my sister."

Glenn glanced sideways at Liam. It was obvious that the man was nursing his usual severe hangover. In just the few days that Glenn had been in Medicine Bow, Liam had been drunk every evening and there was a wild and reckless air about him that caused men to avoid his company.

"Here they come," Liam said, twisting around along with the crowd that filled Megan's tent saloon.

Glenn was a six-footer and could peer over most

of the guests and what he saw brought a smile to his lips. Aileen looked magnificent. She wore a dress that she'd ordered from St. Louis and it was peach-colored with white lace to match her white gloves. Her reddish-brown hair had been brushed to a shine and her face was radiant with happiness. Glenn had never seen Aileen look so lovely. She was escorted into the tent by the courtly Henry Harrison Armbruster. Probably Liam should have given his sister away but Glenn knew that Aileen would not have risked him being drunk and ruining this ceremony. Besides, Henry Harrison was a man of dignity and charm.

The groom was no less impressive. Dr. Thaddeus Wiseman towered over everyone and was resplendent in a dark blue suit, white shirt, and collar. A splash of color was evident because someone had found a rose for the doctor to wear in his lapel.

Megan entered the tent with little Jenny and Glenn thought them every inch the present and the future beauties of their proud Irish heritage. Just looking at Megan caused Glenn to ache with desire. She was more beautiful than a rainbow, softer than a sunset gentle across the hills. If Glenn allowed himself to think about how Megan had chosen Thaddeus over himself, it filled him with despair. Instead, he was determined to reflect on his second chance to win her love.

The crowd was all smiles as the wedding party came to a halt before the minister from Cheyenne. At that moment, everyone fell silent. The Reverend Vincent Holloway was a short, barrel-chested man with a booming voice and an impressive command of the Bible. Glenn listened attentively as Holloway began to speak.

"Dear friends and family, we are gathered here today

to witness the holy marriage of Miss Aileen O'Connell and Dr. Thaddeus Wiseman, two Christians who have come to stand before God as a testimony to their love and devotion to His laws and His love. In this most holy of sacraments, we see how the Lord binds together a man and a woman so that all the world can witness their undying commitment to the bonds of marriage. Today, it brings us great joy to . . ."

"Jezus Christ!" Liam hissed. "This pious windbag is going to prattle on forever!"

"Hush!" Glenn snapped with asperity. "Don't ruin your sister's happiest day. Just look at her face, man. Have you ever seen her so joyful?"

Liam looked and his anger cooled. "She does look happy. She and little Jenny deserve the best and, by gawd, that sawbones better give it to 'em. What really galls me is how that dandy Peter Arlington is hangin' on to Rachel. Look at 'em! You'd think they were a couple of lovebirds but he don't really give a damn about Rachel. He's leavin' for California and I'll bet he don't even tell her good-bye."

"Shh!"

Glenn was aware that people were turning to stare at Liam with hostility because his voice was a real distraction. Liam glared back defiantly and reached inside his coat pocket to produce a silver flask that he uncorked and noisily sampled.

"Barkman, are you starin' at me!" Liam demanded of a man close by.

"Liam, please!" Glenn implored as more heads turned and Reverend Holloway momentarily lost his train of thought. "You're going to ruin the wedding ceremony."

But Liam was spoiling for a fight. "Fat man, if you got something to say, we can step outside and settle the issue!"

The heavyset man was Carl Barkman, the owner of a mercantile that had been following the tracks right from the beginning at Omaha. Barkman had a reputation for being honest and hardworking. The portly man was Megan's friend and had been her unfailing supporter during the whiskey price war. He was also a very proud and outspoken gentleman.

"You're drunk," Barkman said with disgust. "Mr. O'Connell, why don't you have the decency to leave this happy occasion?"

Liam's face darkened and his lips drew back from his teeth. "All right," Liam choked, "let's settle this, you overstuffed toad!"

Up in front, the Reverend Holloway became so distracted that his voice faltered just when he was supposed to ask Aileen if she took Thaddeus to be her lawfully wedded husband. The bride and groom turned to glare at Liam like everyone else. Glenn knew that he had to get Liam outside and cool him down before the fool did something crazy, like attack Barkman with his fists or even his six-gun.

"Come on," Glenn said, pushing between the two men who looked ready to start swinging. "Liam, let's get a drink and start celebrating early."

Liam struggled to reach Barkman who probably could have given a good account of himself because of his heft. No matter, Glenn was pushing and shoving Liam outside and fighting to keep him from rushing back into the tent and causing further disruption of the wedding ceremony.

"Let go of me!"

"Not unless you promise to simmer down and behave!"

"I'll kill that pompous toad!"

"No," Glenn said, "because you'd probably get your neck stretched and you'd damn sure ruin Aileen's wedding. For chrissakes, man! Think of your sister and little Jenny. Do you want to hurt them?"

Liam shook himself free. "All right," he snapped, "I can settle with Barkman later. Let's get a drink. No one is gonna miss us back there anyway."

Glenn nodded with relief. He was sorry to miss the wedding but he figured he was doing Aileen, Megan, and his friends a favor by getting Liam away from it.

"Where do you want to get a drink?" Glenn asked.

"Ike Norman's place."

Glenn scowled. Ike Norman was a hard, unscrupulous man who had tried to ruin Megan by staging a whiskey price war. He'd simply watered his already poor grade whiskey down while Megan had refused to resort to such dishonesty. Furthermore, Ike ran a crooked gambling hall and his saloon had a notorious reputation for fleecing the Union Pacific rail crews. It was only when General Dodge threatened to have the man run off that Ike finally cleaned up his operation, but he was continually backsliding.

There was also the nefarious Miss Belle King, a cutthroat little vixen whom Megan had once befriended only to have that friendship betrayed by Belle's jealousy. She had joined Ike and become his girl even though she could not have been more than seventeen and Ike was old enough to be her father.

"Why don't we go on down to the Whistle Stop instead," Glenn suggested.

Liam pulled up short. "What's the matter, you don't want to drink with me?"

"It's not that, it's just that I don't much care for Ike Norman and I'm surprised, given the trouble he's caused your sister, that you'd drink in his place."

"Ike's all right. He's tough. That's what people don't like about him. Come on!" Liam urged as they hurried along. "You just need to get to know Ike. He's fine. I've done some work for him and he pays well."

Glenn resigned himself to having one drink and then returning to the wedding reception. Maybe Liam would decide to stay and get drunk at Ike's and do everyone a favor.

"Well, well!" Ike said as they walked inside his tent saloon. "If it ain't the brother of the bride and Mr. Glenn Gilchrist! Why, you're about the last pair I'd expect to come by and visit me and Belle."

Glenn looked over at Belle who was dressed in black knit stockings and a red dress while dealing cards to a pair of bleary-eyed construction workers. She was a soiled dove with the face of an angel and the disposition of a cornered alley cat. She flashed Glenn a look of pure poison and kept dealing over her own stack of chips while the rust eaters clutched the last few dollars of their monthly pay.

"What'll you have?" Ike asked.

"Whiskey," Liam said. "The good stuff."

"Sure."

Ike was a hawk-faced man in his early forties with slicked back hair the color of a raven's wing. Lately, he'd grown a mustache and goatee and taken to wearing a red garter belt around his left bicep.

He poured the drinks and then poured another for himself. "I believe this is the first time you've ever been in my establishment, Mr. Gilchrist."

"That's right."

"You should come more often! Why, I know that you're sweet on Megan, but we have more fun at my place. I got some girls that would like to meet you but you have to leave Belle alone. She's all mine."

Ike laughed and winked.

"I'm sure you do," Glenn said distastefully as he took a sip of the man's whiskey and found it not to his liking.

Ike leaned forward and stroked his goatee. "You know, I once held Miss O'Connell in very high regard."

"I don't think I want to hear any more," Glenn said in a cold voice as he stared into the man's black eyes.

Ike ignored Glenn's remark. "I still admire Megan but she can't seem to understand that we could make some *real* money if we teamed up together."

"Yeah," Glenn said, eyes missing nothing as he studied the dirty sawdust floor and the nearly overflowing spittoons. The entire place smelled to high heaven and made him want to get out fast. And he would have, if he hadn't felt it necessary to nurse his drink and allow Reverend Holloway at least enough time to finish marrying Aileen and Thaddeus without having to worry about Liam.

"Yes, sir," Ike said with a sad shake of his head, "Megan and I could be a whole lot richer by now if she understood the fundamentals of frontier business."

"She understands business just fine," Glenn said in

a cold voice. "She understands that if you treat your customers right, they'll keep coming back."

Norman stiffened. "Let me tell you something, Mr. Gilchrist. What we have out here at end-of-track is a *captive* audience. We've got a crowd that has a raging thirst and plenty of Union Pacific's money to spend. And if we don't get them to spend it in our businesses, they'll damn sure find other places to spend it."

Glenn had heard enough. He slammed his glass down hard and pivoted on his heel.

"Hey!" Liam called. "Ike didn't mean anything! Come on back and have another drink with us!"

"No thanks," Glenn said, heading outside into the clean air that he woofed down in gulps before he hurried back to wish Aileen and her new husband a lifetime of happiness.

CHAPTER
20

"Liam?"

He turned around to see the one man he still admired, Joshua Hood. "What do you want?"

"We need to talk."

Liam reached out for his bottle of whiskey and refilled his glass, sloshing liquor across the top of the bar and not giving a damn. "Mr. Hood, I don't guess we have anything to say to each other."

Joshua's hand shot out and before Liam could react, he felt himself being dragged up to his toes by his shirtfront. He struggled until Joshua's knee slammed into his groin. An explosion of lights flashed across Liam's eyes and he felt his gorge erupt into his throat. He twisted free and vomited into the sawdust.

"You're a goddamn insult to your sisters!" Joshua said, waiting for him to empty his stomach. "I think the whiskey is drivin' you crazy. Isn't that why you're asking for a noose or a bullet?"

Liam wasn't sure. All he knew was that he still wanted to be a Union Pacific Railroad scout and buffalo hunter. To ride wild and free with bold men unafraid to fight Indians. And to kill Peter Arlington and get Rachel back because seeing her fawn all over the rich Bostonian had made him realize how much he wanted her again.

"Come on," Joshua ordered, grabbing Liam by the collar and propelling him toward the front door of Ike Norman's tent saloon. "Let's get some fresh air."

Liam was shaking and suffering from the dry heaves as Joshua dragged him into an alley where they could talk in private. It was dark out and Liam supposed that the wedding reception had long since ended.

"How come you got so crazy at the wedding that Glenn had to haul away your drunken ass?"

Liam thought that it was none of Joshua's business why he was drinking but he was afraid that the buckskinner would knee him in the balls again so he looked up, wiped his cold and sweaty face with the back of his sleeve, and tried to focus.

"Joshua, there ain't nuthin' goin' worth a damn anymore! I lost my girl to that fancy Arlington. Lyin' sonofabitch doesn't want to hear any more of my stories so I'm broke, and you won't hire me back so I got no future working for the Union Pacific Railroad."

"Is that all?"

Liam's eyes flashed with outrage. "How many damned reasons does a man need to get drunk!"

"A man will always find more'n enough reasons to get drunk. Hell," Joshua said with disgust, "I can think of about a hundred. Anybody can. But sooner or later a fella has got to admit that he causes most of his own misery."

"I ain't!" Liam protested. "It's that damned Arlington. He's the one that took my girl."

"Shit," Joshua said with disgust, "Rachel fell all over you for a year and you never gave her the time of day. Then, when someone else comes along and takes an interest in her, you suddenly decide that Rachel ought to be yours. Act like a man!"

"Rachel loved me! I'd even decided to marry her someday."

Joshua expelled a deep breath. "She's gone, Liam. You had your chance and it passed."

"I'm gonna kill Arlington," Liam vowed, shaking his head back and forth. "I don't know when, but I swear it'll happen."

Joshua grabbed him with both hands and shook him until Liam's teeth rattled. Pushing him away, Joshua said, "Arlington may have fancy airs, but that's no reason to kill him. It'll get you hanged, Liam. Is that what you want?"

"I don't give a damn anymore," Liam muttered.

Joshua threw his hands into the air to indicate that he was out of patience. "Megan and Aileen talked a lot about you yesterday and again after the wedding."

"They did?"

"Yeah."

Liam held his breath. Finally, he gulped and said, "So what did they say bad about me this time?"

"They said that you're killing yourself with whiskey and you're going to kill someone else. They said that you're out of control and getting worse by the day."

"Hell, they don't know nothin'!"

"Yeah they do. Liam, you're going to hurt your sisters and little Jenny. I don't want them to have to see you shot, knifed, or hanged. So, for your own good, I'm running you off."

Liam's jaw dropped. He was not sure that he had heard Joshua correctly. "What?"

"I'm running you off," Joshua repeated.

"Well . . . what the hell does that mean?"

"It means that you're going to be leaving tonight."

"But . . . gawddammit, where am I supposed to go!"

"I don't give a damn and neither do your sisters. Just be gone by tomorrow."

"I got no way out of town."

"You got feet, start walking. You can reach the next station at Como by tomorrow morning. I'll give you enough money to buy a train ticket from there back to Omaha. After that, you're on your own."

Liam couldn't believe this wasn't a nightmare. He squeezed his eyes shut, then opened them again. But Joshua didn't go away and Liam's belly sickness kept boiling up in his gullet.

Joshua reached into his pocket and produced a wad of greenbacks. "This ought to buy you a one-way ticket to Omaha."

Liam's hand snaked out and he grabbed the money. He studied the street that seemed to be tilting.

"Start walking," Joshua ordered.

"Right now?"

"Yep. I damn sure ain't going to let you spend my money on more whiskey."

Salty tears filled Liam's eyes. "How come you won't let me ride with you and the boys? I fought that party of Sioux better'n any of 'em. I killed the most Indians! Even more than you!"

"I expect that's true. But you *liked* killing them, Liam. That's the thing that I couldn't stomach. You were laughing when you shot 'em."

"I was?"

"Uh-huh."

Liam took a step back from Joshua. "Killin' 'em came

real easy. I showed you, Willy, and all the rest of the boys that I was better'n anybody with a six-gun."

"Yeah," Joshua said with a shake of his head. "Now git."

Liam sucked in a deep breath and drew himself up to his full height. His gunhand shaded his Colt. Joshua had a knife in his belt but no pistol. "Maybe I won't," he said, feeling a sense of deadly calm.

"Liam, if you go for that gun, I'll kill you," Joshua said. "I don't want to, but I will."

"You might not toe the mark on that one. I know that you're better with a rifle than a gun. I expect you know that I'm the opposite."

"I do."

Liam waited for the man to say something more but when he did not, Liam licked his lips and said, "I got no place else to go. No place but hell."

"Maybe you should find that half-breed girl you saved from a hanging."

"She's with the Cheyenne."

"I know. And they don't have whiskey and they don't live in hell."

Liam was confused. He suspected that Joshua was trying to mess up his mind. "What do you mean?"

"I mean that I was sick once, just like you. Then I went to live with the Cheyenne. I got well with 'em."

"But you're hired by the U.P. to kill 'em!"

"If they attack the train crews, I have no choice. But they healed me inside, Liam. I'd have been dead long ago if I hadn't have gone and lived with 'em because they were the only ones who'd have me around."

"They'd scalp me."

"Not if you can get captured alive and ask to be taken to Running Elk's camp to see Antelope Woman."

"Well . . . well how am I supposed to do that!"

Joshua lifted a small leather pouch from under his buckskin shirt. "Here, wear this and show it to the Cheyenne. Hold it up to 'em before they start shooting and don't forget to make the sign of peace. You know that much sign language."

"Yeah, but . . ."

"It's your only chance," Joshua said quietly as he extended the pouch to Liam. "If you go to Omaha, you'll either drink yourself to death or get killed."

Liam's hand closed over the pouch and he remembered that those were almost Cassie's identical words forecasting his bad death. He opened his mouth to say something but there didn't seem to be anything more to say. And he realized with absolute certainty that he did not want to shoot Joshua because the chief Union Pacific scout was the best man he'd ever known.

"All right," Liam whispered, looping the thong over his own head and letting it hang against his chest. "But what's inside?"

"An aspen leaf."

"Just an old leaf?"

"Yeah. It's a special leaf, though. You see, it's my Cheyenne spirit medicine. You'll need to find your own. The Indians believe that it can be a rock, a flower, any damn thing that strikes you as big medicine."

"What about a bullet?"

Joshua shrugged. "That too."

Liam's fingers fumbled to open the pouch. He got it open and reached inside. It was true. There was nothing but a dried aspen leaf. Brittle as bone and dry as dust. Liam removed it with his shaking fingers and handed it to Joshua. "A man should have his own medicine."

Joshua took the dried leaf and stared at it with a faraway look in his eyes before he ground it between thumb and forefinger. And as Liam stared, Joshua tilted his head back and poured the desiccated leaf into his mouth. A few swallows and then a loud gulp and the medicine was gone.

Liam was sobering up fast. "After seeing that, I don't guess I'll choose a bullet for my medicine," he muttered before he turned and limped slowly away.

CHAPTER

21

At the east end of town, Liam halted to stare out into the night feeling as empty as the sea of dark land he faced. Overhead, the Wyoming moon was a thin wedge of gold and the stars were glittering like quartz. A set of Union Pacific tracks ran eastward like stretched silver wires and finally linked in the inky distance.

Never before had Liam felt so alone and so betrayed. Joshua Hood had given him a one-way ticket to hell and Peter Arlington had stolen Rachel's fickle heart. Willy was the only real friend he'd ever had and now Willy was dead. His two older sisters . . . well, he'd never really been close to either one of them and they'd always treated him like a child.

The off-tune tinkle of a piano floated up behind him and Liam could hear drunken and raucous laughter. These saloon sounds pulled him around like a puppet on a string. He had Joshua's train ticket money and he had a raging thirst. One last fling would not hurt, Joshua Hood be damned.

Liam was clearheaded and testy as he entered the Round House Saloon. It was not one of the better tent saloons and Liam was not a regular customer. He shouldered his way past men and when he arrived

222

at the plank bartop, he growled, "Give me a bottle of whiskey and it better not be that wasp venom you generally pour to the suckers."

The bartender was a short, balding man with a handlebar mustache. "The best will cost you two dollars, Liam."

"You know my name, huh?"

"You've a reputation."

Liam was pleased. He straightened a little and puffed out his chest. "I don't expect that there are any better in these parts when it comes to shuckin' a gun."

The bartender forced a smile. "Two dollars."

Liam pulled Joshua's damned train ticket money from his pants and slapped it down on the plank. "I'm going away," he announced loud enough for everyone to hear. "And I'd like to buy drinks on the house! Your best, bartender!"

Now the bartender's smile turned genuine. Without batting an eye, he scooped up the entire pile of greenbacks and said, "Yes, sir!"

The other patrons of the Round House crowded around Liam as drinks were liberally poured for everyone.

"Where you goin'?" everyone was asking.

"I'm going to . . ." He started to say hell, but instead he mouthed, "Omaha."

"What for?"

"Tired of livin' at the end-of-track. Same ugly women and boring old Wyoming prairie to look at every night and day. Might be I'll ride down to Abilene and visit them new Kansas cow towns sproutin' up like meadow mushrooms. Or could be I'll go all the way to Texas and sell my fast gun to the highest bidder. I'd like to meet Wild Bill Hickok and see how fast the man really is given all the fussin' over he enjoys."

The men around Liam nodded, drank, and poured. There were six bottles of whiskey on the plank top and five of them went fast while Liam clutched the last one just for himself. For about a quarter of an hour he regaled his new friends about his past and his exciting future. Then, when the whiskey was gone and he showed no signs of buying more rounds, the men around him drifted away. Now Liam stood alone and wobbly, nursing his bottle until the bartender told him he was closing the tent up and it was time to leave.

"I guess since I spent all twelve dollars that I can stay until the cock crows, if'n I want," Liam snarled.

"I'm sorry," the bartender replied. "But I'm tired and got to get some sleep. Maybe you should too, if you're riding all the way to Kansas or even Texas."

Liam pushed away from the bar but had to reach back to steady himself. He shook his head, took the bottle, and navigated his way outside. He stared at the eastern horizon. The moon was gone and the stars were fading. Soon, it would be morning and Joshua Hood would find him drunk and broke. When that happened, there would be hell to pay. Joshua would want an accounting and it would most likely be written in blood.

"Maybe I'll just kill him and take his horse and outfit," Liam muttered to himself as he raised the bottle to the sky. "Then again, maybe he'd get lucky and kill me."

Liam wheeled around full circle and gazed up Medicine Bow's almost empty street. It was the same damned tent row that he'd been looking at for nearly two years. There were big tents, little tents, sagging tents, and patched tents. All of 'em were sorry sonsabitches and most had flimsy hitching rails staked into the ground in front of them. A couple of the worst saloons were still operating but Liam was out of time, money, and a friendly welcome.

He swore at the ground between his boots, then lurched full around and staggered over to the nearest hitching rail with horses. Joshua Hood had taught him a thing or two about horses and saddles so Liam took a few moments to study the selection before he chose a tall and muscular pinto with one white eye, a good western saddle, and a scarred but well-oiled old Sharps buffalo rifle with ball, patches, and powder. He checked the pinto's cinch, untied the animal's reins, threw them over its head, and jammed his boot into a stirrup. It was a bitch getting on without spilling all his precious whiskey, but he managed.

"Liam O'Connell damn sure ain't walkin' to Omaha or no place else," he grumbled as he reined the pinto about and booted it in the ribs. The horse jumped forward almost unseating Liam who dropped his whiskey in favor of the saddle horn.

"Sonofabitch!" he cursed, yanking the pinto back onto his haunches and almost toppling into the street.

The whiskey had leaked into the dirt except for two good swallows. Liam cursed again, gulped the dregs, and climbed back into the saddle. He drew his gun and aimed it at the bottle, firing twice. The pinto shied sideways almost dumping him.

"Ya!" Liam shouted, booting the pinto again and galloping away.

Men staggered out of the bad tent saloons but they didn't see Liam because the pinto was already putting space between him and Medicine Bow.

Liam raced east for about a mile and then he pulled up beside the rails and wiped a cold sweat from his forehead. He felt real bad and the world was slowly spinning at a tilt that threatened to spill him to the roadbed. Off to the east, he could detect a faint line of crimson hugging the earth and Liam knew that it would be daybreak in less than an hour. Soon afterward, the owner of the pinto would be trying to raise friends and form a posse to hunt him down and hang him from one of the tall cottonwood trees that crowded the banks of the Medicine Bow River.

And of course, they'd send a telegram down the line to Como and Rock Creek to be on the lookout for a horse thief astride a pinto pony. Liam guessed he was in big trouble. He had no money, no food, and no friends. He was a horse thief and that alone was a dead-sure hanging offense.

"Cassie," he whispered brokenly a moment before he reined the pinto north into Cheyenne country to find Running Elk's village.

Maybe they wouldn't kill him if he did as Joshua said and showed his little leather medicine pouch and made the sign for peace. He could do that, couldn't he?

Sure!

Liam sucked in great lungfuls of pure prairie air and decided that he would either be scalped before nightfall, or else on his way to Cassie . . . or Antelope Woman and the only prayer he had left in this world.

• • •

Liam saw no Indians that entire first day and it was a blessing. He was shaking and sweating so bad for the need of drink that he could barely ride. That night, he camped along a pretty stream but he might as well have camped on the moon because he was so sick that he just tossed and sweated and cursed the black sky. Finally, he awoke to a sun high up in the heavens. Weak but no longer sweating, he undressed and crawled into the stream, welcoming the current's biting cold. He stayed in the water until his teeth rattled and then he crawled out and used the up side of his horse blanket to dry himself. Liam redressed, looped the medicine pouch around his neck, and trembled with fear. He had been insane to come this far north alone. Better to be caught and hanged as a horse thief than to be captured and tortured by the bloody Indians.

He should have resaddled the pinto but Liam was swamped by inertia and despair. He walked a little way up the river and then found a broken arrow embedded in the bark of a fallen tree. Using his knife, he dug and pried at the arrowhead until it came free. The rotting shaft fell away as Liam fingered the arrowhead, wondering about its past.

"My medicine," he said after a few moments, squeezing the arrowhead until it bit into the flesh of his palm and the resulting pain crushed his rising sense of despair. He opened the medicine pouch, dropped the arrowhead inside, and pressed it to his bosom. Then, he went to the pinto and saw that it was gaunt and feverish with thirst.

Liam untied the animal and led it to drink. Afterward, he fashioned a crude halter and lead rope and led the famished pinto out of the trees and onto the prairie so that it could devour the rich spring grass until it was satisfied and its flanks were no longer pinched.

The prairie was incredibly vast and silent. It was so big and empty he doubted that even God could find him. Liam stood beside the pinto and felt the gentle touch of wind on his face. He closed his eyes and the sun warmed his skin. He felt weak but no longer shaky and knew that he needed food before he began to travel in search of Running Elk.

That afternoon Liam shot a fat beaver as it was dragging a branch toward a shallow lagoon that fingered out from the lazy stream. The creature must have weighed at least fifty pounds. Liam had never eaten beaver but Joshua and his scouts had and they spoke highly of the meat, especially the tail. But the tail looked awful so Liam managed to gut the beaver and skin it. He always carried matches and soon had a fire over which he roasted the beaver's fatty carcass until it sizzled and smoked.

For two more days, Liam rested and feasted on the beaver. When he felt strong and clearheaded, he mounted the pinto and rode north, ever on the alert for the first sign of Indians. If he chanced upon the Sioux or even the Arapaho, Liam knew that he was a dead man. He might also meet the Shoshone who had always befriended the first white trappers who followed the beaver-rich waterways into western Wyoming. Maybe it would even be best to chance upon the Shoshone. Liam was in a strange world; he couldn't make up his mind about anything.

It was almost a full week out of Medicine Bow before he spotted a party of mounted Indians. There were only four, but the mere sight of them filled him with such dread that it was all that he could do not to wheel his pinto about and race south. Instead, Liam dismounted and removed the leather medicine pouch and raised it up before him and waited with his bowels churning ice into his veins.

The four Indians pushed their ponies into a hard gallop. As they drew nearer, Liam saw that they were armed with bows and arrows instead of rifles. He took heart knowing that he might even be able to defeat them with his Sharps and six-shot Army Colt. But if he did that, the only door left open for him was the one to hell.

"Peace!" he called. "Peace! Friend. I seek Running Elk of the Cheyenne!"

The Indians skidded their horses to a halt and dismounted at fifty yards distance. The huddled together like gossipy women and kept glancing over at him, then they resumed their rapid, guttural, and obviously lively conversation.

At last, they seemed to have reached a decision. Knocking arrows onto their bowstrings, one stayed with the horses while the other three warily advanced.

"Peace!" Liam said, alternating between making the sign for peace and wagging his medicine pouch in front of his face.

The Indians stopped and raised their bows. Liam paused. Could they kill him from this distance? Could he draw his gun and kill them from this distance? Did it matter anymore?

"Peace," he said, forcing a grin.

The Indians looked at each other and then they lowered their bows and arrows and came forward, also making the sign of peace and saying, "Cheyenne. Cheyenne."

Liam's knees almost broke from a sudden and explosive release of inner tension. He staggered a little and when the Indians came up to him, the tallest one dressed in a beautiful beaded jacket and with the dark brown feathers of an eagle reached out and touched the medicine pouch.

"Would you like it?" Liam asked.

The Indian leader cocked his head a little and shrugged.

"Here," Liam said, lifting the pouch up and over his head and then extending it to the Indian.

The Cheyenne warrior grabbed and squeezed the pouch. Feeling the outline of the arrowhead, he frowned.

"Look," Liam said, opening the pouch and dumping the arrowhead into the palm of his hand.

The Indian studied it and looked to his friends who grinned.

"Arapaho." The youngest-looking warrior's hand flew to the knife at his side and when Liam jumped back in fright, the Indian laughed and made a stabbing motion at an invisible enemy. "Arapaho!"

"I see," Liam said in a voice that sounded shaky even to himself as he drew his hand away from his Colt.

The Cheyenne made it very clear that they thought that he carried the arrowhead because its power was in the killing of the Arapaho enemy. Liam did not think it wise to sign that he had merely found the arrowhead in dead wood.

The Cheyenne with the ponies joined them and soon they were all smiling and admiring each other's horses, saddles, and weapons. Liam thought this was just dandy and he was delighted when he said, "Running Elk," and the four Cheyenne nodded vigorously and pointed to the west.

"Must see Running Elk," Liam said, pantomiming his intentions by forking his middle and index finger over the wedge of his opposite hand to indicate riding a horse west to Running Elk's village.

The four conferred quite earnestly and when they turned back to Liam, they left no doubt that they would be willing to take him to see Running Elk, if he would give them his six-gun, holster, and bullets.

Liam was trapped. If he declined to accept this offer, there was no telling what might happen next. These warriors might get angry and try to kill him. Even if they left him alone, how could he expect to be so lucky to chance upon another friendly group of Cheyenne?

"Yes," Liam said, nodding and patting the weapon strapped to his side.

The leader, whose name sounded like "Natoka," reached for Liam's Colt but he grabbed its handle and shook his head. "First Running Elk."

This did not make Natoka happy. His smile vanished and he scowled and spoke in a harsh, rapid voice that meant nothing to Liam. But after a few minutes of this tirade, Natoka turned and swung onto his horse, then motioned for everyone to do the same. Liam was only too happy to comply.

We are going to find Running Elk and Cassie, he thought, scarcely believing his good fortune. And maybe, just maybe, he could figure a way out of giving his six-gun to these Indians once he had Cassie by his side. She owed him her life, maybe she could give these four Indians something else that they would prize.

CHAPTER
22

They came upon the tiny herd of sleeping buffalo rather unexpectedly and Liam was not prepared for what happened in the next few moments. The Cheyenne drew their steel-tipped arrows and nocked them on their gut bowstrings. There was a hurried conference and Liam was made to understand that he was to use the big-bore Sharps rifle to kill the first buffalo. Afterward, the Indians would attack and kill as many as possible before the herd scattered and ran away.

Liam had shot buffalo before but always with a proven and tested rifle. He had no idea if the Sharps he had taken from Medicine Bow was accurate. Still, it didn't appear that he had any choice but to agree to the plan.

Liam dismounted and hobbled the pinto. He had already checked the rifle and knew that it was ready to fire. Dropping to the earth, he laid a bead on the largest buffalo in the herd, a bull that would weigh about a ton. Feeling the eyes of the Cheyenne boring impatiently into him, Liam squeezed the trigger of the Sharps even as he prayed for a quick and clean kill.

The rifle bucked hard against his shoulder and smoke erupted from its muzzle. Through the smoke, Liam saw the bull stiffen, take four running steps, and then collapse, kicking at the dirt. The Cheyenne whooped with delight and attacked.

Liam jumped to his feet and quickly reloaded his rifle with one eye on the Indians. He had never seen them hunt buffalo but he'd heard Joshua describe what was going to happen. Natoka was on the fastest buffalo pony and he guided it with his knees straight into the herd where he leaned toward a running bull. Liam saw Natoka's arrow disappear into the bull's side, just behind the ribs. He saw the bull stagger but keep running and watched with amazement as Natoka rapidly fired two more arrows into the bull before it somersaulted in death.

Liam remounted his pinto and galloped forward, wanting a better vantage point. He saw that the other three Indians were almost equally skilled. They had each chosen a bull and were unleashing arrow after arrow into their prey while, at the same time, attempting to direct the herd into a milling circle. It was an astonishing display of courage and teamwork between the Indians and their buffalo ponies.

Three bulls died but the fourth and youngest hunter was having difficulty. His arrows had failed to penetrate his victim's lungs and even as Liam watched, the enraged and injured beast stopped, spun, and hooked at its tormentor. Its short but thick horn punched into the pony's side, ripping it open like a bean can. The buffalo was so powerful it lifted both horse and rider, then hurled them to the earth.

Liam shouted and drove his pinto forward knowing that the young warrior was lost even as the dazed Indian tried to climb back to his feet and draw his knife. The bull gored the Cheyenne and tossed him into the air. Liam's rifle boomed as he swept in and the bull staggered, then whirled to face its next tormentor. Liam saw that the young Cheyenne was dying. His belly had been opened and he was trying to cradle his spilling innards. As the wounded bull charged, Liam dropped his empty rifle and drew his six-gun. The Army Colt bucked six times in such rapid succession there was no break in the retort but instead a sound like rolling thunder.

The buffalo never reached Liam. Its massive head was riddled by bullets and it spilled forward, rolling like a mountain.

Liam jumped from the pinto and raced over to the dying young warrior. The Cheyenne hunter gripped Liam's shoulder and stared into his eyes with calmness and without a trace of fear. The Indian squeezed Liam's shoulder and then began to chant while the other warriors gathered around and joined in the death chant. Liam watched as life fled the eyes of the youthful Cheyenne and he heard the man's throat rattle in death.

The chanting continued long after Liam stood up and walked away to check his horse and busy himself to keep from thinking about what he had just witnessed. The handsome young Indian had suffered horribly but died well. He had chanted to his gods in preparation to entering the Indian spirit world and Liam wished him a sweet and swift passage.

That day, the Cheyenne placed their dead companion in the bough of a tree with his weapons and saddle. They sang his death song before they came to Liam and handed him the warrior's eagle feathers.

"You keep 'em," Liam said, pushing them back toward Natoka.

But the Cheyenne was more than insistent and so Liam kept the feathers. They were special, but Liam did not realize how special until they reached Running Elk's camp three days later with as much buffalo hump, tongue, and meat as they could drag on hastily constructed travois.

"Liam!"

He grinned to see Cassie jump up from her work with the other Indian women and rush forward. Liam dismounted and reached out with his hand but Cassie batted it away and hugged him tightly.

"I don't believe this," she said, looking up at his face. "You look . . . wonderful!"

"So do you," he heard himself say. "This Indian life must be agreeing with you, Cassie."

"Antelope Woman," she firmly corrected. "The railroad camp whore named Cassie is dead."

"All right, Antelope Woman."

"Liam O'Connell is also dead. You can't ever go back to them, can you."

It wasn't a question and Liam just nodded.

"Good!" Cassie said with obvious relief and pleasure. "You will be given a Cheyenne name."

"By who?"

Antelope Woman shrugged. "Maybe the warriors who brought you here have already chosen your name."

"Beats me."

Antelope Woman went to the men and began to converse rapidly with them as the tribe listened. Liam just watched. He looked around at the village and saw a lot of dogs and children. The children looked well fed and happy. A lot of them were staring at him as the conversation droned on and on. Some of them were more interested in his rifle and the handsome pinto pony.

Liam grinned. They grinned back. They went around to the travois and one cut off a hunk of raw hump fat and jammed it into his mouth. This boy's mother rushed over and angrily scolded her son.

"It's all right," Liam said. "There's more than enough buffalo meat for everyone. And when it's gone, I'll hunt you up a couple of tons more."

A few minutes later Antelope Woman presented to Liam an older Cheyenne with a crooked nose and a mane of silver hair. His face was wrinkled by the sun and wind, but mostly by age.

"Liam, this is Chief Running Elk," she said.

The chief grinned and Liam saw that he was almost toothless. Liam grinned back and Cassie said, "He tells me that your new name is Big Buffalo Thunder."

Liam blinked. "Big Buffalo Thunder?"

"Yes. That is your new Cheyenne name. The warriors who brought you here gave you that name because of your mighty buffalo rifle."

Liam turned the name over in his mind and decided that he rather liked the sound of it. "Fine," he said, eyes filled with the stately old chief who had begun to talk to Antelope Woman.

Antelope Woman listened respectfully, eyes often flicking to Liam with warmth and intimacy. Finally, the old chief patted Liam's shoulder in an obvious gesture of acceptance and friendship. Liam was extremely relieved but also deeply touched by this simple act of humility. He could see that Running Elk's melancholy brown eyes were partially blinded by the dull cloud of cataracts. It made him feel sadness.

After Chief Running Elk spoke to his people, he turned and walked away. "What else did he say to his village?"

"He has told everyone that you are to be treated as one of us. He has listened to the others say how you killed the bull and stood unafraid before its charge."

"Hell," Liam scoffed, "the truth is that old bull was already dyin' and I just . . ."

"Running Elk says that you are strong medicine."

Liam grinned. "Well, that's good, but . . ."

"And that you will stay and fight Cheyenne enemies."

Liam's grin slipped badly. "You mean . . . the Union Pacific?"

"Yes," Antelope Woman said "You must."

"Or else I'm a goner, right?"

She dipped her chin. "Maybe you won't have to kill any of them. Well, Big Buffalo Thunder, maybe you'll be lucky and just hunt buffalo to help feed our village with that big rifle."

Liam didn't want to think about having to raid the Union Pacific construction or survey crews.

"There is something else that I don't think you understand," Antelope Woman said.

"What's that?"

"Those feathers are a sign that you have taken Two Arrows's place."

"He's the young fella that was killed?"

"Uh-huh. He has many ponies and two wives."

Liam blinked. "You mean . . ."

"Yes."

Liam shook his head back and forth. "I'm staying right here in Running Elk's village."

"You will be allowed to bring Two Arrows's horses and wives to this camp."

"But I don't want 'em!"

Antelope Woman grabbed Liam's wrist and her fingernails bit into his flesh. "Don't you dare say that! When a warrior dies, someone has to care for his family. In this case, it is you."

"Jezus," Liam groaned. "I was sort of hoping that . . ."

"What?" Antelope Woman asked, lowering her voice.

"Well, that you and me could . . . you know, get together."

She stepped back and eyed him closely. "Are you asking me to become your third wife?"

"I can have three?"

"Sure. But you have to provide for us."

"And you'd all expect me to . . ." Liam realized he was blushing.

"That's up to you," Antelope Woman said coyly. "I can't speak for the others, but I'd want a *real* husband."

"Huh!" Liam toed the earth. "Boy," he said with a shake of his head. "I can't even speak Indian and already I've taken on the responsibility for three wives."

"With three wives, not understanding our language might be a big advantage."

When Antelope Woman grinned, Liam barked a laugh because he knew exactly what she meant.

CHAPTER
23

Peter Arlington III waited impatiently as the Union Pacific supply train began to approach the new loading dock at St. Mary's station. A strong prairie wind was blowing dust devils across this part of central Wyoming and Arlington could see blustery storm clouds moving in from the north. It was hot and the prairie pollen was giving Arlington's allergies fits. Soon, in a few weeks at most, he would be leaving this harsh land for a much more hospitable climate.

The locomotive blasted its steam whistle and chugged forward to a final, shuddering halt. Arlington knew that Thomas Durant, vice president of the Union Pacific, was returning from Washington, D.C., where he was involved in a terrible scandal that involved his money-making scheme to pad his own pockets with cash. Durant was under intense fire from the newspapers and Arlington realized that he would have to approach the fiery Union Pacific official with great care lest he be summarily dismissed. Durant had a reputation for being cold and ruthless and Peter Arlington was nervous about this meeting.

Durant was the first of the passengers to disembark. He was an average-looking gentleman, with a bushy

mustache and scraggly chin whiskers. His most notice-
able characteristics were his dark, penetrating eyes and
intense, restless energy.

"Sir!" Arlington called. "Mr. Durant? May I have a
word with you?"

Durant turned and glared. He recognized Arlington
and barked, "No more interviews! I've nothing more to
say about the Credit Mobilier except that it is perfectly
above board and legal in every respect."

"I'm sure it is," Arlington said, catching up with
the impatient man and matching his stride. "I know
that the eastern newspapers have been giving you fits.
That's why my father has telegraphed me asking for
an interview that would focus on the favorable aspects
of this epic endeavor and point out that you, sir, have
been unjustly maligned over this Credit Mobilier fi-
nancing business."

Durant pulled up short. "Are you serious?"

"Why of course! I think every man ought to have an
opportunity to defend himself. I'm offering you that
opportunity."

Durant's face relaxed. "When do you want to do the
interview?"

"As soon as possible."

"Good," Durant snapped. "Come to my coach."

"Now?"

"Why not!"

"No reason, sir." Arlington could not believe his good
fortune. Often, it took weeks to gain an interview with
Durant, if one was to be gained at all.

"We might as well start while we walk," Durant said.
"I've a tubful of troubles that need sorting out and my
time is very valuable."

"Yes, sir."

"Shoot," Durant ordered.

Arlington had thoroughly researched Durant's checkered past and had given this hoped for interview a great deal of careful thought. He knew that Durant held a doctorate degree in medicine but had practiced for only a short time. Business and the prospect of wealth had always held far more allure for the doctor than the mundane and penurious livelihood of medicine. A promoter extraordinaire, Durant had wheeled and dealed his way into the halls of the United States Congress and had been instrumental in gaining favorable terms for the builders of the transcontinental railroad.

The extremely liberal Pacific Railroad Act of 1864 had given both the Union and Central Pacific railroads huge tracts of free land bordering both sides of the proposed rails as well as lucrative allowances to do the actual construction work. Yet, despite these generous terms, both railroads were chronically short of funds and constantly on the verge of financial collapse.

"All right," Durant said, "what are your questions?"

"Uh, how do you judge the rate of construction?"

Durant scowled. "It's meeting my expectations. General Dodge is a very difficult and obstreperous man to work with, but he knows his business and he can get the job done. The Casement brothers are without peer."

"Good!" Arlington said, hurrying along.

"Aren't you even going to take some notes?" Durant snapped.

"I will when we come to rest," Arlington said. "But until then, I have an excellent memory."

"You'd better have because I won't stand for being misquoted. And I insist on seeing every word of your copy before you send it back east for publication."

"Yes, sir! Every word." Arlington was about to add further assurances but just then, his twenty-dollar bowler was torn off his head by the wind and went sailing across the prairie. He would have sprinted after it but Durant didn't notice nor would he wait so Arlington swore under his breath and wrote off the damned bowler.

They came to Durant's private Pullman car resting on a side rail. Out of the hard wind at last, an aide took their coats and soon they were settled in a very plush office with heavy mahogany furniture and crystal brandy glasses in their fists.

"Now," Durant said, pausing after a fifteen-minute monologue on his early years and successes.

After lighting a cigar, he continued, "As you can well see, Mr. Arlington, I am a man on a mission and that mission is to keep Congress's toes to the fire so that we receive the money enough to finish this transcontinental railroad. But Congress must realize that our men will not work for free and when their wages are delayed, we have big problems."

"I understand."

"Those men live from one payday to the next," Durant said in a pitying voice. "That's the way that they think. Bad whiskey and sinful women. I'm convinced that they can't spend their money on either one fast enough."

"I've noticed, sir."

"Young man, I'll bet that your father knows how to use money to his advantage just as I do. If he did not, he would not have built a newspaper. What is its name?"

"*The Boston Herald*," Arlington said quickly.

"Hmm, don't think I've heard of that one. Is it a major paper? If it's not then . . ."

"Circulation of over fifty thousand."

"Good! Then I want every one of those fifty thousand readers to know that I am a self-made man. An entrepreneur. A visionary. An honorable man who will not accept defeat or even compromise."

"Yes, sir."

Slightly mollified by Arlington's permissive acceptance of all that he had said, Durant lowered his voice. "This Credit Mobilier is a perfectly legitimate corporation founded and necessary to insure a constant flow of cash into this railroad."

"Of course it is."

Actually, Arlington knew that quite the opposite was true. His own research and inside information left no doubt that the Credit Mobilier was a shameful device whereby big Union Pacific investors and insiders could make huge profits from inflated railroad contracts. It had been set up by the Union Pacific's board of directors to win the very construction contracts that were set by an unsuspecting Congress. These were huge and inflated contracts to lay rails, grade roadbed, dig tunnels, build bridges and locomotive roundhouses both in Omaha and Cheyenne. And since the board of directors was also the ones choosing the contractors, they were merely hiring themselves and reaping outrageous profits.

"This railroad would have gone under before it left Omaha," Durant was saying. "They claim that we're bidding against ourselves, well, we are the most efficient contractors! Who else could come out here and build to our exacting specifications while fighting off the damned Indians?"

"No one," Arlington said dutifully.

"Of course not."

Arlington let the Union Pacific vice president rant on for a while and then he said, "Are you by any chance a hunter, sir?"

"A what?" Durant was thrown off kilter by this unexpected question.

"A hunter. You know, of trophy animals."

"Hell no! Why are you asking me such a damn foolish question?"

"No reason," Arlington said quickly, "except that my father would prize the head of a trophy buffalo. I think that if I could find an escort and bag such an animal for my father, you'd have a powerful voice in Boston."

"I don't need a voice in Boston," Durant snapped. "I need more of 'em in Washington, D.C."

"I understand, but my father does have congressional connections. And I was hoping that you might allow me to join your surveyors out on the line and perhaps take a little hunting trip with your chief scout, Mr. Joshua Hood."

Durant refilled his glass. "Let's cut through the smoke and the rhetoric. As I understand it, your proposition is that I provide you the means to get a trophy for your father, and in return, his newspaper is going to vigorously defend me against my critics. Furthermore, influential people will be asked to support me in Congress. Is that it?"

"Why yes, sir, that about covers it."

"All right," Durant said, "one trophy buffalo head packed in salt and delivered to Omaha in return for your father's support and this article defending me and the Credit Mobilier against those yapping dogs who seek to destroy my reputation."

Durant stood up. "Now, if we are finished with this interview, I have work to do."

Arlington couldn't believe that he had pulled this off! "Thank you, sir. Who shall I expect to contact me about going out to the survey parties and the hunt?"

Durant drained his glass. "I'll order Glenn Gilchrist to take you with him the next time he goes out. Do you know our assistant chief surveyor?"

"Very well."

"Good. You remind me of him. I think you'll get along well together."

"I'm sure of it."

Arlington extended his hand in farewell but Durant had turned away and was shuffling through a stack of papers.

"Thank you, Dr. Durant."

"Good day, Mr. Arlington," the man said without looking up.

Outside Durant's special Pullman coach, Peter Arlington clapped his hands together with delight. He made his way through the windy, dusty street of St. Mary's until he came to Megan's tent saloon. Pushing inside, he looked for Rachel or Glenn Gilchrist. Seeing neither one, he spotted Henry Harrison.

"Can I buy you a drink!"

"You know perfectly well that I never touch hard liquor."

"Then how about something else?"

Henry Harrison smiled. "I am fond of sarsaparilla."

"I'll get a bottle for you," Arlington said, hurrying to the bar.

"You look like the cat who swallowed the canary," Harrison said when his young Boston friend returned with their drinks. "Good news?"

"Very! Glenn and I are going out to a survey camp. And along the way, I might even shoot a trophy buffalo."

"I'm sure he'll be less than delighted," Henry remarked.

"That might be, Mr. Armbruster, but I am very delighted."

"Obviously. Have you told Rachel about this great adventure that you are about to undertake?"

"No, where is she?"

"Probably in the storeroom getting more liquor stocked for tonight. It's payday, you see."

"Oh, I'd forgotten."

Henry chuckled. "Believe me, I haven't forgotten. Things have been rather slow this past week."

Arlington paused. "Why does a man of your skill stay in a tent saloon?"

"What do you mean?"

"Why aren't you getting rich on California's Barbary Coast or dealing cards on a Mississippi riverboat? In short, why aren't you in a place where wealthy sporting men gather to test their gambling skills?"

Henry shuffled the cards without realizing it. They were a smooth blur in his little hands. "I like Megan, Rachel, and Aileen," he said. "They've become like my daughters. I always wanted daughters but was never blessed that way."

"Any sons?"

"One. Killed playing cards in New Orleans."

"I'm sorry."

Henry forced a sad smile. "He was cheating. Dealing from the bottom of the deck with marked cards. An Armbruster—can you imagine! And after all the years that I'd schooled him. Told him again and again that a real professional doesn't need to resort to cheating. And he was good enough to have made a fine living with an honest deck."

"Then why . . ."

"Greed," Henry said with a sad shake of his head, "is the thing that gets men killed. Very few men realize their limitations or enjoy the simple pleasures."

"And you do?"

"Yes," Henry said, "I do. I like being a part of this grand railroad adventure. I like the construction workers and I never take all their money. Quite often, I even allow them to win so that they can enjoy their other pleasures. But most of all, Mr. Arlington, I like my girls and I keep a watchful and protective eye on all three of them."

Arlington was not sure, but he thought that he detected a slight warning in Henry's voice. "Are you saying that I had better be careful with Rachel?"

"She loves you and you're using her," Henry said, each word chipping off like flint. "I can't help her about that. Just don't deceive her and don't leave her with child."

"I would never do such a thing!" Arlington feigned shock and indignation, but Henry didn't seem to notice.

"Oh, yes you would," Henry said. "Just don't."

Arlington felt the man's demeanor change and a stiffness settling in between them. "Excuse me. I've got to find Rachel and Glenn Gilchrist."

"Good day," Henry clipped, the cards moving restlessly in his nimble fingers.

CHAPTER
24

Glenn was not pleased about being assigned to escort Peter Arlington out to the advance survey crews where the newspaperman would write a few articles and try to kill a trophy buffalo for his father in Boston.

Standing before Durant, whom he'd never liked, Glenn argued, "It's too dangerous out there, sir. I can't possibly guarantee Arlington's safety. And as for this 'trophy buffalo' that he's so damned set on bagging, I don't understand why Peter doesn't just hire a company of professional hunters and go out on his own."

"Never mind that, just do what I've ordered," Durant snapped from his desk chair.

Glenn wasn't willing to drop the matter. "But, sir, if Peter is killed or injured, his family could sue this railroad."

"Enough!" Durant shouted, coming to his feet. "Mr. Gilchrist, either you work for this railroad and do as you are ordered, or you are fired. Make up your mind. Which is it?"

"Dr. Durant, I've been a loyal and hardworking employee since the day I hired on in Omaha."

"No you haven't," Durant countered furiously. "Do you really think that I've forgotten how you informed those Irish widows that they should hold this railroad liable for the deaths of their families when the Missouri River flooded? That we should actually compensate them for an act of God!"

"It was the least we could do!"

"We owed them nothing!"

Glenn couldn't believe that a few thousand dollars of Union Pacific compensation to the destitute families who'd suffered terrible loses in that spring flood was still a festering point with Durant. The monies paid to widows like Megan and Aileen had been a pittance compared to their hardships. And yet, this rich, scheming, and conniving promoter still held Glenn at blame for supporting a just, humanitarian payment.

Durant's voice shook. "I should have fired you long ago, Gilchrist."

"Then do it!"

"No!" Durant's eyes burned with hatred. "You're going to have to quit, which will prove that you're afraid to take Arlington out on the plains and that you've never had the stomach for doing the really dangerous work. And by the way, those coal samples you gathered?"

"What about them?"

"Our engineers require more. They want samples from a secondary deposit."

"Why?"

Durant shrugged. "I don't know or care. You can either agree to do as you're told, or quit."

"I won't quit," Glenn heard himself vow.

"Then you have your orders," Durant said coldly.

Glenn turned on his heel and stomped out of Durant's private Pullman coach. He was seething with anger that nearly exploded when he almost ran into Peter Arlington who was waiting outside.

"I couldn't help but overhear you two," Arlington said. "I'm sorry. I didn't specifically ask that you be assigned to accompany me."

"Nice to hear," Glenn snapped, "because I have no use for this trophy hunting business. Killing buffalo for food is necessary, risking your life to shoot something and pack its head in salt so that it can be bolted to an office wall makes no sense to me."

"Then I suggest that you take Dr. Durant's advice and quit," Arlington said, his own voice becoming chill.

"Go to hell."

"No." Arlington said quietly. "I'm going to visit your forward survey crews, do a little writing and hunting, then return to Boston. How soon can we leave?"

Glenn clenched his fists at his sides in useless anger. Arlington had Durant in his pocket and there was no sense in bucking the tide. With luck, he could find a new coal deposit, get the man's trophy buffalo head packed east, and be finished with this entire sorry business in less than two weeks. After that, perhaps Durant would leave him alone and let him do his own work without further interference.

"We'll leave right at daybreak," Glenn announced.

"What must I bring?"

"Supply all your own gear and horses. I'll take care of the rest."

"We'll need a wagon and a couple hundred pounds of salt or brine." Arlington smiled. "And, Glenn, you'll need a wagon anyway to bring back those new coal samples."

"Anything else?"

"Nope."

"What about the Malloy brothers?"

"They'll not be happy, but they'll be coming," Arlington said. "I figure we can use all the rifles we can get out there just in case we run into a Cheyenne war party."

Glenn had to agree. "Just as long as everyone understands that since I'm responsible for this party, I give the orders."

"Sure," Arlington said with an indifferent shrug.

Glenn hurried away. He had a lot of things to do in a short period of time before he went to say good-bye to Megan.

That evening, Glenn coaxed Megan out of her tent saloon for a walk in the moonlight. He told her about Thomas Durant's still smoldering resentment concerning the awards for damages and loss of life during the terrible springtime flood along the Missouri River.

"So," Megan said as they strolled out where the moon was bright and the sound of the rough tent city was less distracting, "Thomas Durant still blames you."

"No doubt about it."

"Well," Megan said, "I always knew that Durant still blamed me for raising such a fuss. He'll cross the street rather than tip his hat or offer a greeting when we meet. Aileen says he treats her the very same way."

"He's not worth worrying about."

"Oh, but he is!" Megan said, stopping to turn her face up to Glenn. "He could fire you."

"It wouldn't be the end of the world. I could find other engineering or survey work."

"But not at the end-of-track."

"No," Glenn admitted. "I'd have to leave."

Megan took his hand and they continued walking. "And where would you go?"

"I haven't given it a thought."

"You could go back home. I'm sure that your father and mother would welcome you with open arms and that there would be at least a vice presidency in your father's bank."

"Oh, at least," Glenn said with an amused smile. "But after this . . ." His hand swept out to encompass the vast sweep of dark prairie. "After this grand western adventure, I would go crazy sitting at a desk shuffling papers and making cold and calculating financial decisions. I shudder at the thought of overseeing ledgers and profit and loss statements and deciding whether or not to grant some poor devil a loan knowing I'd make more money if he fails and our bank repossesses all his assets."

"I see." Megan glanced sideways at him. "It sounds as if you've been ruined for more traditional ways of earning a living."

"I have been," Glenn admitted. "I confess that I'm frustrated at times working for the Union Pacific. I never have liked Durant, but I greatly admire General Dodge, Sam Reed, and the Casement brothers. It would be very hard to leave this epic race across the West and return to the safety and comfort of eastern high society."

"Then you shouldn't."

Glenn stopped and looked closely at Megan because she sounded as if she were driving at something he'd not yet figured out for himself. "What choice would I have otherwise, if Durant decides to fire me tomorrow?"

"You could go to California," Megan said without a

moment's hesitation, "and work for the Central Pacific Railroad. I'm sure that they would—"

"Work for our rivals!" Glenn took a back step. "Megan, you can't be serious!"

"I am," she insisted. "More and more I hear talk about this race and how *our* railroad is so much better than *their* railroad. And how we have to beat them because it would be so insulting to let those little 'yellow heathens' show up the proud Irish."

"Whoa!" Glenn called with a laugh. *"You're* Irish."

"Of course, and I've never even met a Chinaman but I don't think they ought to be ridiculed or made fun of just because of their size, habits, or color. From what I've heard, they are very industrious."

"And where did you hear that?"

"Peter Arlington told me."

"I see. I wonder where he came to know the Chinese. I wouldn't think there were any in Boston."

"I don't know about that," Megan said. "But anyway, if Durant were stupid enough to fire you, go to work for the Central Pacific and do it with a clear conscience. If it's western adventure you crave, I'm sure there is plenty to be found in the high Sierras."

"You're serious, aren't you."

"Of course I am! There are times when I think I'd sell my saloon for a few hundred dollars and a chance to pack up and go to California. I don't have to worry about Aileen anymore. There's nothing that is holding me back now."

"What about me?" Glenn asked, pulling her close. "I know I wasn't your first choice. That hurts but not enough to make me want to give up winning your love."

Megan sighed and laid her head against his chest. Glenn breathed in the perfume of her hair. He whispered, "If it's California that you want, Megan, just say the word and I'll take you there."

She looked up, eyes large and luminous. "You'd really do that?"

"I'd take you anywhere."

Megan lifted on her toes and kissed him. It wasn't just the usual quick buss that he'd previously had to settle for, either. It was a long, hard, and very serious kiss that sent a surge of passion coursing through Glenn's veins. Her body seemed to melt into his and he could not seem to get enough of her.

"Megan," he choked, "I want you!"

Megan drew back, bosom heaving. "I didn't expect that to affect me so," she said breathlessly. "It took me by surprise."

"Not me. I knew that, if we kissed, something would happen. Megan, if . . ."

Before he could say anything more, Megan placed her fingers over his lips. "Don't," she pleaded, "don't spoil the moment. If something is meant for us, it will happen."

"But how can you be sure! We need to *make* our dreams come true, not wait for a miracle. Marry me, Megan! Marry me tomorrow and we'll leave for California."

"No," she said with a smile. "There are too many people that would be hurt by such a sudden decision. There's Rachel and Henry Harrison and Victor."

"Give them your tent saloon! They're capable people. Rachel is going to have her heart broken anyway by Peter Arlington. He doesn't love her and never will.

Give her your saloon and let her make her own independence. Just like you did."

In reply, Megan kissed him again, only this time slow and sweet. "When you return, we'll talk some more. And maybe we really will marry and go to California."

"That would suit me right down to the ground," he said. "I could use a change."

"And what about working for the Central Pacific Railroad?"

"I'd have to think about what you said," Glenn decided after a long pause. "I'd have to give it a hell of a lot of serious consideration."

Megan nodded with understanding for she admired loyalty. "We'd better go back now."

"All right," he said, taking her hands. "But I want you to promise me just one thing."

"What?"

"That you won't fall in love with anyone else before I can return."

Megan laughed out loud and it was music to Glenn's ears. It took every bit of his willpower not to reach out and crush her again in his arms and then make love to her right out on this open, starlit prairie.

They left early the next morning. Glenn drove the wagon while Arlington and the two hulking Malloy brothers rode horses. Arlington had plenty of firepower, two extra Winchester repeating rifles as well as saddlebags stuffed with ammunition. There were boxes of supplies that they would empty and could pack with the hoped for new samples from a second coal deposit Glenn knew he had better find. Both Megan and Rachel saw them off. Glenn held Megan close and kissed her once more before he climbed up into the wagon and gathered his reins. Rachel tried to throw her arms around Peter's neck and hold him close but he seemed distracted and in a hurry to leave. Rachel was weeping softly when they headed out of St. Mary's into the predawn blackness, leaving behind the construction camp with its towering, triple-decker bunkhouses a loud symphony of snoring.

Five miles out of St. Mary's and just as the sun was rising, they came upon a big Union Pacific camp of bridge builders. These men were responsible for constructing everything from high trestles across big rivers, to hundreds of small trestles across the many gullies that the roadbed would cross. The next afternoon they came upon a hundred-man company of road graders who were using horses, mule scrapers, and hand dump carts.

"Any sign of Indians?" Glenn asked the foreman as they stopped for a moment.

"They hit us once last week and killed three of our men before driving off about forty head of livestock." The foreman shook his head and looked disconsolate. "I sure hope they stay away for a while."

"Me too," Glenn said. "We're going up to the forward surveyors' camp. Any idea how far ahead they're working?"

"About thirty miles. They'll sure be glad to see you. I wouldn't want to be that far with as few of them as they have. I'm surprised that the Indians don't wipe 'em out to a man."

Glenn agreed. As assistant chief of surveyors, he well understood the extreme dangers his peers faced every day spent out at the Union Pacific's vanguard.

In Nebraska, they'd had a lot of support from the United States Army, but it had been sadly lacking on the empty, unsettled plains of central Wyoming.

They continued on and made a cold camp that night beside a steam where the bridge builders would have another trestle to construct because of the almost certain springtime flooding that turned even small streams into raging torrents.

"We haven't seen one buffalo yet," Arlington complained after Glenn had set the night watch. "Not a one."

"Doesn't surprise me," Glenn said. "There's just too much activity along the survey line for buffalo to stay in this vicinity. I think we're going to have to range out from the surveyors' camp and I'm hoping that Joshua Hood is there to meet us."

"But we'll go even if he's not," Arlington said quickly.

"Yeah," Glenn replied, remembering his orders. "But I don't care what Durant said, my main objective is to find a second coal deposit and gather samples. Your buffalo shoot is real secondary."

"That's where you are wrong," Arlington disagreed. "And it would be a shame to see you lose your job over a small misunderstanding."

"There's no misunderstanding," Glenn replied testily. "If we see buffalo while out hunting coal, you can pick the biggest in the herd and kill it. But if we don't see any herds, you're just going to have to go back empty-handed. Otherwise, we risk losing our scalps to become a Cheyenne trophy."

Arlington looked at the Malloy brothers and then stared out into the twilight. "I just have a feeling that this is all going to turn out fine," he said to no one in particular.

Glenn went to bring the wagon horses in and tie them up for the night. He didn't see any need to make a big point of the matter, but Peter Arlington's feelings or hunches didn't matter one bit. This was Cheyenne country and only fools would go riding around in it looking for a giant buffalo to shoot and behead. The entire subject was a sore point with him and he imagined that Joshua Hood would have little more patience concerning the matter.

After the Malloy brothers had left their camp to stand sentry duty until midnight, Arlington leaned over and said, "Glenn?"

"Yeah?"

"You ever think about working for the Central Pacific Railroad instead of this one?"

"Why do you ask?"

"I very much suspect they need experienced surveyors and railroad engineers. I know you're out of favor with Mr. Durant. I just thought that you might be considering a change of scenery."

"As a matter of fact, I have been. But only if Durant fires me."

"He wouldn't do that. You're too valuable. Besides, General Dodge and the Casement brothers would raise hell."

Glenn smiled. "I'd hope so. Good night, Peter."

"Good night. See you at midnight."

"Yeah," Glenn said as he pictured Megan's face shining down at him from the starry heavens.

CHAPTER
25

When Glenn saw the surveyors' camp, everything looked just fine. The canvas tents were rippling in the stiff wind and it appeared that the surveyors had simply gone off for the day and were late to return as evening approached. But as Glenn's supply wagon drew within a half mile of the camp, an uneasy feeling overcame him and he pulled the team of wagon horses up sharply.

"What are you stopping for?" Ennis demanded.

"There should be at least one surveyor left to guard the camp at all times," Glenn said. "That's the rule and it's a good one."

"Well, maybe they forgot the damned rule or . . . or they were shorthanded," Emory said, wiping a sheen of sweat from his brow. "Anyway, I'm half-starved to death and I reckon that they'll have food for us. Maybe even some whiskey."

"No whiskey out here," Glenn said, eyes still riveted on the empty tents. "None allowed."

"Damnation!" Ennis hissed. "Don't see how the Union Pacific expects men to stay clear the hell out here without some whiskey! Come on!"

Glenn guessed the surveyors had just been careless or forgetful. There was always too much work to do but he'd have to remind them to leave at least one guard in camp when they went off to survey. Otherwise, even a few Indians would have free rein to loot and burn out the camp.

Ennis and Emory Malloy were big, rough men and they spurred their weary horses into a gallop and raced ahead. Peter Arlington seemed to be gripped with indecision and held back beside the wagon. His horse didn't like being left behind and started giving him fits.

"Go on ahead," Glenn called, "I'll be along."

Arlington nodded and set spurs to his hot-blooded Thoroughbred gelding. It was a magnificent bay although fractious and difficult to control. The animal surged forward, chomping at the bit and angry that it was being left in the wake of the Malloys' scrub horses.

"Hee-yaw!" Glenn said, snapping the lines on his own four-horse team because he was also eager to reach the surveyors' camp and get some food and rest. Tomorrow he might have to go buffalo or coal hunting, but that was tomorrow.

Glenn was still about three hundred yards distant from the camp when the Malloy brothers jumped from their horses and challenged the silent tents.

"Anybody here!" Ennis shouted, leading his horse over to the nearest tent and parting the canvas flap to peer inside.

Ennis disappeared. Emory had been gawking around and now, with his brother suddenly missing, he went over to the tent where his brother had been standing. Glenn saw Emory draw back the canvas flap to see what his brother was doing inside.

Emory screamed, hands fluttering to the war ax buried in his forehead. Glenn's jaw dropped. The Malloy horses reared and whirled to race toward Glenn and his wagon.

Emory toppled like a felled tree. Peter Arlington sawed on his reins.

"Peter!" Glenn shouted as the easterner tried to drag his high-spirited horse to a stop.

But the horse was hard-mouthed and it ran another sixty or seventy yards with Arlington's terrified shouts and curses fading across the prairie as the tents unloaded a horde of Indians who had been waiting in ambush.

Glenn's hand flew to his rifle and the Winchester repeater came up smooth and fast but not before the Indians unleashed a volley of arrows, several of which struck at Peter Arlington. Glenn saw the young easterner list badly in his saddle. The Thoroughbred gelding screamed and went off-stride as several arrows thudded into the pain-crazed animal.

"Glenn!" Peter cried, dropping his six-gun and trying to keep his horse on its feet.

Glenn fired his Winchester knowing he was going to miss but hoping to distract the Indians long enough to reach Arlington before the man and his horse collapsed.

"Glenn, help!" Arlington cried as another flight of arrows took wing and the Indians charged the easterner.

The Thoroughbred was dying and it was a wonder it did not fall. Arrows as thick as porcupine quills were hanging off of its body. Arlington also took another in the thigh and was now leaning precariously. His reins were dragging and he choked his saddle horn with both hands. The Thoroughbred tried to run but an arrow in the gut brought it up short.

Glenn whipped his team forward and when Arlington's Thoroughbred groaned and collapsed, Glenn leaned back and brought the wagon skidding into a whiplike turn.

"Grab my hand!" Glenn shouted.

But Peter Arlington couldn't stand, much less reach for help. He did manage to climb to his hands and knees. Glenn jumped from the wagon and scooped up Arlington and threw him into the wagon. The team of horses had already begun to run before Glenn could leap back into the driver's seat and he had to grab the back of the flying wagon. The wagon almost got away from him but Glenn was so frightened that he found enough strength for one last burst of speed and was able to throw himself up into the bed.

There was no time to help Peter. Glenn crawled into the driver's seat only to discover that the lines were trailing under the horses. He glanced back and saw the Indians were racing to catch up to their ponies.

For a moment Glenn was seized by panic. He whirled around on his seat and shouted, "Peter!"

The man attempted to speak. Crimson bubbles formed on Peter Arlington's lips and his face was as pale as a cemetery headstone.

"Peter, we've got to get out of this wagon and onto those horses or we're finished!"

The man tried to rise but he had no strength. As the wagon bounced over the prairie, Peter was tossed about in the wagonbed like a loose pine pole. Glenn was sure that the man was going to be thrown overboard and he jumped back to grab and pinion him to the floor.

Staring up at him, Arlington tried to speak again.
Glenn knew that the man was hanging on to life by
a thread. He looked back and saw that several of the
Indians were already boiling out of a ravine where they
had kept their horses hidden.

"Glenn!"

He looked down and saw Peter grasping at a letter
jammed into his inside coat pocket. "Please!" the man
choked.

Glenn tore the letter free and shoved it into his own
pocket. "Peter," he begged, "we've got to *ride*!"

Peter nodded and his lips drew back in a death grin
an instant before he went limp.

Glenn swore in helpless fury and yanked the man's
fancy six-gun from his holster before shoving it into his
waistband. He climbed into the wagon's seat, took a
deep breath, and threw himself forward to land heavily
across the back of the left wheel horse. For a moment
Glenn tottered and almost fell under the wagon.
Clawing desperately, he managed to cling to the sweaty
animal's back and then to reach down for the trailing
lines. It seemed to take forever to bring the team to a
standstill, but it probably took less than a minute.

Glenn didn't even dare to look back at the onrushing
Indians. He could hear them and he knew that they
were coming hard. He swiftly uncoupled the four wagon horses. There was a tangled mass of harness still
binding the animals together but no time to sort things
out. From the sounds of the Indians, Glenn thought that
they must be right on top of him. There wasn't even
time enough to grab the precious Winchester repeating
rifle resting in the wagonbox.

Glenn figured he had less than one minute to unhitch the team from the wagon and make the ride of his life. He made the most of that minute and jumped back onto the wheel horse.

"Yaw!" he screamed, sawing on the tangled harness to point the four horses east toward the protection of the nearest Union Pacific crew. He whipped the sweating animals back into a desperate run.

"Yaw!"

No longer encumbered by the wagon, the team ran as if their tails were burning bushes. Glenn had handpicked each animal for its speed and endurance and now he was counting on that earlier judgment to save his life.

"Yaw! Yaw!" he shouted as the wagon horses ran with their ears back. Glenn was deathly afraid that the animals' flying legs would become entangled in harness and all of them would somersault into a crippling pileup.

But, somehow, that never quite happened.

After a mile, Glenn dared to twist around and he could see that the Indians were swarming over Peter Arlington's pincushioned body and the abandoned Union Pacific wagon with its booty of food and supplies. The new Winchester repeating rifle alone would be a great prize.

When the horses began to falter, Glenn slowed them to a trot. They were heavily lathered and gasping for breath.

"Pace!" he shouted at the brilliant canvas of a glorious western sunset. "Pace yourself, Gilchrist, or they'll overtake and scalp you yet!"

Darkness and a heavy cover of clouds to block the moon and starlight saved him. Glenn swapped horses all night long and kept them moving as hard as they could travel. When he dismounted at a small stream and let the animals drink, he climbed to a low rise of ground and watched the sunrise burn across the land. He saw no Indians and he finally allowed himself to breathe easy.

Feeling shaky with hunger and thirst, Glenn joined the exhausted team for a drink and then he remounted and reined for high ground where he could see anything coming up from behind. Hours later he finally came upon the huge camp of road graders. When they saw him and the heavily lathered team horses, the men rushed to grab their rifles.

Glenn was so tired his legs buckled when he slid off his horse. In a few words he told the Union Pacific workmen what had happened and about the ambush at the surveyors' camp.

"The bastards must have killed them to a man!"

"There's not much question about that," Glenn agreed.

"How many were there?"

Glenn frowned. "I didn't have time to count, but there were at least thirty. Maybe quite a few more. Everything happened so fast that there wasn't time to even think."

"Too bad about your eastern friend," the foreman said. "And I'll bet General Dodge raises hell with the Army for not providing the kind of protection that our survey crews should have been getting all along."

"Yeah," Glenn said, as the full impact of the loss started to hit him in force. He'd lost a lot of friends in the survey crew, good, hardworking men with ideals and ambitions. Many of them had come from the East in search of a new life and adventure. They had been among the elite of the Union Pacific and would be extremely difficult, if not impossible, to replace.

"I need some food and coffee," Glenn said to no one in particular, "and then I need a fresh horse to carry me to the end-of-track. Durant, Dodge, and the Casement brothers will want to know about this as soon as possible."

The foreman nodded and said, "This way to the mess tent, Mr. Gilchrist. I was planning to send a heavily armed and escorted supply wagon back to the train for fresh provisions. You might as well ride along in safety and comfort."

Glenn felt too wrung out to argue. He guessed he might even climb into the back of the wagon and sleep along the way.

CHAPTER
26

Ike Norman and Belle King had argued for weeks and now they were finally in agreement; something had to be done about all their saloon and gambling business that was shifting over to patronize Megan's Place.

"Henry Harrison has won the trust of the big-stakes gamblers," Ike complained. "All we're getting here are the penny-ante players and even those are disappearing! Last night's winnings was less than fifteen dollars."

"I know," Belle said harshly. "The more we rig the games, the worse things get. And, Ike, I don't see how in the hell you can add any more water to our house whiskey. It already tastes like weak tea. Our keg beer is so watery that it doesn't even foam."

"We're either going to have to get rid of Megan and Henry Harrison, or fold up our tent and go back to Omaha broke and with our tails between our legs," Ike said, his lean face grim with resolve.

Belle leaned forward on their bed, breasts almost spilling out of her low-cut silk dress. A cold smile formed on her bright red lips. "How?"

Ike shrugged as if he were talking about the weather instead of lives. "Belle, I guess we've got no choice but to burn Megan out."

"Hell, that won't work! She'd just buy a new saloon tent and start up business all over again. Her customers would probably even take up a collection and get her fixed up bigger and better than ever."

"Then we figure out some way to ruin her reputation."

"Any ideas?"

"As a matter of fact," Ike said, "I do have an idea. We kill Henry Harrison, burn her out, and make it look like they had a fight. One of us just happens to arrive first and witness Megan pulling the trigger and knocking over a lamp that starts the fire."

Belle looked skeptical. "And you think that people would believe that?"

"What choice would they have?" Ike demanded. "And who cares if Megan's friends suspect we're behind the affair? They wouldn't be able to prove anything. And the damage would already be done."

Belle tipped her head to one side and considered every aspect of Ike's plan. "It's not bad," she admitted.

"What do you mean, 'it's not bad'?" Ike laughed. "It's a brilliant way to get rid of the two thorns in our sides and bring back our customers."

"How do we actually kill Henry Harrison?"

"Easy enough," Ike said. "We just wait until tonight. Megan and Armbruster are always the last to leave after accounting for their night's profit. We sneak into their saloon, catch Megan from behind and knock her out cold, then shoot Henry Harrison."

Belle stood up and reached for one of the Mexican cigarettes that she had taken to smoking. Lighting it, she began to pace back and forth. "That's a whole lot easier said than done. Henry Harrison doesn't look like much, but I know for a fact that he carries at least one derringer and he's a damned quick and accurate shot."

"So I've heard. But if I knock Megan over the head and use her as a shield, he'll have no choice but to raise his hands in order to spare her life. And then, I'll shoot the little bastard."

"Why not knife him?" Belle suggested. "That way, there won't be any sound to bring people running. We can take their money and set their tent on fire with both of them inside."

Ike blinked with surprise. "You really do hate Megan."

"There's no love lost between us, that's for sure. But the main thing is that we can't afford to let Megan live. She'd know it was us that killed Henry Harrison."

"But she'd have no proof."

Belle blew a smoke ring and stabbed a bull's-eye through it with her forefinger. "Proof or not, we can't have anyone pointing a finger at us, Ike. If we do this, it has to be all the way. Both of them dead."

"I never killed a woman, Belle." Ike didn't like the idea one little bit. Unlike Belle, he didn't hate Megan, in fact, he admired her tenacity and grit. But business was business and his was slipping away fast.

"I haven't killed anyone." Belle walked over to a bottle of whiskey that she kept at their bedside. She took a long, shuddering drink and when she spoke, her voice was very husky. "But it's either them or us. So I guess now is as good a time to kill as any."

"You'll kill Megan?"

Belle took another drink. "We've tried to buy her out, she thumbed her nose at us. We even offered to form a partnership so that we could all make more money. But what did she do? She made us feel like dirt and wouldn't even listen to what we were offering. Yeah, Ike, I can kill Megan."

"Good," he said, looking away. "We'll do it tonight."

"All right," Belle said, reaching for the bottle.

"No more drinking tonight," Ike ordered. "We ain't going to mess this up. We could get ourselves shot or hanged if something goes wrong."

Belle pouted but didn't make a fuss. Ike was right. Murder was very serious business.

It was well after midnight when they closed their own tent saloon and sent their last few unhappy customers packing. Ike had made sure that neither he nor Belle had much to drink, though their nerves were raw as fresh meat.

"Let's go," he said, hand brushing the six-gun shoved into his belt.

"Jezus," Belle said breathlessly, "my stomach is twisted tighter than a wrung-out rag!"

"Just don't lose your nerve on me," Ike warned. "Once we step into that tent and they see us, there is no turning around. We either kill them and burn their saloon, or we wind up swinging from a rope."

"Yeah," Belle said in a low, tight voice. "And I'm too damned young and pretty to get hanged."

Ike glanced at her. Belle was real young and pretty, but so was Megan O'Connell and Ike was glad that he wasn't going to have to be the one to punch her ticket. He had agreed that he would try to stab Henry

Harrison to avoid a gunshot, but he hadn't quite been able to bring himself to ask Belle how she intended to eliminate Megan.

Although it was after one o'clock, Megan's Place still had plenty of customers and Ike couldn't help feel a pang of envy as he and Belle settled in behind her place to wait until the saloon emptied for the evening. Damn Megan's stubborn independence! She alone was to blame for what was about to happen.

"You want to know how I'm going to kill Megan?" Belle asked.

Ike thought a minute, then shook his head because he realized he didn't want to know. Furthermore, he found himself repulsed by Belle's cavalier attitude.

"Why don't we just shut up and wait," Ike said. "I don't want to talk anymore."

Belle leaned closer. Her perfume filled his senses and she laid her hand up on his thigh. "I don't feel any better about this than you do, Ike. But Megan had her chances and chose to treat us bad. It ain't our fault that she didn't want to work together."

"Yeah, yeah."

"Look," Belle said, hand rubbing up and down. "As soon as we kill 'em and set fire to Megan's saloon, let's go back to our place, get drunk, and make love the rest of the night. How'd you like that, big boy?"

Ike realized with a jolt that he wouldn't like it at all. How could you stab a person to death one minute and make love the next? The prospect actually made him shiver with revulsion.

"Leave me alone, Belle."

"What the hell is the matter with you!"

"Just . . . just shut up!"

She recoiled. "I think that *you're* the one that's losing your nerve! You're starting to worry me."

Ike almost walked out on Belle. It would mean that he would lose his saloon and everything that he'd worked for since Omaha, but for the briefest of moments, it didn't matter. He'd been crazy to even consider killing Henry Harrison and burning Megan out. Crazy with worry and resentment born of jealousy because Megan O'Connell had clearly bested him in the tough saloon business.

"Look!" Belle whispered. "Megan is closing for the night."

Ike edged back deeper into the shadows. He could see up the alley between the tents and the customers were leaving.

"We'll give it another ten minutes, just to be on the safe side. If Rachel is in there with them, we walk by as if we're out for a stroll in the moonlight. Agreed?"

Belle nodded because they'd already decided that this was the best thing to do. Killing Rachel might just incense the entire construction camp so badly that there'd be hell to pay for everyone.

The minutes passed very slowly. When Ike guessed they had passed, he whispered, "All right. Let's go!"

He and Belle began to stroll toward the front of Megan's Place. They could see two silhouettes through the canvas and hear Megan and Henry Harrison as they worked to close up the place for the night.

"How much did you win tonight?" Megan asked her gambler.

"About a hundred."

"Nice work."

"Thanks," Henry Harrison said. "I probably could

have gone for the jugular and taken in a bigger pot, but why? The money will be back there tomorrow night."

"Sure it will," Megan agreed.

Ike and Belle came to the door. Ike drew his six-gun, cocked back the hammer, and stepped inside. He took eight quick strides and was halfway across the interior of the tent saloon before he was noticed.

"One word and you're dead," Ike hissed, cocking his six-gun. "One little squeak and I'll riddle you both."

"What do you want?" Megan demanded. "Ike. Belle. Are you both crazy?"

"No," Ike said. "We're just desperate. Raise your hands and turn around slowly. Henry, don't even think about going for a derringer."

Henry Harrison pushed back in his chair from the poker table where he'd been counting up the night's winnings. "Ike, I don't know what you have in mind, but it *is* crazy."

"Turn around."

Henry Harrison and Megan exchanged glances and they both reached the same conclusion that if they were going to be shot, they'd rather die fighting. As if an unspoken signal for action flashed between them, Megan threw herself toward the nearest cover but Henry Harrison attacked. The little man was surprisingly quick and a derringer was starting to materialize as he crossed the line of fire that put himself directly in front of Megan.

Ike had a knife in his belt but using it was suddenly out of the question. Like most gamblers, he'd had to become a quick and deadly marksman and he fired without aiming. He saw Henry Harrison take a bullet in the head and collapse over his card table. Poker chips and cash cascaded to the floor around the little gambler.

Ike shot him again for good measure.

Belle screamed and ran toward Megan with a derringer in her fist. She fired twice but Megan was up and moving.

"Belle! Let's go!" Ike shouted, grabbing a kerosene lamp and hurling it at Henry's overturned card table. The lamp exploded in a shower of glass and flame. "Come on, Belle!"

But Belle had followed Megan into her storeroom. Ike heard screams and two shots. He raced toward the storeroom and collided with Belle. Her face was ghostly, her eyes bulging with excitement. "She's dead! No witnesses now. Let's go!"

Ike didn't need any urging. He knew that even at this late hour, men would come running to investigate. Drawing his knife, he slashed open the back wall of the tent and bulled his way through.

"Dammit, Ike, you'd better wait for me!"

"Come on!"

Ike could see the bright orange glow of the fire as it spread across the sawdust floor and then soared up the canvas wall. He'd seen tent saloons go up in flames before and it took only moments before they were an inferno.

"Goddammit, come on!" he shouted, grabbing Belle and pulling her through the canvas wall.

They ran hard up the alley hearing men shout. A block away they halted and pressed into the shadows as the silhouettes of men flew past, many carrying sloshing water buckets.

"We did it!" Belle whispered. "We did it!"

Ike swallowed hard and managed to nod his head.

Belle grabbed and hugged his neck. Ike wanted to push her away but she still had a gun in her fist and Ike was afraid that she might use it on him and then take his own saloon.

"Ike, we did it!" she squealed, kissing his face and trying to force her tongue into his mouth.

Ike opened his mouth but he gagged, and Belle drew back and the palm of her hand smashed against the side of his face. It was too dark to see her expression, but Ike could feel her hatred and loathing.

"God damn you, Ike!"

He sucked for fresh air and his eyes lifted to the tower of flame that shot up into the sky over the tent city. A fire bell began to clang over and over as the crews were called to stop the advancing flames. If they failed, other nearby tents were almost sure to be destroyed.

No matter. Ike's saloon was far enough away to be safe—but as Belle's malevolence penetrated the darkness between them, was he?

CHAPTER
27

Glenn was one of the first to reach the inferno that had engulfed Megan's Place. "Where is she?" he cried. "Where's Megan?"

"Nobody's seen her!" a man shouted as he hurled a pitifully small amount of water from his bucket. "We heard gunshots and then there was this fire."

"And no one has even tried to—" Glenn didn't waste any more words. He grabbed a sloshing bucket from another arrival who was about to hurl it at the flames.

"Hey!" the man shouted in protest.

But Glenn didn't have time to explain. Pouring the bucket over his head so that he was drenched, Glenn plunged through the same rent in the canvas that Ike and Belle had passed only minutes earlier.

The heat was almost unbearable. Thick smoke boiled against what was left of the tent's top and Glenn knew that smoke and poison gases would kill him instantly if he inhaled their deadly vapors. Holding his breath, Glenn tried to shield his face as he stumbled around half-blind and searching everywhere for Megan.

The saloon was burning out of control. Everything was on fire. Bottles of liquor were exploding in liquid flames, their corks disappearing like little cannonballs into the smoky air. Glenn saw Henry Harrison's body being consumed by flames and he staggered forward but the heat drove him back again. He could feel his hair starting to curl and scorch.

"Megan!"

The roar of the inferno smothered his cry.

"Megan!"

Glenn threw himself to the sawdust floor. He buried his face in his hands and sucked in a fresh lungful of air. His shirt and pants began to smoke. Taking a deep breath, he retreated, crabbing away from the intensifying heat and flames.

It was a miracle that he found Megan. She was lying facedown in the storeroom, half wedged in between barrels of whiskey. One side of her head was smeared with fresh blood and Glenn was sure that she was already dead. A whiskey barrel standing beside Megan was bullet riddled and emptying itself into the sawdust. Glenn knew the liquor would ignite like a can of kerosene.

He grabbed Megan's arm and dragged her to the back of the tent where his knife quickly cut them an escape.

"Look!" someone yelled and pointed as Glenn struggled to drag Megan out of the burning tent saloon.

A dozen men raced forward to pull Glenn and Megan away until they were a safe distance from the conflagration.

"Get Dr. Wiseman!" came the call. "Get the doctor!"

Glenn felt for Megan's heartbeat. His fingertips were burned but he didn't notice as he found her pulse.

"She's alive!" he breathed. "Megan is alive!"

"You're both damned near charred," a rough construction worker said, shaking his head. "I swear to God and the Virgin Mary that you're a pair of miracles."

Glenn didn't know about any miracles. All he knew for sure was that he was now starting to feel the searing pain of his burns and trembling to think of their miraculous escape from a fiery hell.

Megan's eyelids, hair, and eyebrows were badly singed and her face was crimson from the heat. She roused and touched Glenn's arm. "You saved my life. Wasn't it you?"

"Me and my guardian angel," he told her with a smile that hurt because his face felt like dry and splitting rawhide. "Megan, it's going to be all right. Everything is going to be all right."

Megan sobbed as memories flooded across her pain. "But Henry Harrison is dead! He threw himself at them so that I had a chance to run for my life."

"Threw himself at who?" Joshua Hood asked, pushing other men aside to crouch beside Glenn and Megan.

She looked up at Joshua, tears spilling down her blistered cheeks. "It was Ike Norman and Belle King," Megan said in a halting voice. "They burst into our tent just as we were closing up for the night. They'd already made up their minds to kill us both."

Glenn and Joshua exchanged glances and just then Dr. Wiseman and Aileen broke through the ring of gawking spectators.

"Megan!" Aileen cried, collapsing beside her sister and hugging her fiercely. "Oh, Megan!"

"I'm all right now," Megan choked. "But poor Henry Harrison is dead! Ike Norman shot him and then Belle chased after me with a gun in her fist."

She touched the side of her head and saw the fresh blood. "I knew that I'd been hit. I thought sure that I was dying. After that, I must have blacked out completely."

"Move aside, everyone!" Dr. Wiseman ordered, shoving people out of his way as he knelt beside Megan to examine her injuries. "Someone get me a lantern! I need good light!"

A lantern was raised and Aileen gasped to see the way her sister's beautiful skin was already starting to blister.

"Aileen, get my bag open and hand me that sulfuric ointment. Hurry!"

Aileen snapped out of her shock. Quickly she had her husband's medical kit open and was applying the ointment to a piece of surgical gauze. Thaddeus's examination was brief but thorough.

"You've also been shot, Megan," Thaddeus pronounced as he wiped the ointment on her face and eyelids. "You've a very nasty bullet crease across your temple and a slug is still lodged in the triceps of your upper arm. I think that it will be easy enough to remove. Did Ike Norman do this?"

"No, it was Belle."

Glenn tried to sit up but was seized by a fit of terrible coughing.

Thaddeus gently pushed him down. "You're not going anywhere, Glenn. If you've inhaled smoke, and it sounds as if you have, you're certainly not out of the woods yet."

Joshua Hood straightened and without a word turned and walked away, pushing aside the massing and anxious crowd. He figured that Ike and Belle would be trying to escape and he'd be damned if he'd allow that to happen. Joshua bulled his way through the crowded, eerily lit street now swarming with railroad construction workers. Men had only to see the expression on his face and they quickly stepped aside. Ragged bucket brigades were hastily formed and hundreds of railroad workers struggled to ensure that the fire did not engulf the entire tent city, especially their precious stock of whiskey.

Joshua headed straight for Ike's saloon and gambling hall. If Ike and Belle felt certain that they'd killed both their intended victims, they'd still be around. But if not, Joshua knew that they'd probably be in a high state of alarm and preparing to flee for their lives before they were caught by an enraged mob and strung up from the nearest cottonwood tree.

When Joshua approached Ike's saloon, it was dark but a huge guard dog inside the tent was barking furiously. Maybe the dog sensed Joshua hovering outside or maybe it was just upset by the thickening taste of smoke. Either way, Joshua was going inside to find Ike and Belle. He drew his Bowie knife and slashed the canvas open, then shifted his knife to his left hand and drew his six-gun.

The big guard dog charged before Joshua could get more than one leg inside. Joshua heard its low, menacing rumble and felt its fangs clamp down powerfully on his thick leather boot top. He kicked out but the savage beast would not let go. Unwilling to open fire, Joshua reversed the grip on his Army Colt and pistol-whipped the dog twice before its grip was broken and the beast finally collapsed.

Except for the stunned dog, the saloon was empty.

Joshua knew, however, that Ike and Belle slept in a very plush back room complete with its own private bar and plantation-sized four-poster bed. He'd seen both many a time when the latest tent city was broken down in preparation for yet another leapfrogging move west.

Gun throttled in his fist, eyes trying to probe the dim interior of the tent, Joshua hurried forward in long, silent strides and when he came to the back-room door, he paused to listen. He could hear voices and by pressing his ear to the wood, Joshua made sense of the conversation.

Belle and Ike were having a terrible fight. Their voices were strained hisses; they sounded to Joshua like a pair of angry vipers.

"You're a coward!" Belle accused. "Ike, you've lost your nerve!"

"Oh, yeah? Well at least I didn't act like a cold-blooded killer! Why, I think you actually seemed to enjoy shooting Megan."

"I did! I hated that high and mighty bitch!"

"This isn't going to work out between us," Ike pronounced. "I don't want you around anymore."

"Then leave!" Belle cried. "But if you do, this place is mine!"

"The hell you say!"

"Get out! We're finished!"

Joshua heard a strangled curse and Ike's cry of alarm. "Belle, no!"

Before Joshua could react, two gunshots exploded behind the door. Joshua threw himself into the room. Ike was on his knees, hand clutching his six-gun as he struggled to lift it and take aim. Cool as well water, Belle shot him once more.

At the same instant Joshua's own gun lifted. Belle was quicker than a cat. Her pistol swung around and they both fired at the same instant. Joshua felt a hard jar and was knocked back a step. His left shoulder went numb and his Bowie knife spun harmlessly to the floor. They both fired again and through the black-powder gunsmoke Joshua saw Belle crash over backward. Her head struck a fancy French dresser and she rolled brokenly to rest beside Ike Norman who recoiled from her body.

Joshua pointed his gun at Ike. "You killed Henry Harrison. Shot him down and then set Megan's Place on fire to hide the murder."

Ike twisted his head up. The saloon owner was still choking the butt of his gun but there was no strength or purpose left. Joshua stepped over to the dying man and tore the gun from his hand. "Ike, when you sleep with a viper like Belle, you'd better expect to get bit."

"Yeah," Ike whispered.

"Why'd you do it?"

"Losin' everything. Goin' . . . bust, Joshua."

"Better bust than dust."

Ike's lips worked at a reply but there wasn't enough breath left in the man so he closed his eyes and died without a shudder.

Joshua went over to Belle and studied her body for a moment. He was surprised at how small and delicate she appeared. In death, Belle looked like a fresh-faced schoolgirl. The hard lines in her expression were missing, and if you didn't think too much about what she had become since turning against Megan, you could imagine that Belle was still as innocent and pure as a Sunday school virgin.

Joshua collected Belle's gun and shoved it into his waistband. He took a step and felt dizzy enough to lean against a bureau of drawers. Holstering his own six-gun, he reached across his body and his powerful fingers bit into his shoulder to stanch the flow of his own blood.

"Damn the both of you," he muttered as he walked heavily back to the front of the saloon. It seemed to take forever. He could hear the sound of a fire bell ringing and wondered if the whole damn town would go up in flames. Probably not, because there wasn't much of a wind tonight to spread the towering flames that were still feasting at Megan's Place.

Joshua stepped over the guard dog that was showing signs of recovery and beginning to growl.

"Dog, you're one mean sonofabitch, ain't ya," Joshua said with admiration as he climbed back outside and went to find the doctor.

CHAPTER
28

"Megan, I've been summoned by Dr. Durant," Glenn said two weeks after the inferno and shootings. "It's a meeting that I don't feel very easy about."

Megan looked up from her bed. She was recovering nicely. Her blistered skin was pink and healthy again, and except for her singed eyebrows and eyelids, she looked unaffected by the recent tragedy.

"Perhaps Dr. Durant has something good to tell you," Megan suggested hopefully. "After all, you were honored as a hero for saving me."

"That's true, but Durant wasn't present. No, Megan, the man has always had it out for me. He decided that I was his enemy way back in Omaha and nothing is going to change. I swear he's out to get me."

"Well," Megan said, "I know how much regard and admiration General Dodge and the other Union Pacific officials hold for you. Durant's attitude simply proves that we can never satisfy everyone."

Glenn took her hand, only recently free of bandages. "I love you, Megan. If you'd died along with Henry Harrison, I would have died too."

"I know. And we'll become man and wife. I promise, Glenn. When the time is right, we'll be wed."

Glenn leaned over and kissed Megan, then stood up and nervously fingered his tie. He really did have an uneasy premonition about this hastily called private meeting with the Union Pacific's vice president. "Do I look presentable?"

"More than presentable. You look devilishly handsome."

"Megan, you have a touch of the Irish blarney."

"Do you mind?"

"No." Glenn reached for his suit coat. "Wish me well with Dr. Durant, my dear."

"It will be fine. He's a doctor and will probably just inquire about our health and heartily congratulate you for becoming a local hero."

"That would be nice, but totally unexpected."

Glenn left Megan and walked up the street. It was a fine day with big, billowing cumulus clouds stacking toward heaven. He supposed that later in the afternoon it would probably thunder and shower. At this time of the year, the prairie grass was a wavy green ocean and the rails of the Union Pacific stretched forever in both directions. Very soon now, this tent city would be jumping ten or fifteen miles westward to end-of-track. That was fine. By then, Megan would be strong enough to travel.

Glenn passed the burned-out shell of Megan's Place. It had been completely destroyed but everyone had wholeheartedly agreed that Megan could have Ike's saloon as a just compensation. It was bigger and could be made into a first-class tent saloon. Rachel had already taken over its operation in Megan's absence and was doing a wonderful job. She had Victor to help as well as another young man who had been injured by a dropped rail and who could no longer do heavy construction work. The only thing missing was Henry Harrison and he was simply irreplaceable. Just thinking of how Henry had traded his life in a desperate attempt to save Megan caused Glenn's throat to ache.

As he walked gloomily toward Durant's plush Pullman coach, Glenn was greeted by dozens of passing men, foremen as well as rust eaters. He saw affection and respect in their eyes and it lifted his flagging spirits above the dark thoughts of Henry Harrison's death and his impending meeting with Dr. Thomas Durant.

Glenn realized that he had matured from a naive college boy into a man who had been tested by the transcontinental challenge and not found wanting. He'd fought Indians, blizzards, and rough men. Most important, he'd finally won Megan's heart and would become her husband, the father of their children. Every one of Glenn's dreams and ambitions had come true while the Union Pacific had toiled, bled, and fought its way across Nebraska and deep into Wyoming. It was a grand, grand adventure with danger and challenges aplenty yet to be overcome.

Glenn knocked on the door of the Pullman coach and was bade to enter. Dr. Durant was alone, seated at his desk. His greeting was terse and there was no offer of brandy or exchange of pleasantries. The man's animosity was palpable.

"Sit down," Durant ordered.

Glenn removed his hat and took a seat. He could feel his armpits leaking with dread and anxiety.

Durant came to his feet. He clasped his hands

behind his back, glared down his nose at Glenn, and announced, "You failed me very badly in the matter of Peter Arlington, Mr. Gilchrist."

"What?"

"I hold you responsible for his death."

"Now wait a minute, sir! It was your idea that . . ."

"How well did you know the man?"

Glenn clamped his mouth shut. He was so angry and hurt by this unfair attack on his character that it was difficult to find the means or power to speak. "Not well."

"Do you recall that sealed letter that you took off his body and presented to me?"

"Of course!"

"Do you have any idea as to its contents?"

"How could I? You just admitted that it was sealed."

Durant began to pace back and forth with increasing agitation. "I dutifully sent a telegram to Mr. Arlington's father, care of *The Boston Herald*. And guess what?"

"I'm not in the mood for guessing games, Doctor."

"I wouldn't imagine so." Durant stopped, pivoted, and shouted, "There is no *Boston Herald*!"

Glenn bounced to his own feet. "What!"

"That's right. And don't look so surprised," Durant hissed, voice dripping with contempt. "I think you knew all along that our charming Mr. Peter Arlington the Third was a Central Pacific Railroad spy."

"You must be out of your mind!"

"Am I?"

Durant marched over to his desk and snatched up a letter. Arlington's letter. The letter that he had taken from the dying man while under Indian attack. "Listen to this, Mr. Gilchrist."

Glenn sat back down. A sense of foreboding overcame him and he felt like a man standing on a scaffold with a noose around his neck. Guilt or innocence meant nothing. Only a black void awaited him.

"The letter is written to a Mr. Harry Loudermilk, care of the Central Pacific Railroad. It reads:

'Dear Mr. Loudermilk: I believe that the progress of the Union Pacific will meet or even exceed our worst fears. The U.P. is laying track at the rate of three miles a day and that figure is expected to hold steady through the remainder of this year. The survey route across the remainder of Wyoming appears to be flat with few rivers or other geographic obstacles. I have been consulting very closely with Assistant Chief Surveyor Glenn Gilchrist. He is an amiable and cooperative fellow who has given me all the necessary information I need to predict that the U.P. rails will enter the Utah Territory and the Wasatch Mountains by next spring. At that time, attempts will be made to enlist the support of Brigham Young, leader of the Church of the Latter-Day Saints. If this assistance is won, we can surely expect that our U.P. rivals will redouble their efforts to claim the Great Basin and Nevada Territory as their prize.'"

Durant stopped reading and looked up, eyes filled with loathing. "Mr. Gilchrist, I don't need to read any more of this damning evidence. It is quite clear for anyone to see that you conspired to assist a railroad spy. That you provided Peter Arlington, or whoever he really was, everything he needed to know to pass on to the Central Pacific Railroad."

"That's a lie!" Glenn shouted, coming to his feet.

"No it isn't," Durant said coldly. "It's true. I don't suppose that you actually broke any laws, but you are a man without loyalty. Will you present a letter of resignation to this railroad or must I tell General Dodge and the other officers that you consorted with our Central Pacific adversaries?"

Glenn's fists doubled at his sides and it was all that he could do to keep from attacking the fool. "I resign."

"Good choice. Collect your pay and be gone by tomorrow."

Glenn couldn't believe what was happening. His whole being revolted at this terrible injustice. He felt himself dropping through the gallows and choking on Durant's noose. He wanted to scream in rage and to throttle the Union Pacific's vice president but he felt as if his shoes had been cast in buckets of cement and he could not move.

"I'm going to prove you are an idiot," he managed to whisper. "I'm going to prove that I had nothing to do with any conspiracy nor did I know that Peter Arlington the Third was anything other than what he presented himself to be."

"Get out of my sight, Mr. Gilchrist!"

"With pleasure," Glenn swore as he wheeled and stormed outside.

Ten minutes later he was at Megan's bedside, telling her about the charges and his forced resignation as an alleged Central Pacific Railroad spy.

"But that's ridiculous!" Megan cried. "You've been extremely loyal to this railroad. You've repeatedly risked your life in its service. These charges can't be proven. At worst, you were deceived by Peter—as we all were—Durant included!"

"I know," Glenn said miserably. "But the fact of the matter is that I have been banished. I've a cloud on my name and I mean to clear it."

"But how?"

"I'm finished with the Union Pacific," Glenn said darkly. "But I can redeem my good name by finding this Harry Loudermilk fellow conspirator and demanding that he absolve me of any complicity with the Central Pacific Railroad."

"You're going to California?"

"Where else can I clear my good name and redeem my honor? I can't return to my family. There would be questions and I'd not be able to lie about the reasons for my sudden discharge from the Union Pacific."

Glenn balled his fists. "Yes, I *am* going to California."

"Then I will go with you."

"Megan, I . . ."

"I'm coming," she insisted, throwing her arms around his neck. "You know that I've always dreamed of going to California. And now I shall simply get there a few happy years earlier than expected."

"But you've a saloon to run! A sister and friends. People depend on you."

"I'll make Rachel my working partner. She can run Megan's Place or whatever she wants to call it. I trust her. She's become an excellent businesswoman."

"But you've only had a few weeks to recover from your injuries and . . ."

Megan stilled his protest by reaching up and pulling his face down to hers. She kissed his lips, her breath hot and sweet, her body soft and willing. After a moment she breathed, "Please, Glenn, no more reasons why I can't go with you. Just fix me up a wagon and take me along to California."

"It's a long, perilous journey. We'll need to hook up with a wagon train for safety and even then we will be traveling in constant danger."

"Life itself is dangerous," Megan said with a smile. "You saved my life, remember? Do you really think I'd let you run off to California to clear your name without taking me along to help?"

"I guess not."

"Of course not!"

"When do you want to leave?"

"By tomorrow. Isn't that what Durant ordered?"

Glenn's expression clouded. "To hell with Durant's orders!"

"This last time," Megan said, "let's obey them. And someday, we'll return with a sworn statement from Harry Loudermilk and demand a public apology from Dr. Durant."

"His pride would never allow it."

"Then we'll get even."

"How?"

Megan's fingers caressed his face. "Glenn, we'll join the Central Pacific and make the doctor regret the day that he attempted to ruin your good name."

"I like that. I like that very much!"

Glenn started to say more, but then Megan was pulling him down and kissing all his California plans for vindication clean away.